HE FELT HIMSELF BEING WRENCHED AND FLUNG—

AS IF ACROSS SOME IMAGINABLE DISTANCE OF TIME OR SPACE . . .

The aged face of the man who called himself James Rater Bailey had worn a snarl when they left him alone in the cell with Doug. His gnarled fingers clutched at the tattered charms he always wore about his throat and he muttered something, as if praying to the devils it had been said he worshipped.

Doug has never sought help, knowing he could expect none. It had been a fair fight after he was attacked, and the hoodlum's death had been an accident. Doug could have escaped if he had not called for an ambulance. But he had not asked for mercy even after he had learned the drunk was the son of the state's Governor. He had faced their gas chamber without pleading.

"Doug." The old man's voice had been urgent. "I came to help you—for your grandfather's sake."

Doug snorted. "Miracles don't work against cyanide."

"Doug, listen. You won't believe me—nobody ever did. But take this!" A tiny capsule had fallen from his crooked hand.

Now, fighting the spasms from the deadly gas, Doug seemed to be dreaming . . . of another time and place . . .

GORDON R. DICKSON

THE LAST DREAM

Copyright © 1986 by Gordon R. Dickson

A Baen Books Original

Baen Publishing Enterprises
260 Fifth Avenue
New York, N.Y. 10001

First printing, March 1986
  Second printing, September 1988

ISBN: 0-671-65559-0

Cover art by James Warhola

Printed in the United States of America

Distributed by
SIMON & SCHUSTER
1230 Avenue of the Americas
New York, N.Y. 10020

ACKNOWLEDGMENTS

These stories have appeared previously, in a somewhat different form, as follows:

"St. Dragon and the George," *The Magazine of Fantasy and Science Fiction*, September 1957. © Fantasy House, Inc., 1957.

"The Present State of Igneos Research" and "Ye Prentice and Ye Dragon," *Analog*, January 1975. © Conde Nast Publications, Inc., 1974.

"A Case History," *The Magazine of Fantasy and Science Fiction*, December 1954. © Fantasy House, Inc.

"The Girl Who Played Wolf," *Fantastic*, August 1958. © Ziff-Davis Publishing Co., 1958.

"Salmanazar," *Magazine of Fantasy and Science Fiction*, December 1957. © Mercury Press, Inc., 1962.

"With Butter and Mustard," *The Magazine of Fantasy and Science Fiction*, December 1957. © Fantasy House Inc., 1957.

"The Amulet," *The Magazine of Fantasy and Science Fiction*, April 1959. © Mercury Press, Inc., 1959.

"The Haunted Village," *The Magazine of Fantasy and Science Fiction*, August 1961. © Mercury Press, Inc., 1961.

"The Three," *Startling Stories*, May 1953. © Better Publications, Inc., 1953.

"Walker Between the Planes," *Worlds of Fantasy #2*, 1970. © Universal Publishing and Distributing Corp., 1970.

"The Last Dream," *The Magazine of Fantasy and Science Fiction*, July 1960. © Mercury Press, Inc., 1960.

CONTENTS

CONTENTS

EDITOR'S INTRODUCTION

by Sandra Miesel

All real living is making—of truth and beauty, of goodness and love. "If you are not making," said a wise man, "you cannot possibly be happy because it is the destiny of every man to be a maker." What remains potential in the many is actual in the artist. Then he in turn offers his work and shares his happiness with the many.

In his well-known analysis of fantasy, J.R.R. Tolkien describes the literary artist as a subcreator who gives the Secondary World he makes "the inner consistency of reality." By realizing imagined marvels, he builds a place that commands active belief, not the mere suspension of disbelief. To visit such a Secondary World is to find our dreams of loveliness, horror, and whimsy come true. A measure of the enchantment that refreshes us there may return to the Primary World with us and awakens splendors in everyday things. Once we have wandered in the forests of Faerie, "a tree is a tree at last" even if it grows beside a car-clogged city street.

It is a blessing that fantasy "fans fresh our wits with wonder" lest we smother in mundane chaos and corruption. Values only fleetingly glimpsed in our Primary World stand out clearly in a well-made Secondary One. Thus it can offer a satisfying vision of moral harmony unattained here. In particular, fantasy speaks to our sense of justice. We want to see the ogre slain, the witch bested, the cripple healed, the prince and princess live happily ever after. Nihilists who delight in letting "doom come and dark conquer" pervert the very essence of fantasy and mock the longing for joy that animates it.

What is made in fancy may yet be made in fact. Humorously or grandly, humbly or nobly, modern fantasy carries on the work of mankind's oldest stories. It leads each of us readers beyond ourselves to discover that each of the Hero's thousand faces is our own.

> *J.R.R. Tolkien "desired dragons with
> a profound desire." Yet even the keen-
> est draconophile must set some limits
> to intimacy.*

St. Dragon and the George

A TRIFLE DIFFIDENTLY, JIM ECKERT RAPPED WITH HIS CLAW
on the blue-painted door.

Silence.

He knocked again. There was the sound of a
hasty step inside the small, oddly peak-roofed house
and the door was snatched open. A thin-faced old
man with a tall pointed cap and a long, rather
dingy-looking white beard peered out, irritably.

"Sorry, not my day for dragons!" he snapped.
"Come back next Tuesday." He slammed the door.

It was too much. It was the final straw. Jim
Eckert sat down on his haunches with a dazed
thump. The little forest clearing with its impossible little pool tinkling away like Chinese glass wind
chimes in the background, its well-kept greensward
with the white gravel path leading to the door
before him, and the riotous flower beds of asters,
tulips, zinnias, roses and lilies-of-the-valley all
equally impossibly in bloom at the same time about
the white finger-post labelled S.CAROLINUS and point-

3

ing at the house—it all whirled about him. It was
more than flesh and blood could bear. At any minute now he would go completely insane and imagine he was a peanut or a cocker spaniel. Grottwold
Hanson had wrecked them all. Dr. Howells would
have to get another teaching assistant for his English Department. Angie . . .

Angie!

Jim pounded on the door again. It was snatched
open.

"Dragon!" cried S. Carolinus, furiously. "How
would you like to be a beetle?"

"But I'm not a dragon," said Jim, desperately.

The magician stared at him for a long minute,
then threw up his beard with both hands in a
gesture of despair, caught some of it in his teeth as
it fell down and began to chew on it fiercely.

"Now where," he demanded, "did a dragon acquire the brains to develop the imagination to
entertain the illusion that he is *not* a dragon? Answer me, O Ye Powers!"

"The information is psychically, though not phys-
iologically correct," replied a deep bass voice out
of thin air beside them and some five feet off the
ground. Jim, who had taken the question to be
rhetorical, started convulsively.

"Is that so?" S. Carolinus peered at Jim with
new interest. "Hmm." He spat out a hair or two.
"Come in, Anomaly—or whatever you call yourself."

Jim squeezed in through the door and found
himself in a large single room. It was a clutter of
mismatched furniture and odd bits of alchemical
equipment.

"Hmm," said S. Carolinus, closing the door and
walking once around Jim, thoughtfully. "If you
aren't a dragon, what are you?"

"Well, my real name's Jim Eckert," said Jim.

"But I seem to be in the body of a dragon named Gorbash."

"And this disturbs you. So you've come to me. How nice," said the magician, bitterly. He winced, massaged his stomach and closed his eyes. "Do you know anything that's good for a perpetual stomach-ache? Of course not. Go on."

"Well, I want to get back to my real body. And take Angie with me. She's my fiancée and I can send her back but I can't send myself back at the same time. You see, this Grottwold Hanson—well, maybe I better start from the beginning."

"Brilliant suggestion, Gorbash," said Carolinus. "Or whatever your name is," he added.

"Well," said Jim. Carolinus winced. Jim hurried on. "I teach at a place called Riveroak College in the United States—you've never heard of it—"

"Go on, go on," said Carolinus.

"That is, I'm a teaching assistant. Dr. Howells, who heads the English Department, promised me an instructorship over a year ago. But he's never come through with it; and Angie—Angie Gilman, my fiancée—"

"You mentioned her."

"Yes—well, we were having a little fight. That is, we were arguing about my going to ask Howells whether he was going to give me the instructor's rating for next year or not. I didn't think I should; and she didn't think we could get married—well, anyway, in came Grottwold Hanson."

"In *where* came *who?*"

"Into the Campus Bar and Grille. We were having a drink there. Hanson used to go with Angie. He's a graduate student in psychology. A long, thin geek that's just as crazy as he looks. He's always getting wound up in some new odd-ball organization or other—"

"Dictionary!" interrupted Carolinus, suddenly.

He opened his eyes as an enormous volume appeared suddenly poised in the air before him. He massaged his stomach. "Ouch," he said. The pages of the volume began to flip rapidly back and forth before his eyes. "Don't mind me," he said to Jim. "Go on."

"—This time it was the Bridey Murphy craze. Hypnotism. Well—"

"Not so fast," said Carolinus. "*Bridey Murphy . . . Hypnotism . . . yes . . .*"

"Oh, he talked about the ego wandering, planes of reality, on and on like that. He offered to hypnotize one of us and show us how it worked. Angie was mad at me, so she said yes. I went off to the bar. I was mad. When I turned around, Angie was gone. Disappeared."

"Vanished?" said Carolinus.

"Vanished. I blew my top at Hanson. She must have wandered, he said, not merely the ego, but all of her. Bring her back, I said. I can't, he said. It seemed she wanted to go back to the time of St. George and the Dragon. When men were men and would speak up to their bosses about promotions. Hanson'd have to send someone else back to rehypnotize her and send her back home. Like an idiot I said I'd go. Ha! I might've known he'd goof. He couldn't do anything right if he was paid for it. I landed in the body of this dragon."

"And the maiden?"

"Oh, she landed here, too. Centuries off the mark. A place where there actually were such things as dragons—fantastic."

"Why?" said Carolinus.

"Well, I mean—anyway," said Jim, hurriedly. "The point is, they'd already got her—the dragons, I mean. A big brute named Anark had found her wandering around and put her in a cage. They were having a meeting in a cave about deciding what to do with her. Anark wanted to stake her out for a decoy, so they could capture a lot of the local people—only the dragons called people *georges*—"

"They're quite stupid, you know," said Carolinus, severely, looking up from the dictionary. "There's only room for one name in their head at a time. After the Saint made such an impression on them his name stuck."

"Anyway, they were all yelling at once. They've got tremendous voices."

"Yes, you have," said Carolinus, pointedly.

"Oh, sorry," said Jim. He lowered his voice. "I tried to argue that we ought to hold Angie for ransom—" He broke off suddenly. "Say," he said. "I never thought of that. Was I talking dragon, then? What am I talking now? Dragons don't talk English, do they?"

"Why not?" demanded Carolinus, grumpily. "If they're British dragons?"

"But I'm not a dragon—I mean—"

"But you *are* here!" snapped Carolinus. "You and this maiden of yours. Since all the rest of you was translated here, don't you suppose your ability to speak understandably was translated, too? Continue."

"There's not much more," said Jim, gloomily. "I was losing the argument and then this very big, old dragon spoke up on my side. Hold Angie for ransom, he said. And they listened to him. It seems he swings a lot of weight among them. He's a great-uncle of me—of this Gorbash who's body I'm in—and I'm his only surviving relative. They penned Angie up in a cave and he sent me off to the Tinkling Water here, to find you and have you open negotiations for ransom. Actually, on the side he told me to tell you to make the terms easy on the georges—I mean humans; he wants the dragons to work toward good relations with them. He's afraid the dragons are in danger of being wiped out. I had a chance to double back and talk to Angie alone. We thought you might be able to send us both back."

He stopped rather out of breath, and looked hopefully at Carolinus. The magician was chewing thoughtfully on his beard.

"Smrgol," he muttered. "Now there's an exception to the rule. Very bright for a dragon. Also experienced. Hmm."

"Can you help us?" demanded Jim. "Look, I can show you—"

Carolinus sighed, closed his eyes, winced and opened them again.

"Let me see if I've got it straight," he said. "You had a dispute with this maiden to whom you're betrothed. To spite you, she turned to this third-rate practitioner, who mistakenly exorcized her from the United States (whenever in the cosmos that is) to here, further compounding his error by sending you back in spirit only to inhabit the body of Gorbash. The maiden is in the hands of the dragons and you have been sent to me by your great-uncle Smrgol."

"That's sort of it," said Jim dubiously, "only—"

"You wouldn't," said Carolinus, "care to change your story to something simpler and more reasonable—like being a prince changed into a dragon by some wicked fairy stepmother? Oh, my poor stomach! No?" He sighed. "All right, that'll be five hundred pounds of gold, or five pounds of rubies, in advance."

"B-but—" Jim goggled at him. "But I don't have any gold—or rubies."

"What? What kind of a dragon are you?" cried Carolinus, glaring at him. "Where's your hoard?"

"I suppose this Gorbash has one," stammered

Jim, unhappily. "But I don't know anything about it."

"Another charity patient!" muttered Carolinus, furiously. He shook his fist at empty space. "What's wrong with that auditing department? Well?"

"Sorry," said the invisible bass voice.

"That's the third in two weeks. See it doesn't happen again for another ten days." He turned to Jim. "No means of payment?"

"No. Wait—" said Jim. "This stomach-ache of yours. It might be an ulcer. Does it go away between meals?"

"As a matter of fact, it does. Ulcer?"

"High-strung people working under nervous tension get them back where I come from."

"People?" inquired Carolinus suspiciously. "Or dragons?"

"There aren't any dragons where I come from."

"All right, all right, I believe you," said Carolinus, testily. "You don't have to stretch the truth like that. How do you exorcize them?"

"Milk," said Jim. "A glass every hour for a month or two."

"Milk," said Carolinus. He held out his hand to the open air and received a small tankard of it. He drank it off, making a face. After a moment, the face relaxed into a smile.

"By the Powers!" he said. "By the Powers!" He turned to Jim, beaming. "Congratulations, Gorbash, I'm beginning to believe you about that college business after all. The bovine nature of the milk quite smothers the ulcer-demon. Consider me paid."

"Oh, fine. I'll go get Angie and you can hypnotize—"

"What?" cried Carolinus. "Teach your grandmother to suck eggs. Hypnotize! Ha! And what about the First Law of Magic, eh?"

"The what?" said Jim.

"The First Law—the First Law—didn't they teach you anything in that college? Forgotten it already, I see. Oh, this younger generation! The First Law: *for every use of the Art and Science, there is required a corresponding price.* Why do I live by my fees instead of by conjurations? Why does a magic potion have a bad taste? Why did this Hanson-amateur of yours get you all into so much trouble?"

"I don't know," said Jim. "Why?"

"No credit! No credit!" barked Carolinus, flinging his skinny arms wide. "Why, I wouldn't have tried what he did without ten years credit with the auditing department, and *I* am a Master of the Arts. As it was, he couldn't get anything more than your spirit back, after sending the maiden complete. And the fabric of Chance and History is all warped and ready to spring back and cause all kinds of trouble. We'll have to give a little, take a little—"

"GORBASH!" A loud thud outside competed with the dragon-bellow.

"And here we go," said Carolinus dourly. "It's already starting." He led the way outside. Sitting on the greensward just beyond the flower beds was an enormous old dragon Jim recognized as the great-uncle of the body he was in—Smrgol.

"Greetings, Mage!" boomed the old dragon, dropping his head to the ground in salute. "You may not remember me. Name's Smrgol—you remember the business about that ogre I fought at Gormely Keep? I see my grandnephew got to you all right."

"Ah, Smrgol—I remember," said Carolinus. "That was a good job you did."

"He had a habit of dropping his club head after a swing," said Smrgol. "I noticed it along about the fourth hour of battle and the next time he tried it, went in over his guard. Tore up the biceps of his right arm. Then—"

"I remember," Carolinus said. "So this is your nephew."

"Grandnephew," corrected Smrgol. "Little thick-headed and all that," he added apologetically, "but my own flesh and blood, you know."

"You may notice some slight improvement in him," said Carolinus, dryly.

"I hope so," said Smrgol, brightening. "Any change, a change for the better, you know. But I've bad news, Mage. You know that inchworm of an Anark?"

"The one that found the maiden in the first place?"

"That's right. Well, he's stolen her again and run off."

"*What?*" cried Jim.

He had forgotten the capabilities of a dragon's voice. Carolinus tottered, the flowers and grass lay flat, and even Smrgol winced.

"My boy," said the old dragon reproachfully. "How many times must I tell you not to shout. I said, Anark stole the george."

"He means Angie!" cried Jim desperately to Carolinus.

"I know," said Carolinus, with his hands over his ears.

"You're sneezing again," said Smrgol, proudly. He turned to Carolinus. "You wouldn't believe it. A dragon hasn't sneezed in a hundred and ninety years. This boy did it the first moment he set eyes on the george. The others couldn't believe it. Sign of brains, I said. Busy brains make the nose itch. Our side of the family—"

"*Angie!*"

"See there? All right now, boy, you've shown us you can do it. Let's get down to business. How much to locate Anark and the george, Mage?"

They dickered like rug-pedlars for several minutes, finally settling on a price of four pounds of gold, one of silver, and a flawed emerald. Carolinus got a small vial of water from the Tinkling Spring and searched among the grass until he found a small sandy open spot. He bent over it and the two dragons sat down to watch.

"Quiet now," he warned. "I'm going to try a watch-beetle. Don't alarm it."

Jim held his breath. Carolinus tilted the vial in his hand and the crystal water fell in three drops— *Tink! Tink!* And again—*Tink!* The sand darkened with the moisture and began to work as if something was digging from below. A hole widened, black insect legs busily in action flickered, and an odd-looking beetle popped itself halfway out of the hole. Its forelimbs waved in the air and a little squeaky voice, like a cracked phonograph record repeating itself far away over a bad telephone connection, came to Jim's ears.

"Gone to the Loathly Tower! Gone to the Loathly Tower! Gone to the Loathly Tower!"

It popped back out of sight. Carolinus straightened up and Jim breathed again.

"The Loathly Tower!" said Smrgol. "Isn't that that ruined tower to the west, in the fens, Mage? Why, that's the place that loosed the blight on the mere-dragons five hundred years ago."

"It's a place of old magic," said Carolinus, grimly. "These places are like ancient sores on the land, scabbed over for a while but always breaking out with new evil when—the twisting of the Fabric by these two must have done it. The evilness there has drawn the evil in Anark to it—lesser to greater, according to the laws of nature. I'll meet you two there. Now, I must go set other forces in motion."

He began to twirl about. His speed increased rapidly until he was nothing but a blur. Then suddenly, he faded away like smoke; and was gone, leaving Jim staring at the spot where he had been.

A poke in the side brought Jim back to the ordinary world.

"Wake up, boy. Don't dally!" the voice of Smrgol bellowed in his ear. "We got flying to do. Come on!"

II

The old dragon's spirit was considerably younger than his body. It turned out to be a four hour flight to the fens on the west seacoast. For the first hour or so Smrgol flew along energetically enough, meanwhile tracing out the genealogy of the mere-dragons and their relationship to himself and Gorbash; but gradually his steady flow of chatter dwindled and became intermittent. He tried to joke about his long-gone battle with the Ogre of Gormely Keep, but even this was too much and he fell silent with labored breath and straining wings. After a short but stubborn argument, Jim got him to admit that he would perhaps be better off taking a short breather and then coming on a little later. Smrgol let out a deep gasping sigh and dropped away from Jim in weary spirals. Jim saw him glide to an exhausted landing amongst the purple gorse of the moors below and lie there, sprawled out.

Jim continued on alone. A couple of hours later the moors dropped down a long land-slope to the green country of the fenland. Jim soared out over its spongy, grass-thick earth, broken into causeways and islands by the blue water, which in shallow bays and inlets was itself thick-choked with reeds and tall marsh grass. Flocks of water fowl rose here and there like eddying smoke from the glassy surface of one mere and drifted over to settle on another a few hundred yards away. Their cries came faintly to his dragon-sensitive ears and a line of heavy clouds was piling up against the sunset in the west.

He looked for some sign of the Loathly Tower, but the fenland stretched away to a faint blue line that was probably the sea, without showing sign of anything not built by nature. Jim was beginning to wonder uneasily if he had not gotten himself lost when his eye was suddenly caught by the sight of a dragon-shape nosing at something on one of the little islands amongst the meres.

Anark! he thought. And Angie!

He did not wait to see more. He nosed over and went into a dive like a jet fighter, sights locked on Target Dragon.

It was a good move. Unfortunately Gorbash-Jim, having about the weight and wingspread of a small flivver airplane, made a comparable amount of noise when he was in a dive, assuming the plane's motor to be shut off. Moreover, the dragon on the ground had evidently had experience with the meaning of such a sound; for, without even looking, he went tumbling head over tail out of the way just as Jim slammed into the spot where, a second before, he had been.

The other dragon rolled over onto his feet, sat up, took one look at Jim, and began to wail.

"It's not fair! It's not fair!" he cried in a (for a dragon) remarkably high-pitched voice. "Just because you're bigger than I am. And I'm all horned up. It's the first good one I've been able to kill in months and you don't need it, not at all. You're big and fat and I'm so weak and thin and hungry—"

Jim blinked and stared. What he had thought to be Angie, lying in the grass, now revealed itself to be an old and rather stringy-looking cow, badly bitten up and with a broken neck.

"It's just my luck!" the other dragon was weeping. He was less than three-quarters Jim's size and so emaciated he appeared on the verge of collapse. "Everytime I get something good, somebody takes it away. All I ever get to eat is fish—"

"Hold on," said Jim.

"Fish, fish, fish. Cold, nasty fi—"

"Hold on, I say! SHUT UP!" bellowed Jim, in Gorbash's best voice.

The other dragon stopped his wailing as suddenly as if his switch had been shut off.

"Yes, sir," he said, timidly.

"What's the matter? I'm not going to take this from you."

The other dragon tittered uncertainly.

"I'm not," said Jim. "It's your cow. All yours."

"He-he-he!" said the other dragon. "You certainly are a card, your honor."

"Blast it, I'm serious!" cried Jim. "What's your name, anyway?"

"Oh, well—" the other squirmed. "Oh well, you know—"

"What's your name?"

"Secoh, your worship!" yelped the dragon, frightenedly. "Just Secoh. Nobody important. Just a little, unimportant mere-dragon, your highness, that's all I am. Really!"

"All right, Secoh, dig in. All I want is some directions."

"Well—if your worship really doesn't . . ." Secoh had been sidling forward in fawning fashion. "If you'll excuse my table manners, sir. I'm just a mere-dragon—" and he tore into the meat before him in sudden, terrified, starving fashion.

Jim watched. Unexpectedly, his long tongue flickered out to lick his chops. His belly rumbled. He was astounded at himself. Raw meat? Off a dead animal—flesh, bones, hide and all? He took a firm grip on his appetites.

"Er, Secoh," he said. "I'm a stranger around these parts. I suppose you know the territory.... Say, how does that cow taste, anyway?"

"Oh, terrruble—mumpf—" replied Secoh, with his mouth full. "Stringy—old. Good enough for a mere-dragon like myself, but not—"

"Well, about these directions—"

"Yes, your highness?"

"I think ... you know it's your cow ..."

"That's what your honor said," replied Secoh, cautiously.

"But I just wonder ... you know I've never tasted a cow like that."

Secoh muttered something despairingly under his breath.

"What?" said Jim.

"I said," said Secoh, resignedly, "wouldn't your worship like to t-taste it—"

"Not if you're going to cry about it," said Jim.

"I bit my tongue."

"Well, in that case ..." Jim walked up and sank his teeth in the shoulder of the carcass. Rich juices trickled enticingly over his tongue....

Some little time later he and Secoh sat back polishing bones with the rough uppers of their tongues which were as abrasive as steel files.

"Did you get enough to eat, Secoh?" asked Jim.

"More than enough, sir," replied the mere-dragon, staring at the white skeleton with a wild and famished eye. "Although, if your exaltedness doesn't mind, I've a weakness for marrow...." He picked up a thighbone and began to crunch it like a stick of candy.

"Now," said Jim. "About this Loathly Tower. Where is it?"

"The wh-what?" stammered Secoh, dropping the thighbone.

"The Loathly Tower. It's in the fens. You know of it, don't you?"

"Oh, sir! Yes, sir. But you wouldn't want to go there, sir! Not that I'm presuming to give your lordship advice—" cried Secoh, in a suddenly high and terrified voice.

"No, no," soothed Jim. "What are you so upset about?"

"Well—of course I'm only a timid little mere-dragon. But it's a terrible place, the Loathly Tower, your worship, sir."

"How? Terrible?"

"Well—well, it just is." Secoh cast an unhappy look around him. "It's what spoiled all of us, you know, five hundred years ago. We used to be like other dragons—oh, not so big and handsome as you, sir. Then, after that, they say it was the Good got the upper hand and the Evil in the Tower was vanquished and the Tower itself ruined. But it didn't help us mere-dragons any, and I wouldn't go there if I was your worship, I really wouldn't."

"But what's so bad? What sort of thing is it?"

"Well, I wouldn't say there was any real *thing* there. Nothing your worship could put a claw on. It's just strange things go to it and strange things come out of it; and lately . . ."

"Lately what?"

"Nothing—nothing, really, your excellency!" cried Secoh. "Your illustriousness shouldn't catch a worthless little mere-dragon up like that. I only meant, lately the Tower's seemed more fearful than ever. That's all."

"Probably your imagination," said Jim, shortly. "Anyway, where is it?"

"You have to go north about five miles." While they had eaten and talked, the sunset had died. It was almost dark now; and Jim had to strain his eyes through the gloom to see the mere-dragon's foreclaw, pointing away across the mere. "To the Great Causeway. It's a wide lane of solid ground running east and west through the fens. You follow it west to the Tower. The Tower stands on a rock overlooking the sea-edge."

"Five miles . . ." said Jim. He considered the soft grass on which he lay. His armored body seemed undisturbed by the temperature, whatever it was. "I might as well get some sleep. See you in the morning, Secoh." He obeyed a sudden, bird-like instinct and tucked his ferocious head and long neck back under one wing.

"Whatever your excellency desires . . ." the mere-dragon's muffled voice came distantly to his ear. "Your excellency has only to call and I'll be immediately available. . . ."

The words faded out on Jim's ear, as he sank into sleep like a heavy stone into deep, dark waters.

When he opened his eyes, the sun was up. He sat up himself, yawned, and blinked.

Secoh was gone. So were the leftover bones.

"Blast!" said Jim. But the morning was too nice for annoyance. He smiled at his mental picture of Secoh carefully gathering the bones in fearful silence, and sneaking them away.

The smile did not last long. When he tried to take off in a northerly direction, as determined by reference to the rising sun, he found he had charley horses in both the huge wing-muscles that swelled out under the armor behind his shoulders. The result of course, of yesterday's heavy exercise. Grumbling, he was forced to proceed on foot; and four hours later, very hot, muddy and wet, he pulled his weary body up onto the broad east-and-west-stretching strip of land which must, of neces-

sity, be the Great Causeway. It ran straight as a
Roman road through the meres, several feet higher
than the rest of the fenland, and was solid enough
to support good-sized trees. Jim collapsed in the
shade of one with a heartfelt sigh.

He awoke to the sound of someone singing. He
blinked and lifted his head. Whatever the earlier
verses of the song had been, Jim had missed them;
but the approaching baritone voice now caroled
the words of the chorus merrily and clearly to his
ear:

> "A right good sword, a constant mind,
> A trusty spear and true!
> The dragons of the mere shall find
> What Nevile-Smythe can do!"

The tune and words were vaguely familiar. Jim
sat up for a better look and a knight in full armor
rode into view on a large white horse through the
trees. Then everything happened at once. The knight
saw him, the visor of his armor came down with a
clang, his long spear seemed to jump into his mailed
hand and the horse under him leaped into a gal-
lop, heading for Jim. Gorbash's reflexes took over.
They hurled Jim straight up into the air, where his
punished wing muscles cracked and faltered. He
was just able to manage enough of a fluttering flop
to throw himself into the upper branches of a
small tree nearby.

The knight skidded his horse to a stop below
and looked up through the spring-budded branches.
He tilted his visor back to reveal a piercing pair of
blue eyes, a rather hawk-like nose and a jutting
generous chin, all assembled into a clean-shaven
young-man's face. He looked eagerly up at Jim.

"Come down," he said.

"No thanks," said Jim, hanging firmly to the

tree. There was a slight pause as they both digested the situation.

"Dashed caitiff mere-dragon!" said the knight finally, with annoyance.

"I'm not a mere-dragon," said Jim.

"Oh, don't talk rot!" said the knight.

"I'm not," repeated Jim. He thought a minute. "I'll bet you can't guess who I really am."

The knight did not seem interested in guessing who Jim really was. He stood up in his stirrups and probed through the branches with his spear. The point did not quite reach Jim.

"Damn!" Disappointedly, he lowered the spear and became thoughtful. "I can climb the dashed tree," he muttered to himself. "But then what if he flies down and I have to fight him unhorsed, eh?"

"Look," called Jim, peering down—the knight looked up eagerly—"if you'll listen to what I've to say, first."

The knight considered.

"Fair enough," he said, finally. "No pleas for mercy, now!"

"No, no," said Jim.

"Because I shan't grant them, dammit! It's not in my vows. Widows and orphans and honorable enemies on the field of battle. But not dragons."

"No. I just want to convince you who I really am."

"I don't give a blasted farthing who you really are."

"You will," said Jim. "Because I'm not really a dragon at all. I've just been—uh—enchanted into a dragon."

The man on the ground looked skeptical.

"Really," said Jim, slipping a little in the tree. "You know S. Carolinus, the magician? I'm as human as you are."

"Heard of him," grunted the knight. "You'll say *he* put you under?"

"No, he's the one who's going to change me back—as soon as I can find the lady I'm—er—betrothed to. A real dragon ran off with her. I'm after him. Look at me. Do I look like one of these scrawny mere-dragons?"

"Hmm," said the knight. He rubbed his hooked nose thoughtfully.

"Carolinus found she's at the Loathly Tower. I'm on my way there."

The knight stared.

"The Loathly Tower?" he echoed.

"Exactly," said Jim, firmly. "And now you know, your honor as knight and gentleman demands you don't hamper my rescue efforts."

The knight continued to think it over for a long moment or two. He was evidently not the sort to be rushed into things.

"How do I know you're telling the truth?" he said at last.

"Hold your sword up. I'll swear on the cross of its hilt."

"But if you're a dragon, what's the good in that? Dragons don't have souls, dammit!"

"No," said Jim, "but a Christian gentleman has; and if I'm a Christian gentleman, I wouldn't dare forswear myself like that, would I?"

The knight struggled visibly with this logic for several seconds. Finally, he gave up.

"Oh, well . . ." He held up his sword by the point and let Jim swear on it. Then he put the sword back in its sheath as Jim descended. "Well," he said, still a little doubtfully, "I suppose, under the circumstances, we ought to introduce ourselves. You know my arms?"

Jim looked at the shield which the other swung around for his inspection. It showed a wide X of silver—like a cross lying over sideways—on a red background and above some sort of black animal in profile which seemed to be lying down between the X's bottom legs.

"The gules, a saltire argent, of course," went on the knight, "are the Nevile of Raby arms. My father, as a cadet of the house, differenced with a hart lodged sable—you see it there at the bottom. Naturally, as his heir, I carry the family arms."

"Nevile-Smythe," said Jim, remembering the name from the song.

"Sir Reginald, knight bachelor. And you, sir?"

"Why, uh . . ." Jim clutched frantically at what he knew of heraldry. "I bear—in my proper body, that is—"

"Quite."

"A . . . gules, a typewriter argent, on a desk sable. Eckert, Sir James—uh—knight bachelor. Baron of—er—Riveroak."

Nevile-Smythe was knitting his brows.

"Typewriter . . ." he was muttering, "typewriter . . ."

"A local beast, rather like a griffin," said Jim, hastily. "We have a lot of them in Riveroak—that's in America, a land over the sea to the west. You may not have heard of it."

"Can't say that I have. Was it there you were enchanted into this dragon-shape?"

"Well, yes and no. I was transported to this land by magic as was the—uh—lady Angela. When I woke here I was bedragoned."

"Were you?" Sir Reginald's blue eyes bulged a little in amazement. "Angela—fair name, that! Like to meet her. Perhaps after we get this muddle cleared up, we might have a bit of a set-to on behalf of our respective ladies."

Jim gulped slightly.

"Oh, you've got one, too?"

"Absolutely. And she's tremendous. The Lady Elinor—" The knight turned about in his saddle and began to fumble about his equipment. Jim, on reaching the ground, had at once started out along the causeway in the direction of the Tower, so that the knight happened to be pacing alongside him on horseback when he suddenly went into these evolutions. It seemed to bother his charger not at all. "Got her favor here someplace—half a moment—"

"Why don't you just tell me what it's like?" said Jim, sympathetically.

"Oh, well," said Nevile-Smythe, giving up his search, "it's a kerchief, you know. Monogrammed. E. d'C. She's a deChauncy. It's rather too bad, though. I'd have liked to show it to you since we're going to the Loathly Tower together."

"We are?" said Jim, startled. "But—I mean, it's my job. I didn't think you'd want—"

"Lord, yes," said Nevile-Smythe, looking somewhat startled himself. "A gentleman of coat-armor like myself—and an outrage like this taking place locally. I'm no knight-errant, dash it, but I *do* have a decent sense of responsibility."

"I mean—I just meant—" stumbled Jim. "What if something happened to you? What would the Lady Elinor say?"

"Why, what could she say?" replied Nevile-Smythe in plain astonishment. "No one but an utter rotter dodges his plain duty. Besides, there may be a chance here for me to gain a little worship. Elinor's keen on that. She wants me to come home safe."

Jim blinked.

"I don't get it," he said.

"Beg pardon?"

Jim explained his confusion.

"Why, how do you people do things overseas?"

said Nevile-Smythe. "After we're married and I have lands of my own, I'll be expected to raise a company and march out at my lord's call. If I've no name as a knight, I'll be able to raise nothing but bumpkins and clodpoles who'll desert at the first sight of steel. On the other hand, if I've a name, I'll have good men coming to serve under my banner; because, you see, they know I'll take good care of them; and by the same token they'll take good care of me—I say, isn't it getting dark rather suddenly?"

Jim glanced at the sky. It was indeed—almost the dimness of twilight although it could, by rights, be no more than early afternoon yet. Glancing ahead up the Causeway, he became aware of a further phenomenon. A line seemed to be cutting across the trees and grass and even extending out over the waters of the meres on both sides. Moreover, it seemed to be moving toward them as if some heavy, invisible fluid was slowly flooding out over the low country of the fenland.

"Why—" he began. A voice wailed suddenly from his left to interrupt him.

"No! No! Turn back, your worship. Turn back! It's death in there!"

They turned their heads sharply. Secoh, the mere-dragon, sat perched on a half-drowned tussock about forty feet out in the mere.

"Come here, Secoh!" called Jim.

"No! No!" The invisible line was almost to the tussock. Secoh lifted heavily into the air and flapped off, crying. "Now it's loose! It's broken loose again. And we're all lost . . . lost . . . lost . . ."

His voice wailed away and was lost in the distance. Jim and Nevile-Smythe looked at each other.

"Now, that's one of our local dragons for you!" said the knight disgustedly. "How can a gentleman of coat armor gain honor by slaying a beast like that? The worst of it is when someone from the Midlands compliments you on being a dragon-slayer and you have to explain—"

At that moment either they both stepped over the line, or the line moved past them—Jim was never sure which; and they both stopped, as by one common, instinctive impulse. Looking at Sir Reginald, Jim could see under the visor how the knight's face had gone pale.

"In manus tuas Domine," said Nevile-Smythe, crossing himself.

About and around them, the serest gray of winter light lay on the fens. The waters of the meres lay thick and oily, still between the shores of dull green grass. A small, cold breeze wandered through the tops of the reeds and they rattled together with a dry and distant sound like old bones cast out into a forgotten courtyard for the wind to play with. The trees stood helpless and still, their new, small leaves now pinched and faded like children aged before their time while all about and over all the heaviness of dead hope and bleak despair lay on all living things.

"Sir James," said the knight, in an odd tone and accents such as Jim had not heard him use before, "wot well that we have this day set our hands to no small task. Wherefore I pray thee that we should push forward, come what may, for my heart faileth and I think me that it may well hap that I return not, ne no man know mine end."

Having said this, he immediately reverted to his usual cheerful self and swung down out of his saddle. "Clarivaux won't go another inch, dash it!" he said. "I shall have to lead him—by the bye, did you know that mere-dragon?"

Jim fell into step beside him and they went on again, but a little more slowly, for everything seemed an extra effort under this darkening sky.

"I talked to him yesterday," said Jim. "He's not a bad sort of dragon."

"Oh, I've nothing against the beasts, myself. But one slays them when one finds them, you know."

"An old dragon—in fact he's the granduncle of this body I'm in," said Jim, "thinks that dragons and humans really ought to get together. Be friends, you know."

"Extraordinary thought!" said Nevile-Smythe, staring at Jim in astonishment.

"Well, actually," said Jim, "why not?"

"Well, I don't know. It just seems like it wouldn't do."

"He says men and dragons might find common foes to fight together."

"Oh, that's where he's wrong, though. You couldn't trust dragons to stick by you in a bicker. And what if your enemy had dragons of his own? They wouldn't fight each other. No. No."

They fell silent. They had moved away from the grass onto flat sandy soil. There was a sterile, flinty hardness to it. It crunched under the hooves of Clarivaux, at once unyielding and treacherous.

"Getting darker, isn't it?" said Jim, finally.

The light was, in fact, now down to a grayish twilight, through which it was impossible to see more than a dozen feet. And it was dwindling as they watched. They had halted and stood facing each other. The light fled steadily, and faster. The dimness became blacker, and blacker—until finally the last vestige of illumination was lost and blackness, total and complete, overwhelmed them. Jim felt a gauntleted hand touch one of his forelimbs.

"Let's hold together," said the voice of the knight. "Then whatever comes upon us, must come upon us all at once."

"Right," said Jim. But the word sounded cold and dead in his throat.

They stood, in silence and in lightlessness, waiting for they did not know what. And the blankness about them pressed further in on them, now that it had isolated them, nibbling at the very edges of their minds. Out of the nothingness came nothing material, but from within them crept up one by one, like blind white slugs from some bottomless pit, all their inner doubts and fears and unknown weaknesses, all the things of which they had been ashamed and which they had tucked away to forget, all the maggots of their souls.

Jim found himself slowly, stealthily beginning to withdraw his forelimb from under the knight's touch. He no longer trusted Nevile-Smythe—for the evil that must be in the man because of the evil he knew to be in himself. He would move away . . . off into the darkness alone . . .

"Look!" Nevile-Smythe's voice cried suddenly to him, distant and eerie, as if from someone already a long way off. "Look back the way we came."

Jim turned about. Far off in the darkness, there was a distant glimmer of light. It rolled toward them, growing as it came. They felt its power against the power of lightlessness that threatened to overwhelm them; and the horse Clarivaux stirred unseen beside them, stamped his hooves on the hard sand, and whinnied.

"This way!" called Jim.

"This way!" shouted Nevile-Smythe.

The light shot up suddenly in height. Like a great rod it advanced toward them and the darkness was rolling back, graying, disappearing. They heard a sound of feet close, and a sound of breathing, and then—

It was daylight again.

And S. Carolinus stood before them in tall hat and robes figured with strange images and signs. In his hand upright before him—as if it was blade and buckler, spear and armor all in one—he held a tall carven staff of wood.

"By the Powers!" he said. "I was in time. Look there!"

He lifted the staff and drove it point down into the soil. It went in and stood erect like some denuded tree. His long arm pointed past them and they turned around.

The darkness was gone. The fens lay revealed far and wide, stretching back a long way, and up ahead, meeting the thin dark line of the sea. The Causeway had risen until they now stood twenty feet above the mere-waters. Ahead to the west, the sky was ablaze with sunset. It lighted up all the fens and the end of the Causeway leading onto a long and bloody-looking hill, whereon—touched by that same dying light—there loomed above and over all, amongst great tumbled boulders, the ruined, dark and shattered shell of a Tower as black as jet.

III

"—why didn't you wake us earlier, then?" asked Jim.

It was the morning after. They had slept the night within the small circle of protection afforded by Carolinus' staff. They were sitting up now and rubbing their eyes in the light of a sun that had certainly been above the horizon a good two hours.

"Because," said Carolinus. He was sipping at some more milk and he stopped to make a face of distaste. "Because we had to wait for them to catch up with us."

"Who? Catch up?" asked Jim.

"If I knew *who*," snapped Carolinus, handing his empty milk tankard back to emptier air, "I would have said *who*. All I know is that the present pat-

tern of Chance and History implies that two more
will join our party. The same pattern implied the
presence of this knight and—oh, so that's who they
are."

Jim turned around to follow the magician's gaze.
To his surprise, two dragon shapes were emerging
from a clump of brush behind them.

"Secoh!" cried Jim. "And—Smrgol! Why—" His
voice wavered and died. The old dragon, he suddenly noticed, was limping and one wing hung a
little loosely, half-drooping from its shoulder. Also,
the eyelid on the same side as the loose wing and
stiff leg was sagging more or less at half-mast.
"Why, what happened?"

"Oh, a bit stiff from yesterday," huffed Smrgol,
bluffly. "Probably pass off in a day or two."

"Stiff nothing!" said Jim, touched in spite of
himself. "You've had a stroke."

"Stroke of bad luck, I'd say," replied Smrgol,
cheerfully, trying to wink his bad eye and not
succeeding very well. "No, boy, it's nothing. Look
who I've brought along."

"I—I wasn't too keen on coming," said Secoh,
shyly, to Jim. "But your granduncle can be pretty
persuasive, your wo—you know."

"That's right!" boomed Smrgol. "Don't you go
calling anybody your worship. Never heard of such
stuff!" He turned to Jim. "And letting a george go
in where he didn't dare go himself! Boy, I said to
him, don't give me this *only a mere-dragon* and *just
a mere-dragon*. Mere's got nothing to do with what
kind of dragon you are. What kind of a world
would it be if we were all like that?" Smrgol mimicked (as well as his dragon-basso would let him)
someone talking in a high, simpering voice. "Oh,
I'm just a plowland-and-pasture dragon—you'll
have to excuse me, I'm only a halfway-up-the-hill
dragon—*Boy!*" bellowed Smrgol, "I said, you're a

dragon! Remember that. And a dragon acts like a dragon or he doesn't act at all!"

"Hear! Hear!" said Nevile-Smythe, carried away by enthusiasm.

"Hear that, boy? Even the george here knows that. Don't believe I've met you, george," he added, turning to the knight.

"Nevile-Smythe, Sir Reginald. Knight bachelor."

"Smrgol. Dragon."

"Smrgol? You aren't the—but you couldn't be. Over a hundred years ago."

"The dragon who slew the Ogre of Gormely Keep? That's who I am, boy—george, I mean."

"By Jove! Always thought it was a legend, only."

"Legend? Not on your honor, george! I'm old— even for a dragon, but there was a time—well, well, we won't go into that. I've something more important to talk to you about. I've been doing a lot of thinking the last decade or so about us dragons and you georges getting together. Actually, we're really a lot alike—"

"If you don't mind, Smrgol," cut in Carolinus, snappishly, "we aren't out here to hold a parlement. It'll be noon in—when will it be noon, you?"

"Four hours, thirty-seven minutes, twelve seconds at the sound of the gong," replied the invisible bass voice. There was a momentary pause, and then a single mellow, chimed note. "Chime, I mean," the voice corrected itself.

"Oh, go back to bed!" cried Carolinus furiously.

"I've been up for hours," protested the voice, indignantly.

Carolinus ignored it, herding the party together and starting them off for the Tower. The knight fell in beside Smrgol.

"About this business of men and dragons getting together," said Nevile-Smythe. "Confess I wasn't much impressed until I heard your name. D'you think it's possible?"

"Got to make a start sometime, george." Smrgol rumbled on. Jim, who had moved up to the head of the column to walk beside Carolinus, spoke to the magician.

"What lives in the Tower?"

Carolinus jerked his fierce old bearded face around to look at him.

"What's *living* there?" he snapped. "I don't know. We'll find out soon enough. What *is* there—neither alive nor dead, just in existence at the spot—is the manifestation of pure evil."

"But how can we do anything against that?"

"We can't. We can only contain it. Just as you—if you're essentially a good person—contain the potentialities for evil in yourself, by killing its creatures, your evil impulses and actions."

"Oh?" said Jim.

"Certainly. And since evil opposes good in like manner, its creatures, the ones in the Tower, will try to destroy us."

Jim felt a cold lump in his throat. He swallowed.

"Destroy us?"

"Why no, they'll probably just invite us to tea—" The sarcasm in the old magician's voice broke off suddenly with the voice itself. They had just stepped through a low screen of bushes and instinctively checked to a halt.

Lying on the ground before them was what once had been a man in full armor. Jim heard the sucking intake of breath from Nevile-Smythe behind him.

"A most foul death," said the knight softly, "most foul . . ." He came forward and dropped clumsily to his armored knees, joining his gauntleted hands in prayer. The dragons were silent. Carolinus poked with his staff at a wide trail of slime that led around and over the body and back toward the Tower. It was the sort of trail a garden slug might have left—if this particular garden slug had been two or more feet wide where it touched the ground.

"A Worm," said Carolinus. "But Worms are mindless. No Worm killed him in such cruel fashion." He lifted his head to the old dragon.

"I didn't say it, Mage," rumbled Smrgol, uneasily.

"Best none of us say it until we know for certain. Come on." Carolinus took up the lead and led them forward again.

They had come up off the Causeway onto the barren plain that sloped up into a hill in which stood the Tower. They could see the wide fens and the tide flats coming to meet them in the arms of a small bay—and beyond that the sea, stretching misty to the horizon.

The sky above was blue and clear. No breeze stirred; but, as they looked at the Tower and the hill that held it, it seemed that the azure above had taken on a metallic cast. The air had a quivering unnaturalness like an atmosphere dancing to heat waves, though the day was chill; and there came on Jim's ears, from where he did not know, a high-pitched dizzy singing like that which accompanies delirium, or high fever.

The Tower itself was distorted by these things. So that although to Jim it seemed only the ancient, ruined shell of a building, yet, between one heartbeat and the next, it seemed to change. Almost, but not quite, he caught glimpses of it unbroken and alive and thronged about with fantastic, half-seen figures. His heart beat stronger with the delusion; and its beating shook the scene before him, all the hill and Tower, going in and out of focus, in and out, *in* and *out* . . .

. . . And there was Angie, in the Tower's doorway, calling him . . .

"*Stop!*" shouted Carolinus. His voice echoed like a clap of thunder in Jim's ears; and Jim awoke to his senses, to find himself straining against the barrier of Carolinus' staff, that barred his way to the Tower like a rod of iron. "By the Powers!" said the old magician, softly and fiercely. "Will you fall into the first trap set for you?"

"Trap?" echoed Jim, bewilderedly. But he had no time to go further, for at that moment there rose from among the giant boulders at the Tower's base the heavy, wicked head of a dragon as large as Smrgol.

The thunderous bellow of the old dragon beside Jim split the unnatural air.

"*Anark!* Traitor—thief—inchworm! Come down here!"

Booming dragon-laughter rolled back an answer.

"Tell us about Gormely Keep, old bag of bones! Ancient mudpuppy, fat lizard, scare us with words!"

Smrgol lurched forward; and again Carolinus' staff was extended to bar the way.

"Patience," said the magician. But with one wrenching effort, the old dragon had himself under control. He turned, panting, to Carolinus.

"What's hidden, Mage?" he demanded.

"We'll see." Grimly, Carolinus brought his staff, endwise, three times down upon the earth. With each blow the whole hill seemed to shake and shudder.

Up among the rocks, one particularly large boulder tottered and rolled aside. Jim caught his breath and Secoh cried out, suddenly.

In the gap that the boulder revealed, a thick, slug-like head was lifting from the ground. It reared, yellow-brown in the sunlight, its two sets of horns searching and revealing a light external shell, a platelet with a merest hint of spire. It lowered its head and slowly, inexorably, began to flow downhill toward them, leaving its glistening trail behind it.

"Now—" said the knight. But Carolinus shook his head. He struck at the ground again.

"Come forth!" he cried, his thin, old voice piping on the quivering air. "By the Powers! Come forth!"

And then they saw it.

From behind the great barricade of boulders, slowly, there reared first a bald and glistening dome of hairless skin. Slowly this rose, revealing two perfectly round eyes below which they saw, as the whole came up, no proper nose, but two air-slits side by side as if the whole of the bare, enormous skull was covered with a simple sheet of thick skin. And rising still further, this unnatural head, as big around as a beach ball, showed itself to possess a wide and idiot-grinning mouth, entirely lipless and revealing two jagged, matching rows of yellow teeth.

Now, with a clumsy, studied motion, the whole creature rose to its feet and stood knee-deep in the boulders and towering above them. It was man-like in shape, but clearly nothing ever spawned by the human race. A good twelve feet high it stood, a rough patchwork kilt of untanned hides wrapped around its thick waist—but this was not the extent of its differences from the race of Man. It had, to begin with, no neck at all. That obscene beachball of a hairless, near-featureless head balanced like an apple on thick, square shoulders of gray, coarse-looking skin. Its torso was one straight trunk, from which its arms and legs sprouted with a disproportionate thickness and roundness, like sections of pipe. Its knees were hidden by its kilt and its further legs by the rocks; but the elbows of its oversize arms had unnatural hinges to them, almost as if they had been doubled, and the lower arms were almost as large as the upper and near-wristless, while the hands themselves were awkward, thick-fingered parodies of the human extremity, with only three digits, of which one was a single, opposed thumb.

The right hand held a club, bound with rusty metal, that surely not even such a monster should have been able to lift. Yet one grotesque hand carried it lightly, as lightly as Carolinus had carried his staff. The monster opened its mouth.

"He!" it went. "He! He!"

The sound was fantastic. It was a bass titter, if such a thing could be imagined. Though the tone of it was as low as the lowest note of a good operatic basso, it clearly came from the creature's upper throat and head. Nor was there any real humor in it. It was an utterance with a nervous, habitual air about it, like a man clearing his throat. Having sounded, it fell silent, watching the advance of the great slug with its round, light blue eyes.

Smrgol exhaled slowly.

"Yes," he rumbled, almost sadly, almost as if to himself. "What I was afraid of. An ogre."

In the silence that followed, Nevile-Smythe got down from his horse and began to tighten the girths of its saddle.

"So, so, Clarivaux," he crooned to the trembling horse. "So ho, boy."

The rest of them were looking all at Carolinus. The magician leaned on his staff, seeming very old indeed, with the deep lines carven in the ancient skin of his face. He had been watching the ogre, but now he turned back to Jim and the other two dragons.

"I had hoped all along," he said, "that it needn't come to this. However," he crackled sourly, and waved his hand at the approaching Worm, the

silent Anark and the watching ogre, "as you see
... The world goes never the way we want it by
itself, but must be haltered and led." He winced,
produced his flask and cup, and took a drink of
milk. Putting the utensils back, he looked over at
Nevile-Smythe, who was now checking his weapons. "I'd suggest, Knight, that you take the Worm.
It's a poor chance, but your best. I know you'd
prefer that renegade dragon, but the Worm is the
greater danger."

"Difficult to slay, I imagine?" queried the knight.

"It's vital organs are hidden deep inside it," said
Carolinus, "and being mindless, it will fight on
long after being mortally wounded. Cut off those
eye-stalks and blind it first, if you can—"

"Wait!" cried Jim, suddenly. He had been listening bewilderedly. Now the word seemed to jump
out of his mouth. "What're we going to do?"

"Do?" said Carolinus, looking at him. "Why, fight,
of course."

"But," stammered Jim, "wouldn't it be better to
go get some help? I mean—"

"Blast it, boy!" boomed Smrgol. "We can't wait
for that! Who knows what'll happen if we take
time for something like that? Hell's bell's, Gorbash,
lad, you got to fight your foes when you meet
them, not the next day, or the day after that."

"Quite right, Smrgol," said Carolinus, dryly.
"Gorbash, you don't understand this situation. Every time you retreat from something like this, it
gains and you lose. The next time the odds would
be even worse against us."

They were all looking at him. Jim felt the im-
pact of their curious glances. He did not know
what to say. He wanted to tell them that he was
not a fighter, that he did not know the first thing
to do in this sort of battle, that it was none of his
business anyway and that he would not be here at

all, if it were not for Angie. He was, in fact, quite humanly scared, and floundered desperately for some sort of strength to lean on.

"What—what am I supposed to do?" he said.

"Why, fight the ogre, boy! Fight the ogre!" thundered Smrgol—and the inhuman giant up on the slope, hearing him, shifted his gaze suddenly from the Worm to fasten it on Jim. "And I'll take on that louse of an Anark. The george here'll chop up the Worm, the Mage'll hold back the bad influences— and there we are."

"Fight the ogre . . ." If Jim had still been possessed of his ordinary two legs, they would have buckled underneath him. Luckily his dragon-body knew no such weakness. He looked at the overwhelming bulk of his expected opponent, contrasted the ogre with himself, the armored, ox-heavy body of the Worm with Nevile-Smythe, the deep-chested over-size Anark with the crippled old dragon beside him—and a cry of protest rose from the very depths of his being. "But we can't win!"

He turned furiously on Carolinus, who, however, looked at him calmly. In desperation he turned back to the only normal human he could find in the group.

"Nevile-Smythe," he said. "You don't need to do this."

"Lord, yes," replied the knight, busy with his equipment. "Worms, ogres—one fights them when one runs into them, you know." He considered his spear and put it aside. "Believe I'll face it on foot," he murmured to himself.

"Smrgol!" said Jim. "Don't you see—can't you understand? Anark is a lot younger than you. And you're not well—"

"Er . . ." said Secoh, hesitantly.

"Speak up, boy!" rumbled Smrgol.

"Well," stammered Secoh, "it's just . . . what I

mean is, I couldn't bring myself to fight that Worm
or that ogre—I really couldn't. I just sort of go to
pieces when I think of them getting close to me.
But I *could*—well, fight another dragon. It wouldn't
be quite so bad, if you know what I mean, if that
dragon up there breaks my neck—" He broke down
and stammered incoherently. "I know I sound aw-
fully silly—"

"Nonsense! Good lad!" bellowed Smrgol. "Glad
to have you. I—er—can't quite get into the air
myself at the moment—still a bit stiff. But if you
could fly over and work him down this way where
I can get a grip on him, we'll stretch him out for
the buzzards." And he dealt the mere-dragon a
tremendous thwack with his tail by way of con-
gratulation, almost knocking Secoh off his feet.

In desperation, Jim turned back to Carolinus.

"There is no retreat," said Carolinus, calmly,
before Jim could speak. "This is a game of chess
where if one piece withdraws, all fall. Hold back
the creatures, and I will hold back the forces—for
the creatures will finish me, if you go down, and
the forces will finish you if they get me."

"Now, look here, Gorbash!" shouted Smrgol in
Jim's ear. "That Worm's almost here. Let me tell
you something about how to fight ogres, based on
experience. You listening, boy?"

"Yes," said Jim, numbly.

"I know you've heard the other dragons calling
me an old windbag when I wasn't around. But I
have conquered an ogre—the only one in our race
to do it in the last eight hundred years—and they
haven't. So pay attention, if you want to win your
own fight."

Jim gulped.

"All right," he said.

"Now, the first thing to know," boomed Smrgol,

glancing at the Worm who was now less than fifty yards distant, "is about the bones in an ogre—"

"Never mind the details!" cried Jim. "What do I do?"

"In a minute," said Smrgol. "Don't get excited, boy. Now, about the bones in an ogre. The thing to remember is that they're big—matter of fact in the arms and legs, they're mainly bone. So there's no use trying to bite clear through, if you get a chance. What you try to do is get at the muscle—that's tough enough as it is—and hamstring. That's point one." He paused to look severely at Jim.

"Now, point two," he continued, "also connected with bones. Notice the elbows on that ogre. They aren't like a george's elbows. They're what you might call double-jointed. I mean, they have two joints where a george has just the one. Why? Simply because with the big bones they got to have and the muscle on them, they'd never be able to bend an arm more than halfway up before the bottom part'd bump the top if they had a george-type joint. Now, the point of all this is that when it swings that club, it can only swing in one way with that elbow. That's up and down. If it wants to swing it side to side, it's got to use its shoulder. Consequently if you can catch it with its club down and to one side of the body, you got an advantage; because it takes two motions to get it back up and in line again—instead of one, like a george."

"Yes, yes," said Jim, impatiently, watching the advance of the Worm.

"Don't get impatient, boy. Keep cool. Keep cool. Now, the knees don't have that kind of joint, so if you can knock it off its feet you got a real advantage. But don't try that, unless you're sure you can do it; because once it gets you pinned, you're a goner. The way to fight it is in-and-out—fast. Wait for a swing, dive in, tear him, get back out again. Got it?"

"Got it," said Jim, numbly.

"Good. Whatever you do, don't let it get a grip on you. Don't pay attention to what's happening to the rest of us, no matter what you hear or see. It's every one for himself. Concentrate on your own foe; and *keep your head.* Don't let your dragon instinct to get in there and slug run away with you. That's why the georges have been winning against us as they have. Just remember you're faster than that ogre and your brains'll win for you if you stay clear, keep your head and don't rush. I tell you, boy—"

He was interrupted by a sudden cry of joy from Nevile-Smythe, who had been rummaging around Clarivaux's saddle.

"I say!" shouted Nevile-Smythe, running up to them with surprising lightness, considering his armor. "The most marvelous stroke of luck! Look what I found." He waved a wispy stretch of cloth at them.

"What?" demanded Jim, his heart going up in one sudden leap.

"Elinor's favor! And just in time, too. Be a good fellow, will you," went on Nevile-Smythe, turning to Carolinus, "and tie it about my vambrace here on the shield arm. Thank you, Mage."

Carolinus, looking grim, tucked his staff into the crook of his arm and quickly tied the kerchief around the armor of Nevile-Smythe's lower left arm. As he tightened the final knot and let his hands drop away, the knight caught up his shield into position and drew his sword with his other hand. The bright blade flashed like a sudden streak of lightning in the sun, he leaned forward to throw the weight of his armor before him, and with a shout of *"A Nevile-Smythe! Elinor! Elinor!"* he ran forward up the slope toward the approaching Worm.

Jim heard, but did not see, the clash of shell and steel that was their coming together. For just then everything began to happen at once. Up on the hill, Anark screamed suddenly in fury and launched himself down the slope in the air, wings spread like some great bomber gliding in for a crash landing. Behind Jim, there was the frenzied flapping of leathery wings as Secoh took to the air to meet him—but this was drowned by a sudden short, deep-chested cry, like a wordless shout; and, lifting his club, the ogre stirred and stepped clear of the boulders, coming forward and straight down the hill with huge, ground-covering strides.

"Good luck, boy," said Smrgol, in Jim's ear. "And Gorbash—" Something in the old dragon's voice made Jim turn his head to look at Smrgol. The ferocious red mouth-pit and enormous fangs were frighteningly open before him; but behind it Jim read a strange affection and concern in the dark dragon-eyes. "—remember," said the old dragon, almost softly, "that you are a descendant of Ortosh and Agtval, and Gleingul who slew the sea serpent on the tide-banks of the Gray Sands. And be therefore valiant. But remember, too, that you are my only living kin and the last of our line . . . and be careful."

Then Smrgol's head was jerked away, as he swung about to face the coming together of Secoh and Anark in mid-air and bellowed out his own challenge. While Jim, turning back toward the Tower, had only time to take to the air before the rush of the ogre was upon him.

He had lifted on his wings without thinking— evidently this was dragon instinct when attacked. He was aware of the ogre suddenly before him, checking now, with its enormous hairy feet digging deep into the ground. The rust-bound club flashed before Jim's eyes and he felt a heavy blow high on his chest that swept him backward through the air.

He flailed with his wings to regain balance. The over-size idiot face was grinning only a couple of yards off from him. The club swept up for another blow. Panicked, Jim scrambled aside, and saw the ogre sway forward a step. Again the club lashed out—*quick!*—how could something so big and clumsy-looking be so quick with its hands? Jim felt himself smashed down to earth and a sudden lance of bright pain shot through his right shoulder. For a second, a gray, thick-skinned forearm loomed over him and his teeth met in it without thought.

He was shaken like a rat by a rat terrier and flung clear. His wings beat for the safety of altitude, and he found himself about twenty feet off the ground, staring down at the ogre, which grunted a wordless sound and shifted the club to strike upwards. Jim cupped air with his wings, to fling himself backward and avoid the blow. The club whistled through the unfeeling air; and, sweeping forward, Jim ripped at one great blocky shoulder and beat clear. The ogre spun to face him, still grinning. But now blood welled and trickled down where Jim's teeth had gripped and torn, high on the shoulder.

—And suddenly, Jim realized something:

He was no longer afraid. He hung in the air, just out of the ogre's reach, poised to take advantage of any opening; and a hot sense of excitement was coursing through him. He was discovering the truth about fights—and about most similar things—that it is only the beginning that is bad. Once the chips are down, several million years of instinct take over and there is no time for thought for anything

but confronting the enemy. So it was with Jim—
and then the ogre moved in on him again; and
that was his last specific intellectual thought of
the fight, for everything else was drowned in his
overwhelming drive to avoid being killed and, if
possible, to kill, himself. . . .

IV

It was a long, blurred time, about which later
Jim had no clear memory. The sun marched up
the long arc of the heavens and crossed the noon-
ing point and headed down again. On the torn-up
sandy soil of the plain he and the ogre turned and
feinted, smashed and tore at each other. Sometimes he was in the air, sometimes on the ground.
Once he had the ogre down on one knee, but could
not press his advantage. At another time they had
fought up the long slope of the hill almost to the
Tower and the ogre had him pinned in the cleft
between two huge boulders and had hefted its
club back for the final blow that would smash
Jim's skull. And then he had wriggled free between the monster's very legs and the battle was
on again.

Now and then throughout the fight he would catch
brief kaleidoscopic glimpses of the combats being
waged about him: Nevile-Smythe now wrapped
about by the blind body of the Worm, its eye-
stalks hacked away—and striving in silence to draw
free his sword-arm, which was pinned to his side
by the Worm's encircling body. Or there would
roll briefly into Jim's vision a tangled roaring tum-
ble of flailing leathery wings and serpentine bodies that was Secoh, Anark and old Smrgol. Once or
twice he had a momentary view of Carolinus, still
standing erect, his staff upright in his hand, his
long white beard flowing forward over his blue

gown with the cabalistic golden signs upon it, like some old seer in the hour of Armageddon. Then the gross body of the ogre would blot out his vision and he would forget all but the enemy before him.

The day faded. A dank mist came rolling in from the sea and fled in little wisps and tatters across the plain of battle. Jim's body ached and slowed, and his wings felt leaden. But the ever-grinning face and sweeping club of the ogre seemed neither to weaken nor to tire. Jim drew back for a moment to catch his breath; and in that second, he heard a voice cry out.

"Time is short!" it cried, in cracked tones. "We are running out of time. The day is nearly gone!"

It was the voice of Carolinus. Jim had never heard him raise it before with just such a desperate accent. And even as Jim identified the voice, he realized that it came clearly to his ears—and that for sometime now upon the battlefield, except for the ogre and himself, there had been silence.

He shook his head to clear it and risked a quick glance about him. He had been driven back almost to the neck of the Causeway itself, where it entered onto the plain. To one side of him, the snapped strands of Clarivaux's bridle dangled limply where the terrified horse had broken loose from the earth-thrust spear to which Nevile-Smythe had tethered it before advancing against the Worm on foot. A little off from it stood Carolinus, upheld now only by his staff, his old face shrunken and almost mummified in appearance, as if the life had been all but drained from it. There was nowhere else to retreat to; and Jim was alone.

He turned back his gaze to see the ogre almost upon him. The heavy club swung high, looking gray and enormous in the mist. Jim felt in his limbs and wings a weakness that would not let

him dodge in time; and, with all his strength, he
gathered himself, and sprang instead, up under
the monster's guard and inside the grasp of those
cannon-thick arms.

The club glanced off Jim's spine. He felt the
arms go around him, the double triad of bone-
thick fingers searching for his neck. He was caught,
but his rush had knocked the ogre off his feet.
Together they went over and rolled on the sandy
earth, the ogre gnawing with his jagged teeth at
Jim's chest and striving to break a spine or twist a
neck, while Jim's tail lashed futilely about.

They rolled against the spear and snapped it in
half. The ogre found its hold and Jim felt his neck
begin to be slowly twisted, as if it were a chicken's
neck being wrung in slow motion. A wild despair
flooded through him. He had been warned by
Smrgol never to let the ogre get him pinned. He
had disregarded that advice and now he was lost,
the battle was lost. *Stay away*, Smrgol had warned,
use your brains . . .

The hope of a wild chance sprang suddenly to
life in him. His head was twisted back over his
shoulder. He could see only the gray mist above
him, but he stopped fighting the ogre and groped
about with both forelimbs. For a slow moment of
eternity, he felt nothing, and then something hard
nudged against his right foreclaw, a glint of bright
metal flashed for a second before his eyes. He
changed his grip on what he held, clamping down
on it as firmly as his clumsy foreclaws would
allow—

—and with every ounce of strength that was left
to him, he drove the fore-part of the broken spear
deep into the middle of the ogre that sprawled
above him.

The great body bucked and shuddered. A wild
scream burst from the idiot mouth alongside Jim's

ear. The ogre let go, staggered back and up, tottering to its feet, looming like the Tower itself above him. Again, the ogre screamed, staggering about like a drunken man, fumbling at the shaft of the spear sticking from him. It jerked at the shaft, screamed again, and, lowering its unnatural head, bit at the wood like a wounded animal. The tough ash splintered between its teeth. It screamed once more and fell to its knees. Then slowly, like a bad actor in an old-fashioned movie, it went over on its side, and drew up its legs like a man with the cramp. A final scream was drowned in bubbling. Black blood trickled from its mouth and it lay still.

Jim crawled slowly to his feet and looked about him.

The mists were drawing back from the plain and the first thin light of late afternoon stretching long across the slope. In its rusty illumination, Jim made out what was to be seen there.

The Worm was dead, literally hacked in two. Nevile-Smythe, in bloody, dinted armor, leaned wearily on a twisted sword not more than a few feet off from Carolinus. A little farther off, Secoh raised a torn neck and head above the intertwined, locked-together bodies of Anark and Smrgol. He stared dazedly at Jim. Jim moved slowly, painfully over to the mere-dragon.

Jim came up and looked down at the two big dragons. Smrgol lay with his eyes closed and his jaws locked in Anark's throat. The neck of the younger dragon had been broken like the stem of a weed.

"Smrgol . . ." croaked Jim.

"No—" gasped Secoh. "No good. He's gone. . . . I led the other one to him. He got his grip—and then he never let go. . . ." The mere-dragon choked and lowered his head.

"He fought well," creaked a strange harsh voice which Jim did not at first recognize. He turned and saw the Knight standing at his shoulder. Nevile-Smythe's face was white as sea-foam inside his helmet and the flesh of it seemed fallen in to the bones, like an old man's. He swayed as he stood.

"We have won," said Carolinus, solemnly, coming up with the aid of his staff. "Not again in our lifetimes will evil gather enough strength in this spot to break out." He looked at Jim. "And now," he said, "the balance of Chance and History inclines in your favor. It's time to send you back."

"Back?" said Nevile-Smythe.

"Back to his own land, Knight," replied the magician. "Fear not, the dragon left in this body of his will remember all that happened and be your friend."

"Fear!" said Nevile-Smythe, somehow digging up a final spark of energy to expend on hauteur. "I fear no dragon, dammit. Besides, in respect to the old boy here"—he nodded at the dead Smrgol—"I'm going to see what can be done about this dragon-alliance business."

"He was great!" burst out Secoh, suddenly, almost with a sob. "He—he made me strong again. Whatever he wanted, I'll do it." And the mere-dragon bowed his head.

"You come along with me then, to vouch for the dragon end of it," said Nevile-Smythe. "Well," he turned to Jim, "it's goodby, I suppose, Sir James."

"I suppose so," said Jim. "Goodby to you, too, I—" Suddenly he remembered.

"Angie!" he cried out, spinning around. "I've got to go get Angie out of that Tower!"

Carolinus put his staff out to halt Jim.

"Wait," he said. "Listen. . . ."

"Listen?" echoed Jim. But just at that moment,

he heard it, a woman's voice calling, high and clear, from the mists that still hid the Tower.

"Jim! Jim, where are you?"

A slight figure emerged from the mist, running down the slope toward them.

"Here I am!" bellowed Jim. And for once he was glad of the capabilities of his dragon-voice. "Here I am, Angie—"

—but Carolinus was chanting in a strange, singing voice, words without meaning, but which seemed to shake the very air about them. The mist swirled, the world rocked and swung. Jim and Angie were caught up, were swirled about, were spun away and away down an echoing corridor of nothingness . . .

. . . and then they were back in the Grille, seated together on one side of the table in the booth. Hanson, across from them, was goggling like a bewildered accident victim.

"Where—where am I?" he stammered. His eyes suddenly focused on them across the table and he gave a startled croak. "Help!" he cried, huddling away from them. "Humans!"

"What did you expect?" snapped Jim. "Dragons?"

"No!" shrieked Hanson. "Watch-beetles—like me!" And, turning about, he tried desperately to burrow his way through the wood seat of the booth to safety.

V

It was the next day after that Jim and Angie stood in the third floor corridor of Chumley Hall, outside the door leading to the office of the English Department.

"Well, are you going in or aren't you?" demanded Angie.

"In a second, in a second," said Jim, adjusting his tie with nervous fingers. "Just don't rush me."

"Do you suppose he's heard about Grottwold?" Angie asked.

"I doubt it," said Jim. "The Student Health Service says Hanson's already starting to come out of it—except that he'll probably always have a touch of amnesia about the whole afternoon. Angie!" said Jim, turning on her. "Do you suppose, all the time we were there, Hanson was actually being a watch-beetle underground?"

"I don't know, and it doesn't matter," interrupted Angie, firmly. "Honestly, Jim, now you've finally promised to get an answer out of Dr. Howells about a job, I'd think you'd want to get it over and done with, instead of hesitating like this. I just can't understand a man who can go about consorting with dragons and fighting ogres and then—"

"—still not want to put his boss on the spot for a yes-or-no answer," said Jim. "Hah! Let me tell you something." He waggled a finger in front of her nose. "Do you know what all this dragon-ogre business actually taught me? It wasn't not to be scared, either."

"All right," said Angie, with a sigh. "What was it then?"

"I'll tell you," said Jim. "What I found out . . ." He paused. "What I found out was not, not to be scared. It was that scared or not doesn't matter; because you just go ahead, anyway."

Angie blinked at him.

"And that," concluded Jim, "is why I agreed to have it out with Howells, after all. Now you know."

He yanked Angie to him, kissed her grimly upon her startled lips, and, letting go of her, turned about. Giving a final jerk to his tie, he turned the knob of the office door, opened it, and strode valiantly within.

Critics may break butterflies on the wheel, but never dragons.

The Present State of Igneos Research

RESEARCH—SERIOUS RESEARCH, THAT IS—INTO THE SUBject of the large *igneo-eructidae* known familiarly to scholars in the field as "igneos" and to the layman as "dragons," has always been hampered as much by lack of a place to publish results as by the general skepticism of the public—to say nothing of the skepticism of most present-day biologists and zoologists—concerning the existence of this species.

The effect of this has been that efforts to publish in the field have produced activities on the part of the researcher more resembling those of the hero in a late-night spy movie than those of someone engaged in ordinary scholarly investigation. Occasionally, of course, this unorthodox behavior has paid unexpected dividends, as in the discovery of new channels of information, such as the publication in which you are now reading his monograph. True to a long-standing policy of barring nothing from its pages which might be of interest to its admittedly highly-selective readership, Analog has emerged as the one publication of the last several decades which had continuously striven to keep its readers up to date on the latest igneos research.

Occasionally, we must admit, this information has had to be presented in fictional form, even here. But I need not rehearse examples of excellent information on the igneos, reaching this publication's readers from highly qualified workers in the field such as Anne McCaffrey and Poul Anderson, to name only two. Having, however, cited this pair, who by their scholarship and renown are hardly in a position to be shaken by any ordinary attack, let us move along to the main topic. For the subject of this particular paper is not the conditions and problems surrounding igneos research, but a fortunate discovery of a piece of invaluable new evidence which bids fair to shine a powerful, valuable—if not revolutionary—light on the whole species.

This discovery consists of a manuscript that presents an account, in verse, of an encounter between an igneos and a human. It is not, however, merely the account of any random encounter, but details the exact actions of a member of the "Dragon-Runners' Guild" toward one particular igneos, in accordance with the rules of that Guild. The Dragon-Runners' Guild is an organization, the existence of which has been long suspected by researchers into the igneos situation. Now, with this manuscript, proof has at last been obtained that the Guild did indeed exist—and may still, in fact, be not only in existence, but in active existence, even in our present era.

But more of that in a moment. Let us pass on to more solid matters. It is necessary before building conjecture upon fact to give a more precise description of the manuscript, and an account of the information to be deduced from it.

On first examination the narrative appears to be written in something very like Fourteenth Century Middle English. Closer scrutiny, however, reveals two puzzling inconsistencies. One, the chronicler who wrote it was clearly unused to the making of such chronicles. There are variances within the text that show that it was penned with a good deal of carelessness and little thought beyond that of setting down the immediate information it contained. Second, the language used, while it has some of the tricks of spelling common to Middle English in the period mentioned, also shows a meter and rhyme that is only consistent if the words set down are pronounced as a speaker of Modern English would pronounce them.

However, tests of the parchment on which the manuscript was written, and the ink used, have proved that neither parchment nor ink were of any more recent vintage than some five hundred years, and possibly much older. This has left only one possible conclusion, by anyone knowledgeable in the igneos field. That is, that while the manuscript had to be written by someone with a modern ear, it was nonetheless written by such a person while he or she was existing in the Fourteenth Century or earlier.

In short, we must assume that a case of temporal translation (i.e., time-traveling) was involved in the production of this manuscript.

Startling—even self-contradictory—as this may sound to those unacquainted with the work already done in this field, it is quite consistent with other evidence previously published. Those informed about the igneos will undoubtedly recall Ms. McCaffrey's references to, and descriptions of, the phenomenon of temporal translation as achieved by these remarkable creatures, in her earlier papers in this publication. It therefore becomes entirely conceivable that the author of this manuscript was originally of our own modern era.

Once this fact is accepted, the internal evidence of the manuscript delivers up that information which I have—and I believe justly—referred to as revolutionary. For centuries researchers have puzzled over what actually extinguished the race of the igneos. Naturally, among knowledgeable scholars, the mistaken folk-tale notion that the igneos were evil creatures destroyed by human heroes— the "St. George and the Dragon" legend, for example—has long been recognized for the cruel distortion of fact that it is. I, myself, have had a few words to say on this matter in another publication, some seventeen years ago ("St. Dragon and the George," *Fantasy and Science Fiction*, September 1957); and the georgists, I am confident, are a dying breed. For some centuries we in the field have been convinced that igneos-nature was just the opposite of evil; although it is only for the first time, in this manuscript, that we have documentary proof of the fact—documentary proof provided by a human writer.

I refer you to stanza twenty-four, lines one and two, of the manuscript:

"Ye whole world knowes—despyte hys fercer parte
How ech Dragon wythin hathe noble herte . . ."

The important information here lies in the words ". . . hathe noble herte." As I say, anyone expert in the field has long suspected this to be true. But we must ask ourselves, since igneos were noble-hearted, and known by humans to be so, how did canards like the St. George and the Dragon legend get started?

I believe the answer to that can be given simply, in one word. Guilt. As internal evidence in this manuscript makes clear, humans were indeed responsible for the disappearance of the igneos from among us; but not by force of arms. Rather by neglect and inattention, a treatment these noble-hearted creatures could not endure.

As a careful examination of the manuscript will show, a close association between man and igneos was originally considered not merely advantageous, but necessary to the igneos. Observe that the story set down in these lines is that of an igneos revived from a poor state of health by a human. Lacking such human association previously, the igneos Shagoth, as it is noted near the beginning of the poem, has become "fatte" and "styffe," with a temper that "wasse notte gude." He has, in fact, become so debilitated as to lose his natural ability to fly.

Contrast this condition with the accounts of the same igneos, further on in the poem after he has been contacted and exercised by a comparably noble-hearted human—the Prentice (later Knight, still later Baron) Morlet:

"... Above ye rockye strande and cruel sea,
SHAGOTH bete upward, lyght as fethers bee;
Swoopynge and makynge Turnes Immeleman,
And Loope-ve-Loopes, all suche as Dragon
canne ..."

Note, also, how it is later remarked that the now-slim igneos continues to "ronne" and lift "hevie weightes to keepe hym trim" although Morlet, in person, has already parted with him. Above all, note the extremely important lines emphasizing that, as a result of Shagoth keeping up these activities, "all other Dragones envie hym . . ." (!)

To the trained professional eye, lines and line-fragments such as these fit together to make certain unmistakable statements. Shagoth is not just one igneos, left to lead a solitary existence—but all igneos in such condition of human neglect. Morlet is not merely one human, but representative of a whole class of humans who have always concerned themselves with the welfare of the igneos. And the message, in brief, is plain. Igneos require human contact and assistance for their existence in this world. A lack of such contact in recent centuries was obviously a primary reason for their disappearance from among us.

But is this sad conclusion all we can learn from this manuscript? No. There is further information to be gleaned from the lines of poetry; and this indicates almost beyond a shadow of a doubt that the igneos need not be gone from among us for good.

For, I submit humbly, but with the certainty of all my years of scholarship in this field, that these lines, together with other evidence I have mentioned, reveal that the igneos, as a race, have not died out. What they have done is to withdraw temporally from us humans. They have literally hidden themselves somewhere in the temporal continuum, using their ability to travel there.

Where in the temporal continuum are they hiding? The answer to this question must await further research. But no one of intelligence can doubt that the answer is there waiting for us. I submit to you two inescapable conclusions:

One, that this manuscript was clearly written by a modern hand.

Two, that the Dragon-Runners' Guild is proved beyond any reasonable doubt to exist.

The deduction from these conclusions is obvious. The writer of the manuscript must have been himself or herself a member of the Guild—a modern member who was able to return through time to the Fourteenth Century or earlier. Such temporal translations could only have been accomplished with the help of one or more igneos—which means that their race must still exist, in some area removed from our modern present, but from which they are in contact with the Guild. Such Guild-contact can only indicate that the igneos have not completely given up on humanity.

This being the case, however, we may well ask ourselves—can the igneos ever be brought back into contact with the rest of our race, and if so, how?

The poem itself offers an answer. It was the lack of association of noble-hearted humans that caused the igneos to disappear from view, it tells us. But it avoids suggesting that there were no longer any noble-hearted humans in existence. I propose, rather, that it was the noisy vehicles of modern transportation, the overwhelming growth of human cities—in short, the infestation of earth and sky with all the artifacts of what humans call modern civilization—that caused the sensitive igneos to shrink back more and more into isolated areas, where the possibility of their contact with the noble-hearted among our own race was extremely limited.

But now, we have finally come upon a practical means of bringing the igneos out of hiding. It is through such publications as this, that a sufficient number of igneos-minded humans can be located and identified; so that, finding human friends once more available to them, the igneos may possibly be enticed to return among us.

I have been told point-blank by other igneos experts that this prospect is a pipe-dream on my part; that the noble-hearted human is as extinct as the igneos themselves have popularly been believed to be. However, I emphatically reject such pessimism; and I offer to rebut it with the reactions of the readers of this monograph. Let me refer you to the fact that, at its conclusion, the manuscript shows Shagoth and Morlet, although they are now separated, maintaining their friendship through an exchange of correspondence once a year:

> "... Butte yn ye season whenne ye mistletoe
> And holly hangeth hevye on ye bough,
> Ech wrytes to ech a lettere of gude cheere,
> To telle hys friende whatte hym befel thatte
>   yeare."

I stand on my belief that there are among the readers of this publication many of those noble-hearted individuals with whom our time-stranded igneos friends yearn to have contact. And I call on all of you reading this. How many of you would not be willing, like Morlet, to sit down once a year at this holiday season and pen a "lettere of gude cheere" to an igneos friend?

Confident that the positive response to this question will be an overwhelmingly decisive one, I sit back to await the future in an atmosphere of anticipation and high hope.

Ye Prentice and Ye Dragon

Yn frostye season whenne ye mistletoe
And holly hangeth hevye on ye bough;
A deede bothe brave and kindlie once befel;
The tale of whych yn truthe I canne nowe telle.

Ther wasse a Dragon, SHAGOTH, on a clyffe.
I wiss hee wasse a Dragon fatte and styffe;
For thatte since manye settynges of ye sunne
Hee hadde no ferce battaile, nor helthful ronne.

And as bothe Dragones and alle mankinde hathe,
Hys styffnesse fedeth fulle hys anciente wrathe.
By alle of whych I shulde be understoode
To saye of hym, hys temper wasse notte gude.

By cause of thys, hys sore infirmitee,
He sheweth no traveleres ne mercie;
Ande suche grym stories of hym didde resound,
Alle folke of hys clyffe passeth far around.

But at ye tyme of whych I nowe relate
Ther cameth one whose renoun wasse notte grete;

A Prentice onlie, but by stronge oathe bounde,
To ronne alle Dragones, and to keepe them sounde.

And as hys rank, tho gentil, wasse not grete,
Hee had no welth, ne any hy estate;
But that rare charitie to Dragonkinde
Whych Sages praiseth, tyme alle oute of mynde.

MORLET, hys name, a brave and kindlie youth.
When thatte hee knew ye mattere wasse ynsoothe
Of a Dragon's deepe neede, yvowed thatte hee
Shulde see ye SHAGOTH ronninge lyssomlee.

Yet perille was ynough, as welle he wotte,
Sobye hee came at nyghttyme as ythought,
Wher slepeth SHAGOTH yn a rockye neste,
Groanynge for aches thatte paineth stronge hys
reste.

And cleverlye ye Prentice, alle alone,
Beneathe ye necke of SHAGOTH rolled a stone.
So thatte ye Dragon twyst hys necke yn sleepe,
Ye stone from bruysing of his fleshe to keepe.

So slepeth hee wyth twysted necke tyll dawne,
Woke wyth ye sunne and sterteth up anon.
A styffe, and certes, a crookede necke to fynde,
Soe thatte he myghte bye no meanes looke behinde.

Soe payned thys laste condicioun, past beliefe,
Thatte SHAGOTH gan to wepe for verie griefe—
"O sadde a Dragon's lyfe," quod hee, "thatte I
Must suffere soe, and am too fatte to flye!"

But scarcelie hadde he made thys woefulle
moan,
When hee did feele a poke at hys tayle-bone.
Furieuse, hee tryde to turn hys head and see,
Who poked atte hym; but hys styffe necke stopped
hee.

"Hay done!" hee cryed, "Yn Name of Drag-
on's Wrathe!"
Yette MORLET kneweth welle hys Prentice' pathe;
Wherefor hee proddeth SHAGOTH yette once more
And SHAGOTH lepeth from hys neste, aroare.

So wroth ye Dragon wasse, ne recketh hee
Of alle hys aches and alle hys miserie.
"I shalle thys Pokkere shak fro off my tayle,"
Swered hee, "then dryve hym erthwerd lyke a
nayle!"

Rechinge ye open plaine, hee gan gallope
As onlie Dragons canne, withouten stoppe.
At fersom speede hee thundred o'er ye lande,
Ther wasse no distaunce thatte culde hym
withstande.

Meantyme, yonge MORLET, faithfulle to hys
vowe,
Clunge to ye Dragon's tayle, gratefulle enowe.
For hys gude belte, withe whych tyght-bounde
hadde hee,
Hymself to SHAGOTH, leste hee bee throwne free.

So, ryskinge lyfe and lymbe and mortale dethe,

MORLET revowed hys oathe whyle hee hadde
             brethe,
  "I will succour thys Dragon, or wille die.
   Suth dutie ys ye leeste fro suche as I!"

Yet, if yonge MORLET wulde notte bende hys
             wille,
Namor culde SHAGOTH's Dragon's wrathe be
             stille.
  Togethere, they continuede on ther ronne
Through mornynge, noone, and settynge of ye
             sunne.

Acrosse ye wyde plaine, thro ye furthere hilles,
By fieldes and forestes, swampes and rockye rilles,
  Chargeth ye SHAGOTH ynto deepeste nyghte.
Fulle warme wasse hee, ne ached, but felte aryghte.

And as ye yongling dawne gan bleede ye skye,
  SHAGOTH unto hymself asked, "Bee thys I?
  So lyghtlie leping o'er ech hille and dale;
So acheless, fulle of strengthe, ne lyke to fayle?

  "Mayhap thys longe gallope hathe done me
             gude.
 Culdest bee thys Pokkere knewe soe, thatte yt
             wulde?
   Yf soe, mystaken wasse my wrathe anon
I muste admitte to hym thatte I wasse wronge."

Hee turned hys heade—nowe on a supple necke,
  To speke to MORLET. But hee fayled to recke
 Of (juste aheade) a cliffe-edge, sharpe yndeede
From off of whych hee hurtled atte fulle speede

A cliffe ytte wasse, famos fro lande to lande,
For halfe a myle sheere, felle ytte to ye strande
Of ye deepe sea, wyth grete stones alle aboute,
To smashe ye lyfe fro man and Dragon oute.

Ye whole world knowes—despyte hys fercer
parte,
How ech Dragon wythin hathe noble herte;
And yn thys moment whenne fel dethe wasse nere,
Ytte wasse notte for hymself SHAGOTH felte feare.

"Alas!" cryed hee, "ne looked I onne, eftsoone.
I have repayed kyndnesse wyth ferful doome!
Pokkere, t'was thou helped mee—nowe wee muste
dye!"
"NonSense!" quod MORLET. "Needes butte thatte
ye flye."

Grete teares therpon bedewed ye Dragon's
cheek.
"Alas," hee wept, "I am too fatte and weake!"
"Thatte once wasse true," sayd MORLET, "but
namor.
Thy ronne hathe made thee lean and lyght to soare."

"Canne thys bee true?" sayd SHAGOTH. "I
wille trye."
Hee tryed, and lo! Hee founde thatte hee culde flye.
As once hadde hee, when butte a Dragon yonge,
Soarynge above ye erthbounde, everechon.

Ah, grete ye bliss of hygh lordes yn ther toweres,
And grete ther laydes bliss wythin ther bowers;
But no bliss toucheth that whych doth obtayn,
A Dragon fatte, who nowe canne flye agayne!

Above ye rocye strande and cruel sea,
SHAGOTH bete upward, lyght as fethers bee;
Swoopynge and makynge Turnes Immeleman,
Ande Loope-ye-Loopes, all suche as Dragons canne.

So triumphantlee returned hee home by aire,
To hys own clyffe. Partynge wyth MORLET ther,
He didde ye Prentice thanke moste hertilie,
And waved farewel as far as hym culde see.

And soe they parted. Butte since then, ech
dawne,
Earlie, SHAGOTH some lengthie leagues doth
ronne;
Ande lyfteth hevie weightes to keepe hym trim,
Soe thatte alle other Dragones envie hym.

Meantyme, yonge MORLET hath becom a Knyghte.
Yn manye landes hath shone yn gallaunt fyghte
Ande won hym grete honors, untyl ye Kyng
Hath made hym Baronne, as ye mynstrelles sing.

Soe goeth ech, uponne hys separate waye,
SHAGOTH doth aide alle travelleres gone astraye.
MORLET doth rule hys Baronnie, and fyghte
Alle eville Knyghtes, and trounceth them aryght.

Butte yn ye season whenne ye mistletoe
And holly hangeth hevye on ye bough,
Ech wrytes to ech a lettere of gude cheere
To telle hys friende whatte hym befel thatte yeare.

*When art is a product of madness,
what happens when the artist goes
sane?*

A Case History

"YOU LOOK LIKE AN INTELLIGENT YOUNG MAN," SAID THE
gray-haired individual.

"Thank you," the bartender replied. "Another
boilermaker?"

"Make it a double. My nerves are shattered."

"Ninety cents," the barman said, putting it down
in front of him. "For long-term results, however, I
would recommend a psychiatrist."

"I am a psychiatrist," the other answered,
gloomily.

"Oh."

"And there's no use telling me to see someone
else in my own profession," he added. "I can't
afford it. Anyway, it wouldn't help. *Quis custodiet
ipsos custodes?* Or, in other words, who will listen
to the psychiatrist? Nobody but the bartender."

"If you'll excuse me for a moment, the lunch
crowd will be coming in shortly and I've got to get
these glasses washed—"

"Young man," said the psychiatrist, "the patient's name was Elmer."

"Elmer?"

Elmer Grudy was his real name, said the psychiatrist. He is better known under his pseudonymn of Bruce Mondamin, as a leading writer of American fantasy fiction. His speciality was the supernatural spiced with a nice touch of the gruesome, for which certain childhood traumata were directly responsible—but I won't violate professional confidence by going into details. Enough that he was successful and had experienced an unhappy childhood—as who hasn't? Why, in my own case—but I wander from the subject.

As I say, he was successful—up to a certain point. The monsters he was adept at creating in his fiction were uniformly successful in chilling the blood of readers during the early and relatively bleak years of his career when he lived on peanut butter sandwiches and cheap beer. However with the postwar boom in this type of literature, he suddenly began to make money and the first signs of his personal tragedy began to make their appearance. He put on weight, filling out his six foot frame from a skinny 130 to a robust 180 pounds. He moved into better quarters, got a haircut and some new clothes and was observed to smile where he once scowled, to be mildly sociable where he used to be violently antisocial. In short, to give all the sinister indications of being happier than he had ever been in his life before.

I need hardly say that the effect all this had on his writing was disastrous. It was finally and forcibly brought to his attention when his latest story was returned by his most consistent publisher with a curt note, the substance of which was that he clean up a certain passage dealing with the story's Monster—or else—

Elmer looked at the passage indicated, in surprise. He had written it in good faith; and, even looking at it now, he could see nothing wrong with it. The passage went as follows:

"The Thing!*" screamed little Tommy Wittleton, "The Thing in the closet! It's coming out!"*

The Thing came all the way out. It advanced on little Tommy.

"There, there, Tommy," it said, "don't be frightened."

Beaming reassuringly on the little fellow, it produced a large chocolate bar from its pocket and gave it to the boy. Then it took its other hand from behind its back.

"Guess what I have here?" it whispered. Tommy looked. His eyes bugged out.

"The little puppy-dog I wanted for Christmas!" he cried joyfully.

Elmer scratched his head over the passage. It looked all right to him. He worried about it for a week and finally came to see me.

I pointed out the truth to him. He had, unfortunately, become a happy and contented man. It was ruining his work. What he needed was to delve back into his childhood and recapture the old neuroses and psychoses. After some struggle he agreed to try.

Now, Elmer had been raised by a maiden aunt following the early death of both his parents; and this maiden aunt—well, I'll spare you the details. However, the maiden aunt, who was still alive, was the personification of all his early terrors. She lived alone, a complete recluse, in a small town down east. Elmer had not seen her since he had run away from home at the age of fifteen to find freedom and the means of livelihood as general cleanup boy in a flourishing mortuary.

"Go back, Elmer," I told him. "Return in your own mind to the days when you lived with your Auntie Eglantine. Recreate your childhood, and your old skill with monsters will return to you."

Elmer was doubtful, but Elmer tried. He spent long hours walking by himself, or brooding in the cellar of his house (he had a house of his own by this time). He even tried eating sandwiches of stale bread and lard—a favorite of his aunt's during his childhood. But it seemed that he would be without success, until it occurred to him one day to put his unique talents to work on the problem. As a writer, he should be able to dramatize his situation with his pen. Accordingly, he sat down and commenced a story in which a boy like himself was being brought up by an aunt like his aunt; and at the end of the story, the aunt became a hideous monster.

The story was a resounding success. His monster aunt was the most spine-chilling thing to hit the stands and counters in a decade. There was one horrible little bit at the end in which her eyes melted and ran together—but I won't afflict you with the full description. Suffice it to say that the man who set up the galley proofs is now in Bellevue.

Well, the problem appeared solved. Elmer obliged with story after story in which somebody's aunt finished up by becoming a monster. And the aunt he used for his model was always his aunt; and in each story, her appearance became more horrible than ever.

I saw by the reviews in the various periodicals that Elmer was riding the crest of the wave; and I expected to hear no more from him. You can judge my surprise, therefore, when six months later the shattered wreck of a man that called himself Elmer Grudy tottered into my office and collapsed on the couch.

"What's this?" I said.

"Doctor," replied Elmer. "It's all up with me."

By slow degrees I extracted the story from him. Like so many artists he had committed the fatal error of living his own stories too intensely. And his mind was cracking. In a hoarse whisper he told me all.

"Say what you like, Doctor," he husked. "The conviction has been growing on me that my aunt is exactly what I have painted her to be—namely an inhuman monster in human guise. I have fought the notion, but it persists. Ordinary monsters are nothing to me. I used to take imaginary ones to bed with me as a child. But a monster who is at the same time a blood relative—" he shuddered and a look of pure terror came over his face. He clutched at my arm. "In my heart of hearts," he hissed, "I know the truth—that I am still living that story I have written so often. I am still her nephew, no matter under what fictional name I choose to hide myself. She is still my aunt and the close of the story is yet to be enacted. In the end I must return to her. And when I do—" his voice rose to a shriek—"she will turn out to be a monster more horrible than any I have ever described."

"A delusion," I assured him. "Born of overwork and your memories of your childhood."

"No, no," he sobbed. "It's true, I tell you. Even now, in that dark old house of hers, she is moving around inhumanly, a compound of all the forms I have given her in my writing."

Well, I worked with him, but the conviction was too firmly implanted to be removed by ordinary methods. Finally, I had to advance the ultimate suggestion.

"Elmer," I said, firmly, "you can conquer this

obsession of yours only by facing up to it. There is only one way to do this. You must go down and see your aunt."

He collapsed, of course. I brought him around and repeated the suggestion. He collapsed again. However, after several repetitions of this, he finally faced the inevitable and made arrangements to go down to the small town where his aunt lived. It was the greatest mistake of my career.

The psychiatrist sighed.

"Wait a minute," the bartender said. "You aren't going to tell me that when he went down there, he found his aunt actually changed into some sort of horrible being that gobbled him up."

The psychiatrist bristled.

"Of course I'm not going to relate any such ridiculous nonsense!" he snapped. "Elmer had lived with monsters since he was a tiny child. I knew that. The most horrible monster conceivable could never be more than commonplace to such a man. In fact," he added, "it was just that that I was counting on."

The barman stared at him suspiciously.

"I don't believe I understand you," he said. "You mean you actually expected Elmer's aunt to be the monster his weird stories had made her out to be?"

"Naturally," snapped the doctor. "A layman, of course, would reject any such hypothesis on the grounds that it would be impossible. A scientific mind like mine recognises that nothing is impossible. I not only thought it probable that Elmer's aunt had become monstrous, I was sure of it. I had planned Elmer's discovery of this as a form of shock treatment."

The early lunch crowd was beginning to drift in

through the front door of the bar. The barman eyed them nervously.

"Then it didn't happen that way?" he asked, edging away.

"Of course it did! Elmer knocked on the door, was invited in, entered and found himself confronted by an inhuman *thing* which swayed toward him across the carpet and said—reproachfully— 'Elmer! You bad boy! Look what you've done to me!' Immediately, rationality returned to Elmer. He tipped his hat and politely replied, 'Sorry, Auntie,' then returned here to the city."

"I can't understand your being upset, then. He was cured, wasn't he?"

"Oh, he was cured all right," answered the psychiatrist, bitterly. "But I blasted his career in the process."

"I don't see why." Obviously puzzled, the barman stopped his slow retreat.

"I should think it would be obvious," said the psychiatrist, looking up in some surprise. "Elmer's monsters had, even in the beginning, been veiled aunt-images. His success had been founded upon successfully creating monsters out of aunts. Now that he had actually turned his aunt into a monster, the source of his raw material was lost to him. He could no longer write stories in which the aunt turned into a monster. Only one course remained open to him."

"You mean—" the bartender was not an unintelligent young man—"you mean that Elmer is now writing stories in which the monster turns into an aunt?"

"That's exactly what I mean," answered the psychiatrist, moodily. "What else could he do? And, quite naturally, in the process, he is slowly starving to death. I need hardly say," added the learned man, "that there is next to no market for that type of material."

When "the reek and the riot of night is done," certain selected wolves may be fit to be welcomed indoors.

The Girl Who Played Wolf

IT WAS HARRY DECANT WHO STARTED IT. THERE IS NO USE his trying to dodge the responsibility for starting it, for that, at least, is a matter of record. He may or may not have been a thoughtless pawn in the coldly scientific hands of Amos Slizer; but the fact remains that he was the one who first dragged David off to a doctor, he was the one who found out about Amos' private resort, and—so Harry said—talked that eccentric genius into accepting them as guests. And, certainly the most important point of all, it was he who managed their joint introduction to Leona.

It was the introduction that really started things off. Harry and David were sitting on the dock, Harry fishing and David day-dreaming wistfully of meat—thick, juicy steaks, by preference; or, failing that, any kind of solid food that would not exhibit a mad urge to retrace its steps the minute it completed the pleasant journey to his stomach. The Minnesota woods were basking pleasantly in the summer sunshine and faintly over the water came the embattled voices of Amos and that rugged stone wall of scientific conservatism, Angus McCloud, who were ostensibly fishing from a boat. So lay the scene, and David was finding it, in spite of the breakfast which had recently deserted him, all rather comfortable.

He was brought back to reality by the voice of Harry murmuring with admiration in his ear.

"—A super babe."

"Huh?" responded David absent-mindedly.

"Look!" demanded Harry, digging his elbow into David's ribs. "—Coming down the path."

Wearily, David turned his head toward the rutted trail that led down from the slope on which the guest cabins perched. Super babes might be all very well to look at, but at the moment they were running a poor second to day-dreams of tenderloin.

"Where?" he asked.

But Harry had already scrambled to his feet; and David, finding the super babe was not on the path, but already stepping on the shore side of the dock, automatically followed him. So it was, that what with his own abstraction and the confusion attendant on getting to his feet, he did not actually get a good look at Leona until they were standing almost face to face.

What he saw was a lissome redhead in a scarlet bathing suit. She was tall, easily as tall as Harry— which made her just about even with David's chin, and her eyes were as green as the summer woods. At the sight of David she stopped dead, and the two of them stood, transfixed, staring at each other.

Meanwhile, with the ease of long practice, Harry had charged blithely into the business of making himself acquainted.

"Well, well!" he said, heartily. "And, well! You must be one of our fellow guests. Let me extend the hand of friendship and exchange names. I am Harry Decant, and this long, dyspeptic-looking character with the ugly face and large hands is known as David Muncy."

He jogged David with an elbow as a signal to speak up. But the effort was lost. For, suddenly, at the moment of finding himself face to face with the redhead, David had become completely lost in a welter of reactions similar to nothing he had experienced before. His throat had gone dry. His body was tense. The little hairs on the back of his neck had risen tinglingly, and he was possessed of a sudden overwhelming urge to sniff at the newcomer.

"David!" said Harry, jogging him again. "Say hello to the lady."

"Sniff!" sniffed David audibly, leaning forward.

"Dave!" cried Harry.

The redhead drew back half a step, curled her upper lip away from one dainty tooth and snarled delicately.

"Dave!" repeated Harry, grabbing him by the arm and pulling him back. With a start, David came to himself. The odd sensations disappeared in a wave of embarrassment, and he drew back in his turn.

"Excuse me," he mumbled, extending an awkward paw. "I'm glad to meet you."

Cautiously, the girl took it.

"How do you do?" she said in a warm contralto, "I'm Leona Parr, Dr. Slizer's secretary." A feeling of warm pleasure spread over David. He shook her hand warmly. She smiled up at him.

"I'm up here for my health," he said, still holding onto her hand.

"Really," said Leona. "That's too bad."

"Yes," said David, blissfully, "I can't eat solid food."

"How terrible."

"Yes."

"Hey!" said Harry.

They both turned toward him.

"I've got a hand too," he said.

"Oh. Sorry," said David. He thrust Leona's hand rather ungraciously into Harry's. She shook it absent-mindedly.

"It comes from overwork," said David.

"It does?" asked Leona.

"Yes. I was working on my Doctor's thesis in Elizabethan prose and I guess I overdid it."

"You should take better care of yourself."

"Hey!" said Harry.

"I will."

"Yes, do."

"I guess I might as well shove off," said Harry.

"I keep dreaming of meat."

"Poor thing."

"Thick, juicy cuts of meat."

"Well, goodby," said Harry.

"Goodby," said Leona absently. "Fresh meat—raw."

"Raw?" echoed David. "Oh—goodby, Harry."

"Bah!" said Harry, stamping off.

"Much better than cooked," said Leona.

"Do you really think so?" asked David. "I once had an uncle who—"

When the sun went down on the lake, they were still on the dock, and still talking. Leona's bathing suit was still dry.

"Well?" said Harry that evening, in the cabin they shared jointly.

"Well what?" asked David.

"I have," said Harry, sitting up in his bunk and pointing a deliberate finger at David, "known you for twelve years. In all that time, you have been, if you will pardon the expression, a schlump where women are concerned. I say this not to cast any reflection on you, for you are the scholarly type and everyone knows that scholars have a reputation for goggling, stammering, and stumbling in social situations. But, consider, I—" Harry thumped himself emphatically on the chest—"have been working my tongue to the bone for you these last twelve years. If we needed dates, I got both of them. If the conversation lagged over the doughnuts and coffee, I spoke for both of us, filling the air with light chatter and careless banter. And now, all of a sudden, you seem to have blossomed out with this Leona female and become an operator. And I think you owe me an explanation. Have you been goldbricking in lazy treacherous fashion all these years? Or have you suddenly been struck by lightning? Or—" Harry looked at him suspiciously—"what?"

David turned away from the moon he had been contemplating through the cabin window.

"Harry," he said. "Do you know what brought us here?"

"An invitation from Dr. Slizer," answered Harry. "Arranged by yours truly."

"No, Harry," David contradicted with gentle patience. "That's what you think it was. But actually it was fate."

"Fate?"

"Fate," said David, turning back to the window, "that which o'ersees the affairs of men, and turning, twists them to its goals."

"*What?*" yelped Harry. "Fate? Goals? What are you talking about?"

"Oh, that," for a second David looked his normal shy self, "It's a line from a poem I was writing this evening."

"It sounds like Shakespeare," said Harry, suspiciously. "It does not sound like Shakespeare," answered David indignantly, "and anyway, that's beside the point. The point is, Fate had brought Leona and myself together. I almost proposed on the dock tonight. I'll do it tomorrow. We can drive to the nearest Justice and be married in the afternoon. Will you be my best man, Harry?"

"Good God!" cried Harry. "You've been struck by lightning!"

He leaped out of his bunk—a startling figure in maroon pajamas.

"Stay here," he begged. "Promise me you'll stay here until I get back, Dave."

"The world is all one to me tonight," answered David, loftily.

"Well, just stay here," said Harry, and rushed out into the gloom.

The resort was plunged in that absolute blackness peculiar to forested country at night; but the lights of the windows up at the owner's lodge stood out clearly. With only an occasional yelp or curse as his bare feet came into painful contact with stones or twigs, Harry plowed through the darkness to the front door of the lodge and hammered upon it.

"Come in," rasped the irascible voice of Amos Slizer, and Harry burst in to find the two savants arguing over and around a bottle of scotch in the kitchen.

"Have a drink and get your breath back," said Angus, hospitably, offering the bottle, which, incidentally, belonged to Amos.

Harry grabbed at it and poured a couple of good-sized swallows down his throat by way of lubrication.

"That's fine," said Angus, approvingly, "and now that you've got your breath back—"

"I don't know what to think—" began Harry, wildly.

"Now that you've got your breath back," repeated Angus, smoothly, folding his knotted hands together, "perhaps you'll bear me out on a small point of my discussion with Amos, here."

"But David—" began Harry.

"Tush and foosh, David," interrupted McCloud, whose accent betrayed him only when he became irritated. "This is important. Our good friend Amos here—" he leered at the other, who snorted, "has been reading a lot of old wives tales, superstitions and the like. And the result is, they've driven him clear out of his head. They've addled his brains so much he's come up with what the poor soul thinks is a whole new division of knowledge."

"Pay no attention to his phraseology, Devant!" snapped Amos. "He's trying to prejudice you."

"But—" said Harry.

"The result is," continued McCloud, laying a heavy hand on Harry's arm, "that he's taken to believing in witches and ghosts and the like and maintaining that they follow purely natural laws of their own order."

"Para - science!" barked Amos.

"Fool-science! Numbskull science!" roared Angus, suddenly purpling. "Have you any proof, man?"

"I have," said Amos.

"Then why won't you show it to me?"

"Because," crackled Amos. "You're just pigheaded enough to deny the evidence of your own senses."

"Hah!" thundered Angus, gripping Harry's arm and dragging him involuntarily forward half a step. "That's what ye've said before. But I've got you now. Let's see you convince young Harry, here. He's an open-minded pup. Convince him and I'll admit I'm wrong."

Amos brought one bony fist down on the kitchen table with a crash.

"Got you!" he cried. "Why do you think I invited Harry and that friend of his and the girl up here? Eh? Just to get you to make that statement and be forced into abiding by the proof when I produced it. Ha!" He threw back his bony head and roared with laughter.

Angus McCloud's face deepened a good two shades in color.

"A put-up job," he rumbled.

"Not on their part. Not on their part," said Amos. "Harry doesn't know a thing about it, do you, Harry?"

"For Pete's sake!" yelped Harry, finally finding a gap in the conversation. "I've got something important to talk about. David's gone nuts. Clear out of his mind."

"What?" barked Amos, jerking himself upright in his chair and sobering suddenly. "Nuts? Already? What happened? What's he been doing? Why doesn't he take better care of himself? Harry, if you've let him go out of his head, I'll shoot you. What happened?"

"I've been trying to tell you," said Harry, plaintively.

"Well, don't keep standing there telling us you've been trying to tell us," snapped Amos. "Tell us. What's this all about?"

"All right, it was this way," Harry, finding his knees suddenly weak, sat down at the table and took another pull from the bottle. "This afternoon Dave and I met this Leona—"

"Beautiful girl, by the way," said Amos to Angus.

"I've noticed—" said Angus to Amos.

"—and Dave sort of monopolized the conversation right from the start, which isn't like him. Well, I didn't pay much attention to that; but I was talking to him tonight and he tells me he's going to marry her tomorrow."

Amos sighed in relieved fashion and leaned back in his chair.

"Oh, well," he said. "That's nothing to get alarmed about. Young blood—you know—" his voice trailed away vaguely.

"What?" cried Harry.

"Summertime—prime of life—think nothing of it," said Amos soothingly.

"But he asked me to be his best man," bleated Harry, incredulously.

"It'll blow over," said Amos.

"The hell it will," answered Harry, "you don't know Dave."

"Well," said Amos, judiciously, "I suppose I could speak to him. In the morning of course. First thing in the morning."

"Nothing doing," said Harry. "If you know anything about this mantrap that'll make him slow down for a bit, you tell it to him tonight."

"Not tonight."

"Tonight!"

"All right," sighed Amos. "Bring him up here."

"You bet!" said Harry. "Don't move. I'll be right back." He took off from the lodge at a run, which, however, due either to the scotch, or the reassuring effect of Amos' unconcern, slowed down to a more cautious walk which was infinitely kinder on his bare feet. He picked his way down the slope to where the lights of the cabin belonging to David and himself, loomed.

But when he got there, David was gone.

*   *   *

It was high breakfast-time when the prodigal returned. Harry was just finishing his third cup of coffee and looking at Leona with deep suspicion in his eyes, when David wandered in. He was wearing a shirt and pair of slacks, somewhat dirty, rumpled and torn. Harry compared his tangled condition with the bandbox freshness of Leona and the suspicion deepened.

"Where have you been?" he asked.

" 'Morning, darling," said David to Leona.

" 'Morning, dear," replied Leona.

"I said," repeated Harry. *"Where have you been?"*

"Out," replied David, turning to him with a courteously puzzled expression. "In the woods. Is it important? What is the difference?"

"Important?" said Harry, with a bitter laugh. "To me? Hah! No. I wouldn't say it was important. Merely inconvenient. You babble deliriously in the night. I run for help to the lodge and arouse Dr. Slizer and McCloud. Amos implores me to bring you back up to him right away. I go to get you. You're gone. Hah! No, not important. Merely inconvenient, when you're used to people keeping their promises to stay places until you get back to them."

"Oh, did I say that?" inquired David, vaguely.

"You did," said Harry. "Perhaps after you've had breakfast you'll see Dr. Slizer."

"Oh, I don't want any breakfast," said David. "I've already eaten. Some of that raw beef in the icehouse," he turned toward Leona. "You're quite right. It's much better that way."

"Then maybe we can go talk to Amos," said Harry.

"Certainly," consented David. "Be right back, Leona."

"Take your time, dear."

"Hah!" said Harry.

*   *   *

The two savants were sitting on the sun porch. Amos waved Harry and David to chairs as they approached.

"Cigars?" he said.

They shook their heads and sat down.

"Ah, David," said Amos.

"Yes?" said David.

"Harry here tells me you're quite taken with Leona."

"I intend to marry her shortly," said David, nodding his head, "one o'clock this afternoon—or two."

"Humm," said Amos.

"I beg your pardon?" said David.

"The truth is," Amos frowned professionally, "you are making a mistake. You think you're in love."

"I am."

"No," said Amos. "I'm afraid not. In the case of any other two people it could well be love. But in your case I'm afraid that what you think is love, is actually something else."

David blushed.

"No, I don't mean that either," said Amos hurriedly. "The truth is—well—I understand you were out all night last night."

"Well, yes," answered David. "I was."

"Tell me," said Amos, leaning forward confidentially. "While you were out in the woods by yourself, did you have the impulse to—or did you actually—er—bay at the moon?"

"Why," said David, turning a trifle pale, "come to think of it, I believe I did do a little baying."

"At the moon?"

"Yes."

"On any other occasions?"

David squirmed in his chair.

"Well," he stammered. "There was that rabbit."

"What rabbit?"

"Oh, just a rabbit," said David, with a bad attempt at airy unconcern. "I chased it a little way."

"Baying?"

"Well, yes."

"Holy Hannah!" exploded Harry. "Running around the woods at night and howling at moons and rabbits."

"I wasn't howling," said David, with dignity. "I was baying. There's a difference."

"There is, there is," interrupted Amos, hurriedly. "Harry, of course, doesn't understand."

"Damn right I don't," said Harry, belligerently.

"But what's this got to do with me and Leona?" asked David. Amos got up, walked over, and put a fatherly hand on his shoulder.

"My boy," he said, "brace yourself. You and Leona can never be married. Leona is a werewolf."

Angus snorted.

"Angus!" said Amos, sternly. "You promised not to say a word until I was through here."

"But that's ridiculous," said David.

"Is it any more ridiculous than what has happened to you in the last twenty-four hours?" asked Amos. David colored, but stuck to his guns.

"Even if it was true," he said, "I'm not afraid. We'll go see a specialist, or something. Leona and I can never be kept apart." Amos turned his head away sadly.

"Truer words were never spoken," he said. "But not the way you think it. You've only heard half the story. Remember last night. Remember chasing the rabbit. Didn't you notice any change in yourself?"

David's face went totally white.

"Come to think of it—come to think of it—" he choked—"I did. I had a—a tail; and dewlaps."

"You see?" said Amos. "Unknown to yourself all

these years, you have been a were-wolfhound, one of the old breed whose ancestors were developed by the Magicians Anti-Were-creatures Guild of Verona in the early thirteenth century. You are a were-wolfhound, and Leona, being a werewolf, is your natural prey. It is her proximity to you that has made you revert to type. Due to the fine selective breeding of your ancestors, you have felt the were-call early. Leona will feel it in a night or two. She will become a werewolf. You will become a were-wolfhound, and track her down and tear her to bits. The attraction, David, that you feel for Leona, is not the love of a male for a female, but the lust of a hunter for his game."

David fainted.

Later on that day, when David had finally been calmed down and put to bed, Harry slipped away from the first distraught snores of his friend and cornered Amos in the library.

"What're you doing?" he asked.

Amos shook his head, sadly.

"I've been trying to think of some way para-science could be used to obvert the inevitable," he said. "But my knowledge of the field is still too much in the theoretical stage."

"Can't you do anything?"

"I wish I could," said Amos. "I set this little tragedy in motion in a thoughtless impulse to convert Angus to a true scientific curiosity. Now, I'd do anything I could to stop it."

"Well, there must be something we can do."

"What?"

"Can't we lock them up at night, or something?"

"We can try," Amos shook his head dolorously, "but remember, we're not dealing with ordinary humans. Both David and Leona are were-creatures, and nobody can know just what powers they possess."

"Well I don't know about you!" snapped Harry. "But I'm going to keep my eye on Leona, from here on out!"

And so, for the next two days, Leona suffered what can only be referred to as persecution. She took it as long as she could; but finally even her were-will cracked. She sought out Amos in the library and cried on his shoulder.

"There, there," said Amos, nervously, patting her shoulder.

"But it's just awful!" she wailed.

"Come now," said Amos, with the falsely cheerful air of a man who has just heard what his wife claims are burglars downstairs, "are you sure you aren't just imagining things?"

"Certainly not!" sniffed Leona. "It's that Harry. He keeps following me around and saying 'Hah!' darkly."

"Pay no attention," answered Amos soothingly.

"—And David. He keeps putting off getting married, and every time he looks at me and sighs deeply, as if I was somebody dear departed."

"Nonsense," replied Amos. "It's just your imagination. You're overwrought. You haven't—er—been having any strange feelings or impulses lately, have you?"

"Me!" said Leona, indignantly. "Certainly not. Has that Harry been telling stories about me? Oh, I get so mad at him I could tear his throat out!"

"Er—yes," said Amos.

At this moment, there was a knock on the door and Harry breezed in.

"Hah!" he said, noticing Leona in close conversation with Amos.

"You see!" cried Leona, bitterly, and swept out. Harry carefully closed and locked the door behind her.

"Hist!" he said in Amos' ear. Amos jumped back nervously.

"Don't hiss at me!" he snapped.

"I've got it all fixed," said Harry. "They'll be delivered this afternoon. One large steel cage for Leona, and a stout collar with a strong leash for Dave."

"You young idiot!" fumed Amos. "You can't lock a girl up in a steel cage."

"Hah!" said Harry. "Can't I?"

"Don't 'Hah!' at me!" barked Amos irritably. "And anyway it wouldn't do any good. No steel cage will hold a werewolf. It would have to be silver at least."

"Hmm," muttered Harry, a bit crestfallen. "Well, we'd better think of something quick. Time's getting short."

"Nonsense," said Amos, but without his usual spirit, "it probably may not happen for days."

"Hah!" retorted Harry disbelievingly, and went out.

Unfortunately, as it turned out, Harry was justified in his pessimism. That afternoon, Leona was missing. Harry went out looking for her; and came bursting back into the lodge to spoil what was left of the small appetites of the three men sitting around the dinner table—I beg your pardon, two of the three men; Angus McCloud, serene in his scientific skepticism, was eating with his normal appetite, which is to say, like a horse.

"It's started!" cried Harry, slamming the door open. Amos and David leaped like harpooned whales.

"What's happened?" roared Amos, when he had recovered his balance.

"It!" shouted Harry excitedly. "Leona is on the loose. They've found a kid about five miles down the road, torn to pieces."

David turned pale, Amos turned green.

"Oh, no!" groaned Amos. "A little child—"

"Not child!" interrupted Harry, excitedly. "The other kind of kid—son of a goat—you know."

"Thank God," muttered Amos, mopping the perspiration relievedly from his brow. Suddenly, however, his brightening eye caught sight of David sitting at the table, gazing abstractedly at the tablecloth. David was still pale, but there was a slightly puzzled expression on his face, as if he was trying to remember something.

"Oh, oh," groaned Amos. He moved hurriedly over behind David's chair and from this obscure position began to signal frantically to Harry.

"What on earth are you waving your hands for like that?" inquired Harry, in a loud, interested voice.

Amos groaned again, clutching at his forehead in an extremity of despair. Suddenly he took his hands down and began to sing wildly in a cracked voice.

"If a body get a leash

"Comin' through the Rye,

"If a body wear a collar,

"Need anybody cry?"

"Oh, I get it," said Harry cheerfully. "You want the collar and the leash I got to tie Dave up with." And he hurried out.

There was a loud clang from the end of the table where Angus' knife and fork had dropped unheeded on his plate. He was rising to his feet, his face convulsed with wrath.

"By Heaven!" he thundered. "I've been insulted and maligned and controverted by you, Amos Slizer, but I'll be damned if I stand for parodies of Scots' songs. If ye wish to apologize, I will be smoking in the library."

And he stalked out after Harry.

"Kid torn to pieces?" murmured David, wrinkling his forehead at the tablecloth.

Harry came back in with the leash. In response to Amos' frantic signals, he brought them around behind David's chair.

"Kid?" murmured David. "Torn? Teeth? Animal? Wild? Wo—"

"Stop!" yelled Amos, grabbing David by the shoulders. Don't think of it. Think of the girl you love. Think of Leona. Think of her as a beautiful woman—"

"That's silly," interrupted Harry. "He knows as well as we do, she's a were-wolf."

"You fool!" cried Amos. And—

"Werewolf?" roared David, surging to his feet. "Were—grrrh, gnash, gnash. Yowp! Yowp! Yowp!"

"Get the collar on him quick!" panted Amos, who was struggling with the metamorphising David.

"Got it!" grunted Harry, snapping the collar shut. "Sheer good luck the clasp on this happened to be silver." He looked down at David, who was now down on four legs and completing his tail and ears. He made a very good looking hound, indeed. About the size of a St. Bernard, with the dewlaps of a bloodhound and the rather trimmer body of German shepherd or police dog. He was straining at the leash.

"We can't hold him very long," cried Harry; and, sure enough, just at that minute David got all four feet dug in and took off through the house, casually smashing the front door, which happened to be closed, open.

They charged off through the night. Together they made a weird sight, skimming over the ground, the two men being pulled along the path and sometimes through the air, under the light of the rising moon. David's magnificent baying filled the woods.

"We—can't—keep up this pace much longer—" grunted Amos, as he bounded along with fifteen-yard strides.

"Why—" gasped Harry. "Why—don't we just—ride him?"

"Fine—idea," agreed Amos as he drew closer.

Hand over hand they hauled themselves up the leash and assisted each other to seats on David's back. He did not seem to notice the weight, and, as a matter of fact, picked up speed.

"Yowp! Yowp!" bugled David. "Huroo! Huroo!"

He put on the brakes, suddenly, and skidded to a stop.

"What's up?" asked Harry, peering over Amos' shoulder.

"I think," said Amos, cautiously, "that we've reached the dead kid."

"Snuff? Snuff? Snuff?" sniffed David loudly.

"You're right," said Harry. "We have. Do you suppose it's still possible to reason with him?"

"I don't know," said Amos. "We can try." He leaned forward toward one of David's floppy ears. "David!" he said.

"Ruff!" snapped David.

"I don't think he wants to be bothered right now," said Amos, a little timidly.

"Try again," urged Harry.

"David," said Amos.

"Yowp?"

"Stop and think, David. She may be a werewolf, but she is also Leona, the girl you love. When you think of that, doesn't your heart soften toward her?"

"Gruffff—growr!—gnash-rashashash!"

There was a moment of shaken silence on top of David.

"I gather," said Amos, finally, "it doesn't make him feel much different."

Meanwhile, David had been casting around in circles, which grew wider and wider. Suddenly he paused, stopped his circling and plunged off in a straight line, baying with greater energy and intensity than ever.

"What now?" jolted Harry into Amos' ear.

"I think," Amos shouted back, "he's hit her trail."

"Huroo! Huroo! Huroo!" yodeled David.

"This is the end," choked Amos. "She doesn't stand a chance." They plunged on through the night woods, the three of them, David galloping and the other two hanging on for dear life, but nevertheless bouncing clear of David's broad backbone some ninety or hundred times a minute. Up gullies, under pine trees, through underbrush and over huge boulders, they raced, with the moon keeping pace with them, flickering through the trees.

"Hey!" said Harry suddenly. "Aren't we heading back toward the lodge?"

"That's right," ground out Amos, between his clacking teeth, "we seem to be. He'll catch her there. She'll be cornered. And it's all my fault. Why didn't I leave Angus to wallow in his stupidity?"

But at this moment, David checked his headlong flight so suddenly that the two men shot on ahead off his back.

"What's up?" spluttered Harry, coming to a sitting position with his mouth full of moss. He looked around him and was astonished to see Amos on his feet and doing an impromptu war dance.

"Huh?" said Harry, his eyes bugging out.

"Why, don't you see?" chortled Amos. "She's confused her trail. He's all mixed up trying to untangle it. Oh, clever girl, clever girl!"

"And what good," inquired Harry grumpily, "is that going to do us?"

"Why, it'll give us enough time to get to the lodge and head her off. Come on."

"Sniff? Snuff? Snuff?" Sniffed David perplexedly.

"You're right!" said Harry, leaping to his feet. The two men ran off through the woods.

They were still about a quarter mile from the cabin and they covered the distance at the best speed they could manage, which was a slow trot. This, unfortunately, gave them time to think, and memory jabbed them both sharply as they came into the clearing around the resort.

"My heavens!" said Harry, suddenly. "She's a werewolf."

"And Angus is all alone in the lodge!" added Amos, strickenly.

They burst into a clumsy run, approaching the French windows that opened on the library. Across the greensward, as they approached came the rumbling tones of Angus' voice.

"Good girl, nice girl. All right now."

They redoubled their pace and burst through the windows into the library. The sight that struck their eyes brought them skidding to a halt on the library's well-waxed hardwood flooring. Angus McCloud was half bent over by the library table, under which Leona crouched, her eyes shining greenly in the shadow.

"Are you all right?" yelled Harry.

Angus straightened up creakily.

"Of course I'm all right!" he said testily. "Why shouldn't I be?"

"But—but—" stammered Harry, pointing one

shaking forefinger under the table. "Leona—the werewolf—didn't she come in ravening for your throat?"

"She did raven a little bit," said Angus mildly. "But I spanked her with a rolled up newspaper. Now she's gone under the table and won't come out. Who did you say she was?"

"Leona! The werewolf!" shouted Amos, almost beside himself with vexation. "What I've been trying to prove to you. Now don't you believe me, you old idiot?"

To the surprise of both men, McCloud lifted his nose in the air and pointedly ignored Amos, addressing himself instead to Harry.

"In case your friend is interested," he said, "you might remind him that I am still waiting for a suitable apology for his desecration of one of my favorite melodies."

"Holy Hannah!" said Harry. "We haven't time for that. We've got to get Leona out of here before David commits murder." He leaned over and addressed the werewolf. "You hear that, Leona? David'll be here in a minute. Come on out and we'll hide you someplace."

Leona rolled the whites of her eyes up at Angus and stayed put.

"I think," said Amos, "I'm not sure, but I *think* she's waiting for an apology from Dr. McCloud. A fine thing, I must say, Angus, spanking a lady with a rolled-up newspaper."

"She's not a lady, she's a dog," said Angus.

"She's not a dog, she's a werewolf," said Harry. "And if we don't get her out of there inside of the next second or two—oh—oh!"

He held up his hands for silence. And in the distance, approaching with the speed of an express train, they all heard the triumphant yodeling of

David, who had finally gotten the mixed up trail straightened out, and was on his way to the lodge.

"For the last time, Leona," pleaded Harry. "Will you come out? We can—"

"Too late," interrupted Amos.

There was the noise of pounding feet outside and David came crashing bodily through two of the French windows into their midst.

"Huroo! Yowp? Yowp? Yowp?" he yelped.

"If you must know," said Amos, "she's under the table."

"Ruff?" said David, astonished, discovering the crouching Leona and eyeing her with surprise.

"Angus here beat her brutally with a rolled-up newspaper and drove her under the table," said Amos, nastily.

"I did not beat her brutally," protested Angus. "A few whacks with a rolled up newspaper—"

"Arf!" said David, shocked, looking at the older man, accusation in his eyes.

"Go ahead," said Amos, somberly. "She's battered to a pulp. Go in there now and finish her off."

David turned back to Leona; and to all who watched, it was evident that a terrific struggle was taking place within his shaggy breast. The characters in the scene that met his eyes were correct. Here were the humans it was his duty to protect. And here was the werewolf it was his duty to protect them from. But something about the tableau was wrong. It was not the werewolf, savage, bloodthirsty and evil, who stood towering over the shivering, frightened humans; but a human, irascible, brutal and cruel, who stood looming over a shrinking and abused werewolf. There could be no doubt that the revelation of Angus' savagery with the rolled-up newspaper had shaken David's werewolfhoundish heart to the core. Still, duty was duty, and he might have followed the instincts bred into him; but at that moment, it may have been by chance, and it may not—but Leona allowed a sad little whine to escape her.

It was too much for the gallant were-wolfhound. For generations it had been the code of his line to succor and comfort the threatened and attacked. He stretched his head under the table and licked Leona's nose. Then he crawled under himself.

"Thank heaven!" gasped Amos, mopping his brow. "It's going to be all right." He grabbed Harry and Angus by their elbows and hustled them out the door of the library, closing it behind him. "Quiet now," he said. "Just leave them alone."

"Wait a minute," protested Harry, digging in his heels. Noises had begun to emanate from the library. "Listen to that. Maybe they're starting to fight, after all."

"I don't think so," said Amos, firmly, retaining his grasp on the two elbows. "Gentlemen, I must insist. This way, if you please!"

Harry, Amos and Angus were already seated at the breakfast table the following morning, looking somewhat dazed but not unhappy.

"—and so I will accept your apology," Angus was just saying to Amos, "although in the old days singing a parody on Comin' Thro the Rye would have called for claymores at dawn. Ah, good morning, lad."

"Morning," said David, blushing and blinking around the room.

"I see you're fully recovered," said Amos, with satisfaction. "Luckily, I believe I've now stumbled on a new principle in para-science which should enable me to treat both you and Leona and bring this matter under control." He turned to pound Angus affectionately on the back. "Well, how about it, Angus?" he said. "Are you convinced now that para-science exists?"

But Angus had had an evening to think it over.

"Well, now, I wouldn't exactly say that," he replied cautiously. "While this is all very interesting, you must bear in mind I've seen no actual proof that either of the two young people were actually the two beasts I observed last night. No, I'm afraid if you want me to admit I'm convinced, Amos, you'll have to arrange incontrovertible *physical* evidence that Leona and that wolf I left in the library last night with your dog, was one and the same—" He broke off suddenly. Leona had just entered the breakfast room of the lodge. "Ah, good morning, my dear."

But Leona ignored him. Eyes flashing, she marched up to David.

"How dare you?" she cried. "You beast! You hound! You *brute!*"

—And slapped his face.

*Can a Garden of Earthly Delights
flourish with unearthly aid?*

Salmanazar

I SEEM TO HAVE ACQUIRED A SORT OF KITTEN. I CALL IT SAM.

I suppose that doesn't sound too odd, but it
would if you knew me better. I know. I realize all
the nonsense about middle aged bachelors (like
old maids) being supposed to like cats is supposed
to go with a quiet suburban existence and activity
in the local Garden Club. But, I promise you, *I* am
not the type.

In the first place, I don't look fifty. There's not a
grey hair on my head. My existence is far from
quiet. And as for our Garden Club—there is a great
deal more to it than gardening.

We who are in it recognize this. All of us; myself,
Helen Merrivale, Cora Lachese and her contingent,
and (until recently) Achmed Suga—are, if I may
say so, in pivotal position with regard to the junior
organizations. The Hiking Club, the Fund Drives,
the Golden Sixties, and all the host of lesser group-
ings which flourish in a respectable area like Glen
Hills. Indeed, the Garden Club is the H.Q. of Glen

Hills. And, like all elements in which supreme authority is vested, it has its continual, sometimes brilliant and sometimes deadly, internal struggles between opposing chiefs of staff, once external frontiers have been secured.

Oh, indeed I knew—I knew it as long as a year before—that the tide had begun to run against Helen Merrivale, hard-bitten veteran and courageous campaigner that she was. Not one, not two—but five crucial issues, ranging from the placement of the comfort stations at the annual Old-Timers' picnic to the naming of the executive vice-president to the yearly Anti-Trash and Litter Campaign, had gone against her. And what made this doubly awkward was that I was her chief lieutenant.

With all this, however, I suspected nothing when Helen, in August of last year, cleverly managed a nervous breakdown to ensure her honorable withdrawal from the field of combat. I saw her off on a round-the-world trip with my mind occupied only by the disgraceful tactical situation she had dropped in my lap.

Well, I tried to do what I could—but the result was certain. Experienced opponents like Cora Lachese simply do not make mistakes. One by one, I watched my (and Helen's) appointees stripped of their positions of authority in the junior organizations. Though the smile of easy confidence never left my lips during those long and terrible months, I began to make quiet inquiries of travel agencies myself.

How little I knew my leader! She is a great woman, Helen Merrivale. Completely without mercy, of course, but one expects that in such memorable leaders.

Helen returned, quietly and unexpectedly. With her she brought Sam—now why did I write that? She most certainly did not bring Sam. She has no more use for cats or kittens than I do; and at the time Sam could hardly have been more than an embryo. The creature *will* insist on intruding into my writing, as he has intruded into my life. —Now, where was I?

Oh, yes. The first we knew of Helen's return was when we all received mailed invitations to a Home Again party. Attached to my invitation was a note asking me to come early.

I obeyed of course, arriving shortly before the hour. Her sister let me in. Letty. A poor thing by comparison with Helen.

"And where is the dear girl, Letty?" I asked.

"She's waiting for you in the living room," whispered Letty, giving me a strange look. I frowned at her and strode on inside. As I saw the two people waiting there for me, I checked. For an instant. And then I was moving forward with smile and outstretched hand.

I believe I mentioned that I am not the ordinary type of middle-aged bachelor. No grand vizier of an ancient, oriental court, arriving to find his successor waiting by the Emir's chair, could have reacted with more insouciance than myself. And I believe, looking back on it, that at that moment I noticed a spark—just a spark—of admiration in Helen's eyes.

"Horace," she said, "I want you to meet a new, but very dear friend of mine." She turned to the small man at her side. "Mr. Achmed Suga. Achmed, this is Horace Klinton."

I shook hands with him. What the three of us then spoke about in the ensuing moments while the living room gradually filled up with guests, I do not remember. Nor does it matter. The important thing was Suga; as obviously dangerous as he was unprepossessing.

The grip of his hand had been suety. And the

rest of him looked to be of the same material. He was like nothing so much as a little sausage-man. His head, a round grey blob of bulk sausage, seated upon a longer, oblong blob of sausage body. To this larger blob were attached link sausages, two to a limb and sewed tightly together at the elbow or knee joint. Little patties of bulk sausage shaped his hands and feet. I was most cordial to him.

But a natural terminus was approaching to our conversation. And in a moment it had arrived. A stir swept through the room; and a second later, surrounded by her own lieutenants—and a hard-eyed lot they were, as I could testify—Cora Lachese came tramping in.

"Helen!" she cried. And—

"Cora!" echoed Helen. They fell into each others' arms—Helen tall and majestically well-upholstered with regal grey hair, Cora short, stocky and leathery-skinned, with a Napoleonic glint in her dark eyes. A scent of blood was in the air.

"How we missed you!" barked Cora, in her ringing baritone. "Whatever made you stay away so long?"

"The mysterious East," answered Helen. "Its spell got me, my dear! Helpless—I was quite helpless before it." She half-turned toward Suga. "I might have lost myself there forever, if it hadn't been for dear Achmed here."

Cora glanced at the man, and from him to me. I saw her note my own awareness of the fact that I had been supplanted at Helen's side.

"Achmed, this is Cora Lachese, whose praises you've heard me sing so frequently. Cora—Achmed Suga . . ." Helen was saying.

"Haylo, dear lady. Most honored," said Achmed in a thick accent which I had not noticed previously, though it was quite obvious now.

"Achmed will be staying with me several months,"

Helen said. "While he completes his book on Witch-craft in America. We must get him to speak at the Garden Club on the Thugees, or the Assassin's Guild—or one of those other fascinating societies."

"Oh, you study such things, Mr. Suga?" said Cora.

"He is an *adept!*" murmured Helen.

"Please, dear lady," said Achmed, fattily. "Merely I am creature of powers greater than my own."

"Really?" growled Cora. She cocked an eye at Helen. "He's far too valuable for the Garden Club, Helen. We'll have to have him give his little talk to the Old People's Home. I'll tell Marilyn Speedo—"

"Dear Marilyn," murmured Helen again, "where is she?"

We all looked around for Cora's first lieutenant, but she was nowhere to be seen in the room. And at that moment a shriek rang out from the garden beyond the french doors.

We poured out into the garden, all of us. And there lay Marilyn Speedo, dead in a nastursium bed, evidently having just been strangled by a pair of powerful hands.

Quite naturally, this incident cast a pall over the Home Again party. Cora and her group slipped away quite early. A charming funeral was held two days later for Marilyn and during the next few weeks, the police set up patrols about the streets of Glen Hills. However, they had no success by the time the next meeting of the Garden Club was held—on this occasion at the home of Cora Lachese, herself, where custom had shifted it from Helen's home after Helen had left.

Achmed gave us what I must admit was an interesting talk on Hemlock and Related Poisons. I had had no idea, myself, how many lethal substances were available in our fields and woods; and I imagine few of us had, for I saw many of the members taking notes. But after the talk, over the coffee and cakes, the talk inevitably turned to the subject of the murderer, still no doubt lurking among us.

". . . The terrible thing is," said Helen, casting a judicious eye on Cora. "You can never tell *who* he might choose for his next victim!"

"Quite right!" boomed Cora. And, snapping open the sensible leather shoulder bag she had been wearing, rather surprisingly in her own home, she produced a snub-nosed, thirty-two revolver. "Belonged to my little brother Tommy—the one who was a major in the army, you know. Dear Tommy, taught me to shoot like a man—" The revolver went off suddenly, clipping a rather good-sized antler from the deer head overhanging the fireplace. "Oops—how careless of me! Helen, how can you forgive me! It just missed your ear!"

"A miss," said Helen, rather grimly I thought, "is as good as a mile."

"As good as about two inches, in this case, I'd say," replied Cora. "It's remarkable what an eye I have. Tommy never ceased to be amazed at it. Well, what I wanted to show you all were these marvelous little bullets. Something they invented in the first World War, and later outlawed by the United Nations, or some such thing. See—" she took one out and showed it around. "You just cut a deep cross in the soft metal of the nose. When it hits, it spreads out—dum-dum bullets, I believe they used to call them . . ."

While she was showing it around, someone commented on the color of the metal of the bullet itself.

"—Well, yes, as a matter of fact they *are* silver," said Cora. "Rather chic, don't you think? Don't you think so, Helen?"

"Oh, indeed, Cora dear," murmured Helen.

And so our even tenor of life continued—although the murderer was not found. A couple of rather sad suicides occurred, however, to cloud the bright June sunshine—for we were now into mid-summer. Only a week or so after the Garden Club party, Joan Caswell, Cora's second most reliable henchwoman, apparently drowned herself in her own lily pond; and Maria Selzer, the next in line, while doing her morning TV exercises, managed to judo-chop herself on the back of the neck, killing herself instantly.

With this last tragedy a shifting of values became apparent in Glen Hills—many of Helen's lieutenants taking thought evidently on the insecurity of life, and withdrawing from club offices to devote themselves more to home and family. So, perhaps to bring a note of cheer back into all our lives, Cora Lachese chose this moment to announce a gala evening to which all were invited. A Night Lawn Party and Beirfest, with Barbecue.

I must say it was a pleasant evening at first. Cora had produced a most interesting new person—a young man with a heroic name.

". . . Seigfried," Cora called him over as Helen, Suga, and I arrived together. "You must meet him. *Seigfried!* Seig—now, he's gone again. A cultured anthropologist, Helen—from the college over at Inglesby, at the moment. But he's studied abroad for years—oh, there he is!"

She pointed. And we perceived, under the paper lanterns of the lawn party, a tall, shambling young man in a tweed suit. We all moved off to meet him. But I, for one, got waylaid by someone halfway there and never did reach his side. The next I looked he was not to be seen. Neither, for that matter, were Cora or Helen.

However, I quickly ceased to worry about them. The beer Cora had ordered was evidently infernally strong stuff. Either that or I—but I'm sure it was the beer. I have met nobody who was at Cora's that night who did not admit to being a little, at least, uncertain about what went on and what they remember.

In my case, confusion begins later in the evening. Cora had announced an entertainment, while standing by the fire pit where the meat had been barbecued. The fire was mainly red coals by that time. But I remember her flinging up her arms, dramatically in its dim glow, and bellowing out— "Seigfried!"

At that there was a sudden explosion—as I remember—of red smoke from the fire pit. And there leaped into view a figure that no more resembled the youth I had seen, than a sabre-toothed tiger resembles something like—well—Sam. The figure was naked except for a breechclout and feathers, and twice Seigfried's size.

I became aware then of Achmed standing behind me. And at the sight of Seigfried, I saw him start violently and begin to slip away. What possessed me, then, I do not know. But I immediately grabbed him.

"No, you don't!" I cried drunkenly and triumphantly. I had caught hold of his pudgy hand, and he squirmed and pulled against my grasp.

Meanwhile, Seigfried was dancing before the firepit with great leaps and bounds. Suddenly, he yelled at the top of his voice and pointed in the direction of Suga and myself. The whole crowd turned to look.

"Ahani, beja ylar!" yelled Seigfried, or something sounding like that. —And suddenly, without warning, Suga went to pieces.

I mean that literally. I was drunk, of course. It was undoubtedly a hallucination we all had. But one moment, Achmed seemed to be standing there

like any other human being; and the next he began
to come apart. His head tumbled off his shoulders
and went bouncing along the ground like a great,
fat weasel. His body tumbled after, leaping and
rolling and bounding away, thinning out as it went
until it looked like a running hound—and howled
like a hound, too, a hound on the trail of its quarry.
His left arm dropped off; and, hissing like a snake,
began to glide—but why go on? It was a hallucination. There is no need to go into gruesome details.

Yet I cannot forget the way I imagined these—
these *things*, these *parts*, to begin their chase of the
hapless Seigfried. At his first sight of them he had
lost whatever nerve he had originally had. With a
terrified shriek he seemed to turn to flee. But the
parts of Achmed seemed to be everywhere about
the grounds. They hunted him high and low. They
hunted him out of arbors, through summer houses.
They hunted him from the midst of screaming
women where he tried to hide; and finally once
more before the fire pit, they closed in upon him
as if to blanket his shrinking body with their own
shapeless selves.

Together, he and they swayed before the fire in
the half-light of the paper lanterns and the low-
burning coals. And, at that moment, someone who
may have been Cora Lachese—I *thought* I saw her
do it—splashed liquid on the coals. Pit, figures and
all went up in one roaring sheet of white flame.
And I found myself running from that place.

I ran—I assure you I ran all the way home. At
last, in my own home, with the door locked and
bolted behind me, I uncorked a bottle of my fine
manzanilla sherry and drained it from the bottle
like water. It was then I discovered I was carrying
something. Something I had been clutching in my
hand all the while.

It was Sam.

* * *

There is no need to stretch the illusion of that evening out unduly. The next day it was discovered that this youth, Seigfried, had most certainly been unhinged by the long hours of work he had been putting in on his doctorate thesis. Undoubtedly he had been the maniac who had strangled Marilyn Speedo. Almost surely, he had drowned Joan Caswell in her own lily pond. And, while there was some rather firm evidence that he had been teaching a freshman class in anthropology at the time of Maria Selzer's death, yet there was no doubt he was conversant with judo. The official police verdict was an unofficial tribute to Achmed Suga, who—having the adept's resistance to hypnosis—had attempted to restrain the madman, after he had first hypnotized everyone else at the party, and then gone berserk.

—A tragedy culminated by Seigfried's dumping charcoal starter fluid on the live coals of the fire pit and jumping onto them with Achmed clasped to him with maniac strength.

. . . So, we may say this chapter in the history of Glen Hills is finally, if sadly, concluded. Helen and Cora are jointly engaged in reorganization at the moment—a hint having reached us that Mrs. Laura Bromley of an adjoining community is considering a move into our territory—our *turf*, as I like to call it to myself.

And I, myself, am now right hand man to both Cora and Helen. They need me at this time of writing, and the fact is recognized by all. I am a happy man with but one fly in my ointment.

It is Sam. Why I keep the creature . . .

I assure you I have no love for cats.

Nor would I be liable to name one Sam. *Salmanazar*, now—I find that name coming occasionally, trippingly from my lips, when I see the creature. But where the name came from, I have no idea.

Moreover, how could anyone—let alone myself—have any desire to keep a sort of cat which never meows, never purrs, does nothing a cat should do and refuses its milk in favor of a diet of spiders, slugs and filth?

It hates me, I am quite convinced. Also it hates Cora and Helen, judging by the way I see it watching them from a window at times when they pass. Sometimes, also, I see it stalking across the carpet at night like some thick, furry hand, and a shudder takes me.

Besides, on that disgusting and most unnatural diet of its own choosing, there is no doubt but what it is growing . . .

The principle "we are what we eat" ought to impose a certain restraint on consumption.

With Butter and Mustard

"AND HERE WE ARE!" CRIED PETER TIMFOY, EXCITEDLY gazing at the invisible bubble wall that surrounded the Audigel Space Platform. "We made it. Look, Max, look. The ocher sands of Mars. What makes them ocher, Max?" He swallowed and controlled his voice. "Iron rust, I suppose."

"Red lead," snapped Max Audigel, his thicket brows and black beard hidden in a pile of cameras and camping equipment. "It's poisonous. Don't eat any. Get your fat carcass over here and we'll load up for the trip."

"Really?" gulped Peter, coming across the platform. "Red lead? Think of that! I certainly won't taste a single—aw, Max, you're kidding me again. I can tell!"

"Take this, and this, and this. And this. Hang this around your neck. Careful, you idiot! Don't touch the controls in that box at your waist."

"I wish you wouldn't keep calling me an idiot,

Max," said Peter. "Maybe it was only a beer joint but I was a bartender. I belonged to the union."

"Of the jerks, by the jerks and for the jerks," said Max. "Stand still. And remember what I said about that box—it controls your individual atmospheric bubble. I don't give a hang about you, but I don't want that equipment dumped along the way—particularly the cameras."

"Aw, Max. A couple of scientists shouldn't ought to talk that way to each other."

Max stopped. His black beard jutted out like a club. He stood with hands on hips, regarding Peter.

"A couple of what?"

"Aw, Max—"

"How many scientists are there here?"

"Just—just one, Max. You."

"And who invented the Audigel principle?"

"You, Max."

"And what did I bring you along for?"

"Because you don't have any use for other scientists. They're all nitwits—" Peter's voice faltered, died. He looked at the floor.

"Well?"

"To—to fetch and carry, you said, Max—but you were just kidding. You told me when you first came into the joint I had as much science and talent as most Ph.D.'s in the field—"

"No, I was not kidding!" mimicked Max, in a savagely mincing voice. "Now get going, off the edge of the platform, toward that hole in the cliff over there. Go ahead, just step over the edge, idiot. Your personal bubble will merge with the bubble of the platform and let you through. Don't fall down! Why didn't I bring a donkey? It'd have more brains and no delusions of building up its own ego by a parasitic attachment to me."

"I hate you," muttered Peter under his breath,

struggling up from his knees on the sand, and starting out toward the hole in the cliff.

"What?" demanded the harsh voice of Max behind him.

"Nothing, Max."

"Just keep walking. I'll tell you what to do."

They plodded forward across the sand toward the hole in the cliff.

"What's in the hole, Max?"

"A tunnel."

"A tunnel!" Peter tried to crane his neck around and look back at his companion. "How do you know?"

"Because I've been here before. What'd you think?"

"Been here before!" marveled Peter. "Think of that. And all those other scientists back home haven't even got out of the atmosphere yet—oh Max, look! Look at that rosebush away up here!"

"Rosebush!" Max jerked his head around to stare about the landscape. "What rosebush?"

"It—it was right there a moment ago . . ." faltered Peter.

"Rosebush! No, wait—come to think of it, it's probably one of the projections. Pay no attention to it."

"Projections?"

"Pictures! Pictures! You can understand that, can't you? Like on a movie screen—only there's no screen. Also it didn't look like a rosebush."

"It did too, Max. I saw it."

"Well you were wrong," snorted Max. "They didn't know anything about rosebushes. It was just a projection of colored light that reminded you of a rosebush. It wasn't even actually there. If you'd walked into it, you'd have gone right through it."

They went along a few more steps in silence.

"Max?"

"What is it now?"

"Who's *they*, Max?"

"Martians," said Max, briefly.

"M-M-Martians?"

"Watch where you put your feet! Of course, Martians—or whatever the people called themselves that lived here. You don't have to sweat with fright. They're all gone, now."

"G-gone where?"

"That," said Max, grimly, "is what I'm here to find out. That's why I kept my secret of the Audigel Principle. I'm going to be first, from now on. First on Mars. First on all the planets. First to go out among the stars and unlock the secrets they've been hiding. No government interference for me, thanks, so men with half my brains can steal my discoveries, rob me of credit. I'll show them all—"

"—Max!"

"Imbecile!" screamed Max. "What d'you mean? Yelling at me when I'm talking?"

"I . . . I'm sorry, Max."

"Well, what is it?"

"I saw something else, Max. I couldn't see what it was, it was gone so fast—"

"Projections, I tell you! All right, now." Max came around from behind Peter and took the lead. Looking at him Peter was rather surprised to see that Max was himself carrying nothing but a small camera clipped to the belt of his jacket. Otherwise, except for ordinary clothing of pants, shirt and shoes, he was unburdened. "Come on. We've got to go a good ways yet through this tunnel before we come to the city. Don't dawdle."

"I'm not—dawdling—Max," panted Peter.

"I'm not dawdling, Max!" mimicked Max. "No, no, I'm not dawdling! Sweat off about forty pounds and you might be able to walk at a decent pace.

Come on." He turned on a powerful flashlight that searchbeamed down a long, circular walled corridor with walls of highly polished stone, cut straight into the cliffside, and led off.

"Wait for me, Max!"

Peter hurried after him. His insides felt sour and bitter with emotion. He wanted to kick something, but there was nothing around to kick. He fell back on his usual method of consoling himself by thinking what it would be like when he got back from Mars. He would be famous. Audigel and Tomfoy, those two intrepid scientists. He would get rich from television appearances. He would have his own man to do things for him. Come here, you! Bring me my breakfast in bed. Hurry up! I haven't got all day! And how he'd show everybody back at the joint—

"Keep up! Or I'll leave you in the dark!"

"Yes, Max . . ."

Max was so far ahead now, Peter hardly got any help from the flashlight. If the walls weren't so shiny that they bounced some light backward as well as forward, he wouldn't be able to see at all. And the tunnel was widening out now, with other tunnels branching off from it. And there were big, perfectly round holes in the floor to go around— and other things standing in the tunnel to go around too. They might be what Max called them, projections, but Peter wasn't going to walk into them if he could help it. Even if he could walk through them.

"I'm not going to wait for you, so you better make the most of it!"

"I'm coming, Max!" called Peter. "I'm coming just as fast as I can."

And anyway, that *had* been a real rosebush that he saw outside on the sand. He guessed he knew a rosebush from the way it looked. There were the

roses and the leaves, and even the thorns. It had
been a regular rosebush, just like back home outside his rooming house. It had been just about
chest high on him, just about chest—

Peter caught himself suddenly, stepping squarely
into one of the holes along the tunnel floor. He
teetered for a wild, silent moment on the brink—
and then fell.

The shock of his landing was nowhere near as
bad as he had tensed himself for. He had landed
on something firm-textured, yet yielding. Reaching down a cautious hand, he felt it. It was stone-
temperature, the same as the tunnel walls, but
with somewhat the grain and feel of canvas. He
struggled to his feet.

Above him, he could see faintly the dim circle of
the hole itself, the lip perhaps four or five feet over
his head.

"Help!" he cried. "Help! Max!"

The close walls about him seemed to distort and
smother his cries. His voice barely left his lips. It
was absorbed by the pit into which he had fallen.
Above him, the dim reflected light from the torch
up ahead in Max's hand was growing dimmer.
Max had neither heard him, nor looked back to
notice he was missing. Peter's heart leaped into
his throat.

"Oh . . ." he whimpered. Frantically, he groped
about him in the dark. There must be someway to
get up out of here. Something, some handholds to
climb up, a ladder . . .

He bumped his nose on it.

Jerking his head back, he rubbed the small, button shape of the nose, blinking the tears from his
eyes, and moved forward to check again. It was,
indeed, a ladder. A short wooden ladder leaning
against one side of the pit.

Joyfully, Peter scrambled up it, onto firm flooring again. Up ahead of him, the flashlight had been turned in his direction. Max was yelling.

"Where'd you go? Come on up here. I need some of that stuff you're carrying."

Peter broke into a clumsy run. He galumphed forward.

"I fell in a hole," he called.

He found Max standing before a large, ornate piece of grillwork that blocked the tunnel. It was like a large screen of intricately carved ivory, carelessly thrown down in their way.

"Here," snapped Max. "This thing's fallen over on its side since I was here last. I'll have to break it out of the way. Where's that hammer?" He stopped and peered at Peter. "What's that you said? Fell in a hole?"

"Yes, and if I hadn't found the ladder, I'd never have got out, Max."

"Ladder? These people didn't use ladders—or stairs, or anything else."

"Well, there was a ladder in this hole. A wooden ladder."

"Oh, shut up!" said Max. "I've had enough of your stories. Just because you couldn't keep up— Give me that hammer."

He jerked the hammer out of the loop by which it hung from the packsack on Peter's back. A few swift blows of the metal head and the screen collapsed in shards.

"Now come along," snapped Max, punching the hammer back into its loop. "We're almost there."

"Where?" asked Peter, trotting after him. But Max did not answer. And, after a few seconds, an answer became unnecessary, for they turned a blind corner in the tunnel and emerged suddenly into open air.

They found themselves standing in what appeared

to be the heart of a city surrounded by a palisade of small but jagged mountains.

"Look at the screwy buildings," said Peter, marveling.

All about them, some no higher than a single-story cottage, others towering to a height equivalent to eight or ten stories, were walls of every shade and design. Some richly marbled, some single-toned, dull, brilliant, even a few that seemed strangely luminescent for anything in bright sunlight. Streets, or what appeared to be streets, wound crookedly between them.

"So you think they're buildings," said Max, with some satisfaction apparent in his voice.

"Huh?" said Peter. "They *are* buildings, Max."

"Fools, fools—the human race is made up of fools!" But Max did not sound too annoyed. He consented to explain. "These people—Martians if you want to call them that—had no use for buildings. I found out that much when I came here the first time. What they were, I haven't quite settled that. But they didn't *need* buildings. These"—he waved his hand about him—"were objects of art, pieces of virtu."

"Pieces of what, Max?"

Max laughed.

"Come on," he said. "Let's see . . . we go this way . . ." He led off between two of the walls on one of the twisty little streets.

"I'm right behind you, Max."

"Well, stay off my heels, blast it!" barked Max. "Now, come on!"

They penetrated into the multicolored maze of the city, as Peter continued to think of it. As they went along, he began to see what Max had meant about these not being buildings. Some of the walls had gaps in them, or perhaps two walls would not quite come together at a corner. When this happened, Peter was able to look inside. And what he saw was that most of the buildings, or whatever they were, did not have roofs. Or, at least, all they had was a little piece of a roof, though there was one that was all roofed over.

Nor was there any furniture, staircases or windows to be seen inside the walls. Instead, there were all sorts of odd colorful shapes, sitting about apparently at random, or stuck to the walls. Some walls enclosed things that looked like mazes, or masses of cubicles. Some were honeycombed in intricate patterns. Some had a light sort of latticework roofing them in, but were otherwise empty. Only a few had any covering that really blocked out the light of the small sun burning high overhead.

"Gosh, Max," said Peter, "but you know it's kind of peaceful here? Kind of nice."

"Shut up!" snapped Max. "I'm trying to remember the way."

"I just said it was nice, this place."

"*Nice!* Shut up!"

"Yes, Max."

Max was prowling around restlessly, every so often referring to a pencil-drawn map he held in his hand.

"This way," he said. "Now we turn here . . ."

"Max, I'm hungry."

"We'll eat later. Let's see . . . down to the right here . . ."

"Max," said Peter, dreamily, wandering among the walls. It was no trouble to keep up with Max now, with all the pausing and checking he was doing. "Max, you know the old man you used to work for? The one who helped you build the first Platform—the one who was so dumb even if he was a Nobel Prize winner and died just before you got the Platform finished?"

"Shut up!" said Max.

"Well, I was just only thinking how much he'd probably like all these things here," said Peter, hurt. "You said he had all those paintings and carvings he paid so much for."

"I said shut up," said Max. He had come to a full halt. "Something's wrong here."

"Wrong?"

"There's something wrong with this street. It isn't the right way."

Peter was looking up at one of the walls.

"There's a sort of a sign here," he said. "But it doesn't—I mean it's not English."

"Sign?" said Max, whirling around. He looked up on the deep, glowing royal-purple face of the wall Peter was pointing at and saw what appeared to be a short column of something like cuneiform writing inscribed in gold. Max glanced suspiciously from the upright column of markings to Peter, and then back to the column. He muttered under his breath, examining the column.

"We go right," he said at last. And led off. Following, and looking back over his shoulder, Peter could see nothing but the blank purple wall.

"Max—" he started to say. Then shut his mouth. Max was mad enough at him, already.

They continued on deeper into the city, and came up short at last before four towering walls of scarlet enclosing a square. They loomed over the surrounding walls and it was impossible to see if they possessed a roof. There was more cuneiform writing on the wall they faced.

"What does that say, Max?" asked Peter.

"It's the library."

"No kidding?" Peter goggled at the wall. "You're pretty good to read that right off, Max."

"Did you think I'm as dumb as you?" said Max. "My first trip up here when I saw that, I knew there must be an equivalent of the Rosetta Stone around. So I went looking for it.''

"I'm not dumb!"

"Come on!"

Max led the way around the building. Three-quarters of the way around, when they came to the third wall, Peter saw that this one contained a small door set flush with the ground. The door was about five feet in height and about four in width; and it fitted tightly with hardly a seam to mark its outline.

"All right," said Max, as they halted before it. "Stand still."

Peter obediently came to a halt and stood while Max relieved him of all the equipment he had packed on him before they left the Platform. Most of it was camera equipment, but there were a number of other small items, including a thick looseleaf notebook and what looked, when Max took it out of its packaging, like putty.

"What's that?" Peter asked, reaching out for it.

"Don't touch it!" snapped Max. "That's a plastic explosive."

"You going to blow the whole building up?"

"No, you idiot. Only the door."

"Oh." Peter turned and wandered over to the door, leaving Max sorting things and muttering in his beard. The door was, indeed, pretty tightly shut, he saw. There was a keyhole but no key. Maybe, thought Peter, it had dropped on the ground. He searched around the base of the wall and, sure enough, found it about three feet off.

He took it over to Max.

"Here," he said.

"Get away!" growled Max, without looking up.

"But I just wanted to give you—"

"Get away!" roared Max. "And shut up! Don't

bother me. I don't want to hear another word out of you."

Sadly, Peter wandered back to the door. Idly, he tried the key in the lock. It turned, and the door swung open. He went inside. Within, he found himself enclosed by a surprisingly vast single room, whose walls were the outside walls they had walked around, and which towered up to look rooflessly at the sky. But this was not the really surprising thing about the interior; for the inner sides of the walls were as black as shiny basalt, and they were covered, from the point at which they touched the scarlet floor to as far up as the eye could reach, with fine, endless rows of the cuneiform figures embossed in ivory-white. Peter stood back, craning his neck to see how far, far up they actually went.

"You!"

It was Max's voice, bellowing. Peter turned to see Max coming across the scarlet floor toward him, his beard bristling and a wild red light in his eyes.

"What'd you do? How'd you open that door?"

"I only used the key—" Peter shrunk away from him. "I was going to give it to you—"

"Key? What key?"

"The key in the keyhole—"

"*Key!*" screamed Max. "There is no key! There's no keyhole! Do you think I didn't go over that door with a magnifying glass the first time I was here? Did you think I couldn't see just now?" He drew back a fist and drove it suddenly into Peter's face. Peter felt a terrible, crunching pain and fell back, covering his nose with his hands. "I've had enough of your lies. What'd you do?" He hit Peter again, following him up as Peter stumbled blindly backward to get away. "What did you do? Answer me! Answer me!"

He drove Peter finally into a corner between two of the walls and pounded away at him until Peter collapsed in a moaning heap. Finally, Max stood still, hands clenched at his side, breathing hoarsely.

"You won't tell me," he said. "Or you don't know. Oh," his voice sank to a venomous, tearing whisper, *"if you only weren't so damn stupid!"*

Peter said nothing, sobbing against the scarlet floor. He heard Max's footsteps move away from him. After a while, they came back and he heard something dropped with a soft *plop* beside the hands that shielded his eyes.

"There!" grated the voice of Max. "Fill your belly and stay away from me. I've got everything a race ever learned, here at my fingertips. And a greater race than the human one ever was. Can you understand that? Answer me!"

"Yuh . . ." choked Peter.

"This was destined! Can you understand that? It was destined for me to be the first one here, to learn all this. From the first moment I saw the Platform within my grasp—it was destiny driving me. All this was waiting for me, here, left by a race of people that weren't human, that were something even I haven't found out yet. The records I found—the records I found"—Max's voice beat on Peter's ears thickly, like the voice of a man sputtering on soapsuds—"they show them different, different, always different. But now I'm at the heart of it. Here. All the records are here. And you're not to disturb me until I find what I want. Do you hear? Do you hear?"

"Uh-huh," mumbled Peter.

"You better hear. If you bother me—if you cross me—I'll crush you, like some fat slug in my garden. I'll break you. I'll abolish you. I'll destroy you. Take that—"

Peter cried out, huddling away from the hard toe of Max's boot.

"That's better," said the voice of Max. And the sound of his footsteps walked away.

For a while longer, Peter stayed curled up, not daring to move. Finally, he peeked with one tear-wet eye through the spread fingers of his hand. Max was far off, clear across the large single room of the building, down on his hands and knees by the bottommost rows of cuneiform writing. He was copying them on pieces of paper and referring to the looseleaf notebook.

Sniffling, Peter cautiously uncurled and rubbed a blubbery hand across his eyes. He sat up in the corner, with his back against the two walls. His face hurt and his stomach hurt. Something white caught his eye; it was a package of sandwiches done up in a plastic wrapper, lying on the floor by his foot. Sniffing dolefully, he reached out, picked them up, and slowly began to unwrap them. They turned out to be thick slabs of ham carelessly thrust between perfectly dry slices of bread. A sob caught in Peter's throat. Max knew Peter liked a little butter and mustard on his sandwiches; but just because Max didn't care one way or another, he never put anything on them. It was a dirty, dirty trick.

Drearily, he began to comfort himself with small nibbles on the topmost sandwich. It wasn't fair. He took a large bite and chewed on it morosely.

It was all Max's fault. He thought he was the only scientific genius there was. While Peter could remember any telephone number you told him, forever. Or he could look at the numbers on the side of a boxcar once and then, months afterwards, tell you just what they were. Max couldn't do that. And whenever Max couldn't do anything and Peter could, he got mad. Peter never forgot a face or a name, but Max did. Actually, Peter was a bigger genius than Max was—

Peter found his hand was empty, and reached dreamily for another sandwich.

Take right now, for instance. Max couldn't have made it this time without having Peter along to carry the equipment. How'd he be right now, if he didn't have that book and stuff Peter had carried? Suppose Peter had really got stuck in that hole back there. He swallowed and reached for another sandwich.

The ham and bread felt good in his stomach. No wonder he hadn't been able to keep up so well— he'd been weak for food. Yes, Max wouldn't have got very far without him along. No, sir! It took somebody with muscle to carry all that stuff. And that's what Peter had. Why, if he'd wanted to, when Max was pushing him around, a while ago . . .

It took intelligence, too. Peter groped for and found another sandwich. Actually, he was probably more intelligent than Max. He'd found the way in here—that key, and the sign farther back. That was because he was busy figuring things out in the back of his head. Subconsciously, he was quite a genius. Remembering the numbers proved that. He could find a sign or a key or—or something— when Max couldn't. Actually, there was a pattern to all this. Take all those things he'd found. They were facts; and you built a theory from facts. Whenever Peter wanted a fact, he could find one. And it'd be whatever fact he needed. Peter fumbled without looking for another sandwich, but the paper was empty.

That was just like Max. He never made enough sandwiches, either.

But there, see now, this theory—where'd all these Martians go? Well, they all died off. Sure. Except one, maybe, and that one was waiting around to see what they were like . . .

Peter glanced up apprehensively around him, suddenly, but there was nothing to be seen, except Max, busily at work across the empty floor.

. . . But this Martian would like Peter. He wouldn't like Max, because Max wouldn't listen. He'd give Max facts, but Max couldn't see them—like the sign, or the key. You know. That Martian was waiting around for someone like Peter, who was nice. And then he'd make himself into things . . . Peter started to reach automatically for another sandwich and then checked his hand. All gone. And then he'd make himself into things to show Peter he'd be nice if Peter was nice back. Like that ladder. And the sign. And the key. Maybe the rosebush.

Sure, that was probably the Martian right there.

Just one more sandwich would make all the difference.

Peter sighed and looked down at the plastic wrapper on the floor. It was, as he had suspected, empty. But—he leaned forward suddenly—just outside it was another sandwich lying on the bare floor. It must have fallen out when he opened the package.

Grinning, Peter reached out and scooped it up. It was a real thick sandwich. He held it up in front of him and his mouth watered. He opened his mouth—

Sudden doubt struck him.

What if it *was* the Martian? Again? Being a sandwich this time because that's what Peter wanted now?

Cautiously, he lowered the sandwich and considered it.

It *looked* like a sandwich.

But what if it was really the Martian? And what if the Martian wasn't really nice at all? Or what if

the Martian meant to be nice, but didn't really
understand people too well, and didn't really understand what Peter wanted to do to that sandwich when he lifted it up to his mouth? Suppose
the Martian didn't have any eyes or ears or anything like that. Just sort of feelings. So he could
feel what Max was like and didn't bother with
him. And he could feel what Peter was like, and
tried him, and felt Peter's feelings and tried to
check on Peter through things like this, like turning himself into a ladder or a key, or a—

Then if Peter bit into the sandwich the Martian
would find himself being eaten. Then he would be
madder than Max ever was. And then . . . Max said
Martians were greater than humans ever had been.
If one got real mad, it would be terrible, Peter
guessed. Maybe the Martian'd—

Sweating, Peter lowered the sandwich. He
wouldn't bite into that sandwich now. No, sir!

He sat back and looked at the sandwich, sighing.
His face hurt and his stomach hurt, and now he
couldn't have a sandwich that was right before his
eyes. A nice thick sandwich, too. Peter peeked inside it. Just as he thought; this one had butter and
mustard on it, too. And he couldn't eat it. It was a
dirty, dirty trick.

If the Martian didn't want to take a chance on
being eaten, he shouldn't turn himself into a sandwich. It wasn't fair.

Actually, they were all alike, that Martian and
Max. They never thought about you. Just about
themselves. They thought they were the most intelligent. They'd find out some day.

"You!" said Peter to the sandwich. "You don't
scare me!"

The Martian didn't, either. If Peter didn't eat the
sandwich, it was because he just didn't want an-

other sandwich. If—why, if he wanted to—that sandwich would be gone in two bites.

Sitting there like that in front of him!

"You!" said Peter. "You better hear!"

Sitting there like that in front of him to disturb him.

"I'll get what I want," said Peter. "You're not to disturb me until I find what I want. Do you hear? Do you hear?"

He scowled threateningly above the sandwich. He pinched it a little between his fingers and the bread gave.

"Oh, why are you so damn stupid?" he growled.

He lifted up the sandwich, slowly before his eyes. He gnashed his teeth at it.

"Can you understand *that!*"

He shook the sandwich.

"You better hear! I'll teach you!" He pulled the sandwich up in front of his bared teeth. "I'm not scared of you. If you bother me—if you cross me— I'll crush you like some fat slug in the garden."

He looked triumphantly at the sandwich; and it, the Martian, seemed to tremble a little in his grasp.

"I'll crunch you!" he hissed. "I'll abolish you! I'll show you who's boss! I'll *destroy you!* Take *that!*"

He bit viciously into the sandwich. He ate it all down (and it was delicious) and sat there for a long moment after it was gone, holding himself in like a bomb that expects to explode at any minute. But nothing happened, except he felt full at last and strong with good nourishment—better, in fact, than he had ever felt before.

Finally he relaxed. That Martian sandwich had learned its lesson all right. He'd showed it. It just proved what he was like when he decided to ... He looked over at Max and frowned. It was time Max woke up to the fact that Peter wasn't just a pushover, too. Look at Max there, reading that wall. Maybe the wall didn't want to be read. Had Max ever thought of that? It was time somebody straightened him out on a few things.

Filled with a fine new sense of power and fury, Peter got to his feet and marched over to Max. His shadow, falling across the wall, made Max jerk his head up in exasperation.

"*Now* what?" he snarled. Then, suddenly staring at Peter, he checked and the color began to drain out of his abruptly rigid face. Peter, however, did not notice. He was too full of the fine new powerful words bubbling up inside him. He pointed a godlike finger of command at Max, and opened his mouth.

"Human," he said, "go home!"

Although talismans and charms may ward off outer evils, "what rite can exorcise the fiends that dwell behind the eyes?"

The Amulet

HE HAD HIT THE KID TOO HARD, THERE, BACK BEHIND THE tool shed—that was the thing. He should have let up a little earlier, but it had been fun working the little punk over. Too much fun; the kid had been all softness, all niceness—it had been like catnip to a cat and he had got all worked up over it, and then it had been too late. It had just been some drippy-nosed fifteen-year-old playing at running away from home, but the railroad bulls would be stumbling over what was left, back of the toolshed, before dawn.

That was why Clint had grabbed the first moving freight he could find in the yards instead of waiting for the northbound he was looking for. Now that the freight had lost itself in the Ozark back-country, he slipped out of the boxcar on a slow curve and let the tangled wild grass of the hot Missouri summer take the bounce of his body as it rolled down the slope of the grading.

He came to a stop and sat up. The freight rattled

by above him and was gone. He was a little jolted, that was all. He grinned into the insect-buzzing hush of the late afternoon. It took a young guy in shape to leave a moving freight. Any bum could hook on one. He considered his own blocky forearms, smooth with deep suntan and muscle, effortlessly propping him off the soft, crumbling earth; and he laughed out loud on the warm grass.

He felt cat-good, suddenly. Cat-good. It was the phrase he had for himself when things turned out well. Himself, the cat, landed on his feet again and ready to make out in the next back yard. What would the suckers be like this time? He rose, stretching and grinning, and looked over the little valley before him.

Below the ridge, it was more a small hollow than a true valley. The slope of the ridge came down sharp, covered with scrub pine, and leveled out suddenly into a little patch of plowed earth, just beginning to be nubbly with short new wands of grain. A small, brown shack sat at one end of the field, low-down from where he stood now, and in its yard an old granny in an ankle-length black skirt and brown sweater was chopping wood. He could see the flash of her axe through the far, clear air, and the *chop* sound came just behind. And for a moment, suddenly, for no reason at all, a strange feeling of unquiet touched him, like a dark moth-wing of fear fluttering for a second in the deep back of his mind. Then he grinned again, and picked up his wrinkled suitcoat.

"Ma'm," he said in a soft shy voice, "Ma'm, could I get a drink of water from you, please?"

He chuckled, and went down the dip toward the field with easy, long-swinging strides. She was still chopping wood when he came into the yard. The long axe flashed with a practiced swing at the end of her thin, grasshopper-like arms, darkened by the sun even more deeply than his own. The axe split clean each time it came down, the wood falling neatly in two equal sections.

"Ma'm . . ." he said, stopping a few feet off from her and to one side.

She split one more piece of wood deliberately, then leaned the axe against the chopping block and turned to face him. Her face was as old as history and wrinkled like the plowed earth. Her age was unguessable, but a strange vitality seemed to smoulder through the outer shell of her, like a fire under ashes, glowing still on some secret coal.

"What can I do for you?" she said. Her voice was cracked but strong, and the *you* of the question came out almost as *ye*. Yet her dark, steady eyes, under the puckered lids, seemed to mock him.

"Could I get a drink of water, ma'm?"

"Pump's over there."

He turned. He had seen the pump on the way in, and purposely entered from the other side of the yard. He went across to it and drank, holding his hand across the spout to block it so that the water would fountain up through the hole on top. He felt her gaze on him all the time he drank; and when he turned about she was still regarding him.

"Thank you, ma'm," he said. He smiled at her. "I wonder—I know it's a foolish question to ask, ma'm—but could you tell me where I am?"

"Spiney Holler," she said.

"Oh, my," he said. "I guessed I'd been going wrong."

"Where you headed?" she asked.

"Well—I was going home to Iowa, ma'm." His sheepish grin bared his foolishness to her laughter. "I know it sounds crazy. But I thought I was on a freight headed for Iowa. I was going home."

"You live in Iowa?"

"Just outside Des Moines." He sighed, letting his shoulders slump. "Can—can I sit down, ma'm? I'm just beat—I don't know what to do."

"A big chunk like you? Sit down, boy—" her lean finger indicated the chopping box and he came across the yard as obediently as a child and dropped down on it. "How come you're here?"

"Well—" he hung his head. "I'm almost ashamed to say. My folks, they won't ever forgive me. I tell you, ma'm, it's about this pain in my side."

He felt, rather than saw, a dark flicker of interest in her eyes, but when he looked up, her wrinkled face was serene.

"—this pain, ma'm. I had it ever since I was a little kid. The doctors couldn't do nothing for it. And then, my cousin Lee—he's a salesman, gets all over—my cousin Lee wrote about this doctor in St. Louis. Well, the folks gave me the train fare and sent me down there. I got in on a Saturday and the doctor, he wasn't in his office. So I went to this hotel."

He looked at her. She waited, the little breeze blowing her skirt about her.

"Well, ma'm—" he faltered. "I know I should have known better. I was brought up right. But I got sick of that little hotel room and I went out Saturday night to see what St. Louis looked like and—well, ma'm, I got into trouble. It was liquor that did it—unless they put something in my drink—anyway, I woke up Monday morning feeling like the wrath of God and all my folk's money gone." He heaved a groaning sigh.

"And you ain't never going to do it again."

The open sneer in her voice brought his head up with a jerk. She stood, hands on hips above the tight-tucked skirt, grinning down at him. Sudden wrath and fear flamed up in him, but he hid them with the skill of long practice.

"Boy," she said. "You came to the wrong door with your story—set down!" she said sharply, as he started to rise, a wounded expression on his face. "You think I don't know one of old Scratch's people when I meet 'em? Me—out of 'em all? Now how'd you like a drink?"

"A drink?" he said.

She turned and walked across to the half-open door of the house and came back with a fruit-jar, partly filled. She handed it to him. He hesitated, then gulped. Wildcats clawed at his gullet.

She laughed at the tears in his eyes and took the jar from him. She drank in her turn, without any visible reaction, as if the liquid in the jar had been milk. Then she set the jar on the ground and fished a pack of cigarettes from her pocket. She lit herself one, without offering them to him, and stood smoking, gazing away over his head, out over the fields.

"I sent for someone last Tuesday when my Charon was spoiled," she said, musingly. "You can't be nobody but him."

He stared up at her, feeling as if his clothes had been stripped off him.

"You crazy?" he demanded roughly, to get a little of his own back. "You nuts or something?" She turned and grinned at him.

"Well, now, boy," she said. "You sound like you'd be some great comfort to a lone old woman on long winter nights and nothing to do. Quiet!" she snapped sharply, as he opened his mouth again. "Come on in the cabin with me," she said. "I got to check on this."

Warily, confused by a mixture of emotions inside him, yet curious, he rose and followed her in. The interior of the small house was murkily dark, a single room. Some straight-backed chairs stood about a polished wood floor decorated with throw rugs. There was a fireplace and a round-topped, four-legged table. The corners had things in them, but there the shadows were too deep for his sun-dazzled eyes to see. He thought he smelled cat, but there was no cat to be seen; only an owl—stuffed, it seemed—on the mantel over the fireplace.

She bent over. There was the scratch of a match and a candle sputtered alight, illuminating the tabletop and her face, but throwing the rest of the room deeper into darkness. A strange thrill trembled down his spine. He stared at the candle. It was only a candle. He stared at her face—but for all its strangeness, it was only a face.

"Money," she said. "That's what you think you want, eh, boy?"

"What else is there?" he retorted; but the loud notes of his voice rang thin at the end. She burst suddenly into harsh laughter.

"What else is there, he says!" she cried to the room about them. "What else?" The candle flared suddenly higher, dazzling him for a moment. When he could see again, he discovered two things on the table before him. One was a circle of leather string—like a boot shoelace with a small sack attached—and the other was a thin sheaf of twenty-dollar bills, crisp and new, bound about by a rubber band. He looked at the money and his mouth went dry, estimating there must be two or three hundred dollars in the stack. His hand twitched toward it; and he looked up at the old woman.

"Look it over, boy," she said. "Go ahead. Look at it."

He snatched it up and riffled through the stack. There were fourteen of the twenties. His eyes met hers across the table. He noticed again how thin she was, how old, how frail. Or was she frail?

"Only money, boy?" she sneered at him. "Only money? Well, then you got no trouble. You just run me an errand and all that's yours—and as much again when you come back!"

Still he stood, looking at her.

"You want to know?" she said. "I'll tell you what you got to do for that money. You just go get my recipe book from my neighbor, Marie-Elaine."

His voice came hoarse and different from his throat.

"What's the gag?" he said.

"Why, boy, there's no gag," she said. "I done lent my recipe book to Marie-Elaine, that's all, and I want you to fetch it for me."

He considered, his mind turning this way and that like a hunting weasel; but each way it looked there was darkness and the unknown.

"Where does she live?" he asked.

"Her? Over the ridge." She looked at him and leaned toward him across the candle and the table. "Money, eh, boy? Just money?"

"I say—" he gasped, for the smoke of the candle came directly at him, almost choking him. "What else is there?"

"Something else, boy." Her eyes held him. They were all he could see, shining in the darkness. "Something in particular for you, boy, if you want it. You did a fine, dark thing last night; but it's not enough."

"What you talking about?"

"Talking about you. Marie-Elaine, she borrowed my book and my Charon; but she spoiled my Charon. Now she got to get me another, or I take her Azael—don't know what I'm talking about, do you, boy?"

"No—" he gasped.

"I got to play fair with you. Them's the rules. So you take up that amulet there afore you and wear it. No business of mine, if Marie-Elaine can get you to take it off. None of my doings, if you open the book."

His hand went out as if of its own will and picked up the string-and-sack. An odd, sour smell from it stung his nostrils.

"Why'd I want to open your book?" he managed.

"For the pride and the power, boy, the pride and the power." The candle flame flared up between them, blinding him. He heard her, intoning. "Once by call of flesh—once by burn and rash—once by darkness—she'll try you boy. But wear the amulet spite of her and me and the book won't tempt you. There, I've given you fair warning."

The candle flame sank to ordinary size again. Sight of the room came back to him, a slight grin on her face.

He hesitated, standing with the limp, oily leather of the string in his hand. He had feelings about bad spots when he was getting into them—he'd been in enough. Cat-wise, he was. And there was something about this that was whispering at him to get out. Or was it just the moth-wing of fear he had felt as he looked over this hollow? He believed in nothing, not even in witches; but—all that money for a book—and not believing meant not disbelieving ... and that made everything possible. If witches were so— A shiver ran down his back; but hot on it came the sullen bitter anger at this old granny who thought she could use him—*him! I'll show her*, he thought; and the blood pounded hot in his temples. He shoved the bills into his pocket, lifted the amulet, hung it around his neck, and tucked it out of sight into his shirt.

"Yeah. Leave it to me," he said. She laughed.

"That's the boy!" she crackled. "You can't miss it when you see it. A black book with a gold chain and a gold lock to the chain. You'll see it in plain sight. She's got no blindness on you."

"Sure," he said. "I'll get it."

He backed away, turned, and went out the door. He came out into rich, late sunlight. It lay full on the fields; and, in spite of the fact that it was near to sunset, he had to shut his eyes for a moment against its brilliance after the darkness inside.

He turned to the ridge, towering up black with scrub pines above him. A dusty footpath snaked off and up from the cabin and was lost. He was aware of the old woman watching from her cabin door.

"See you," he said, and flipped a hand at her in farewell. But she did not answer; and he turned sullenly away, burning, burning with his resentment.

The first cool breath of dying day filled his lungs as he climbed. He felt the goodness of being alive; and the money was comfortably pressed against his thigh—he could feel it through his pocket with each step up the ridge. But the sourness that had come upon him in his encounter with the old witch stayed with him. The path wound steeply, sometimes taking half-buried boulders like stone steps upward. It had not looked like a very high ridge; but the sun was barely above the horizon when he reached the top.

He stopped to catch his breath and consider whether he should go on, or take the money and cut back to the tracks. Another freight would come soon. Below him, down the way he had come, the shadows were long across the fields of the old woman and the slow curve of the railroad right of way. Before him, the further hollow was half in the shadow of the ridge, and only a small house, very like the old woman's but neater-looking with a touch of something colorful at the windows, stood free of the dark. A sudden thrill of something that was fear, but yet was not fear, ran through him as he stood above the low lands, drowning in the last of the twilight. This was country for witches. He could feel belief coming up into him from the earth under the soles of his surplus army boots. Something evil burnt in the far redness of the descending sun; and the growing breeze of night came out of the shadow of the pines and caressed his cheek with cool, exciting fingers of darkness.

He began with an odd eagerness to scramble down the path along the far side of the ridge. He seemed to go rapidly, but the further hollow was all in twilight by the time he emerged from the pine trees into its open pasture. Overhead, the sky was blood-red with sunset and the roof of the house was tinged with its ochre reflection. A little light glowed yellow behind its windows.

He crossed the meadow and stumbled unexpectedly into a small stream. Wading across, he came up a further slight slope and into the yard of the house. When he was still a dozen feet from the door, it opened; and a woman stood suddenly revealed in silhouette, with the gloaming now too feeble to illuminate her face and the lamp light strong behind her.

He came up to the steps; and as he did so, something large and grey flitted by him and disappeared through the open doorway. It had looked almost like an owl, but the young woman seemed to pay it no attention. He looked up the steps. There were three of them; and they put her head above his own. She was quite young; and her thin, summer dress clung to the close outline of her, revealing a slim, tautly proportioned body.

He stopped, looking up at her.

"Hi," he said. "Say—" a sudden cunningness stilled his tongue as it was about to mention the book he had been sent for—"say, I seem to be lost. Where am I?"

"Not far from Peterborough," she said. She had a low, huskily musical voice. "Come in."

He walked up the steps and she stepped back before him. A light scent of some earthy perfume came to his nostrils and reminded him all at once of how he was a man and this was a woman. The lamplight, as in the old woman's house, blinded him for a second. But he recovered quickly; and when he looked up, it was to see her regarding him from beyond a small table not unlike that other, although this was smaller. There was no owl to be seen. This room, like that in the old woman's house was full of shadows, the main difference being a large yellow cat that sat before a fireplace in which a small fire was burning against the quick coolness of evening. On the mantelpiece above it was a large black book with a gold chain around it, secured by a small gold lock. All this he saw in a glance, but it registered as nothing on his mind compared to the lamplit sight of the young woman.

He had never expected to find her beautiful.

She was tall for a woman, and sheer grey eyes looked at him from under slim black brows. Her hair was the color of the deepest shadows and dropped thickly to curl in one smooth dark wave about her slim shoulders. Her lips had their perfect redness without lipstick and the line of her jaw was delicately carved above the soft column of her neck. Her body was the kind men dream of.

"You're Marie-Elaine," he said, without thinking.

"They call me Marie-Elaine," she nodded.

"You've got a crazy neighbor over the ridge there," he said. "She—" caution suddenly placed its hand on his tongue—"told me your name—but she didn't tell me anything else about you." His voice came out a little thickly with the feeling inside him.

She laughed—not as the old woman had laughed; but softly and warmly.

"She's old," Marie-Elaine said. "She's real old."

"Hell, yes!" he said, continuing to stare at her. And then, slowly, again, he repeated it. "Hell . . . yes . . ."

"You're a stranger," she said.

"Call me Bill." He looked at her across the table. "I was hitching a ride on a freight and the brakeman saw me. I had to drop off by the old lady's place. I got a drink of water from her. She said it was this way to town."

"You must be tired." Her voice was as soft as cornsilk.

"I'm beat out."

"Sit down," she said. "I'll make some coffee."

"Thanks."

He looked about and saw a chair on two slim rockers, spindle-backed and with a thin dark cushion on the seat of it, standing beside the fire. He crossed and sat down in it gingerly—it held. There was a sound of water splashing; and Marie-Elaine came across the room with a kettle. She crouched on the opposite side of the fireplace to swing out a metal arm, hooked at the end, and suspend the kettle from the hook, over the flames. The red flickering light lit up the smooth line of her body all down the clean curve of back and thigh—and the wild blood stirred within him.

"What's Peterborough like?" he said, to be saying something.

"It's a town," she answered. Straightening up, she turned her head and smiled at him, a smile as red as the flames of the fire. "A small town. Strangers don't come, often."

"You like it that way?" he asked, boldly.

"No," she said softly, looking at him. "I like strangers." He felt his heart begin to pound slowly and heavily. "What'd she say about me?"

"Who?" he blinked at her. "Oh, the old bag? Not much." He spread his hands to the fire's warmth. "I didn't get the idea she liked you too well, though."

"She doesn't," Marie-Elaine said. "She hates me. And she's lost her Charon."

"Some of those old bags are that way."

It was a crazy conversation. He checked an impulse to shake his head and clear it. He could talk to a woman better than this. A clink of metal reached his ears. She was lifting the kettle off the hook. Was it boiling already? She carried it away to the further shadows.

He was aware of eyes watching him; and looked down to discover it was the cat. Tall and tawny, it sat upright before the fire, staring at him. Its eyes, half-closed, seemed dreamily to be passing judgment upon him.

"You live here all by yourself?" he asked.

"All by myself." Her voice came back to him and he peered into the dimness, trying to make her out. "Did she warn you about me?"

"Warn?" he said. The cat moved suddenly. He heard the soft sound of paws on the floor and it bounded into his lap. He jumped at the weight of it, then raised his hand to pet it. But it wrinkled its nose suddenly—and spat—and leaped back to the floor again.

"Warn?" he said. "No. What for?"

Marie-Elaine laughed.

"Just talk," she said. She came walking out of the shadows into the firelight, an odd-looking earthenware coffeepot in one hand and two black china cups in the other. She sat down on the settle opposite him, filled both cups and handed one across to him. He took it, hot in his hand.

"How come she's got it in for you?" he asked.

"Oh, it's business," she smiled a cat's creamy smile across the small flame-lit distance between them. "We sell our wares to the same people."

"Yeah," he said. "Your looks wouldn't have anything to do with it?" He watched her to see how the compliment registered. She tilted her face, framed by the dark hair, a little to one side and her shadowed eyes heated his blood.

"My looks?" she murmured.

"You're a doll," he told her, in that sudden harsh voice that usually worked so well for him with women. Her smile widened a little. That was all. But enough.

"Do you want some more coffee?" she asked.

"Pour me." He held out the cup. Her fingers caught and burned against his hand, holding it as she poured the brown liquid into his cup.

"Milk and sugar?" she said.

"Black." He shook his head and drank. The coffee was like nothing he had ever tasted before. Delicious. Staring at the curving china bottom, he realized he had drunk it all without taking his lips from the cup.

"More?" He nodded, and she poured again. He held the cup this time without drinking, warming both hands around it; and looked at her over it. With the coffee in him, the fire seemed brighter and she—standing before him, she had not moved, but now as he watched she seemed, without moving a muscle, to float nearer and nearer, calling to all his senses. His head swam. He smelled the wild, faint savor of her perfume; and, like the candle in the old woman's house, she blotted out everything.

"Tell me—" It was her voice, coming huskily at him.

"What?" he said, blindly staring.

"Would you do something for me?"

"Something? What?" he said. He would have risen and gone to her, but the amulet anchored him like some great weight around his neck.

"You shouldn't ask what," she breathed. "Just anything."

His head spun. He felt himself drifting away as if in some great drunkenness. "You got to tell me first—" he gasped.

Suddenly the enchantment was gone. The room was back to normal, and she was turning away from him with the coffeepot. He leaned a little forward in his chair, toward her, but something had come between them.

"They got a hotel in Peterborough?" he asked.

"No hotel," she shrugged, replacing the coffeepot. "Sleep here," she said indifferently. His chest itched suddenly; and, reaching up to scratch it, his fingers closed around the amulet, through his shirt. Hastily, he dropped his hand again.

"Well, that's nice of you," he said. "I sure appreciate that." The words came out clumsily, and he gulped his second cup of coffee to cover the excitement and confusion in him. The amulet, now that he had noticed it was itching and burning like a live thing. There must be something in it that he was allergic to. He had got all puffed up from poison oak once, on a picnic. When he looked up from the coffee, he saw she was on her feet.

"Here," she said. She picked up the lamp from the table and it lit up a bed against the wall beyond her. "This is where I sleep. But I've another—over here." And she crossed the room, the shadows rolling back before her until against the opposite wall he saw a narrow bunk built of heavy wood and with slats across it, peeping out from under the edges of an old mattress. "I'll get you some bedding."

She turned and went toward a dark door opening in the rear wall of the room. The cat meowed suddenly from near the front door and she spoke over the shoulder. "Let him out for me." Then she had vanished through the rectangle of darkness.

He got up, feeling the relief as the amulet swung out and away from contact with his skin. He walked across to the door, and opened it.

"Here, cat," he said.

It did not come, immediately. Peering through the dimness, he discovered suddenly its green eyes staring at him, unwinkingly. "C'mon! Cat!"

The cool night air blew through the doorway into his face, chilling and antiseptic. Standing with his back to the inner room, he fumbled open the top buttons of his shirt and pulled the little weight of the amulet out. The fire flickered high for a moment behind him, painting the bare wooden door ajar before him and reflecting inward. Looking down, he saw a great, furious rash on his skin where the amulet had rested.

He heard the old witch again, in the back of his mind, chanting—*once by call of the flesh, once by burn and rash.* Sudden fury exploded in him. Did she think she'd frightened him with stuff like that? Did she think he wouldn't dare—?

He yanked, snarling, at the amulet. The cord broke; and he tossed it into outer darkness.

Sudden relief washed over him—and on the heels of it, suddenly, the night became alive. With a thousand voices, whispering, its clamor surged around him, advising him, counseling him, tempting him. But he was too sharp now to be tricked, too wise to be betrayed. Clever, clever, his mind curled and twisted and coiled about on itself like a snake hungry in the midst of plenty and waiting only to make its choice. The heat of his body was gone now, all the lust of his flesh for Marie-Elaine, and only the shrewd mind was left, working. He would show them. He would show them both.

He became aware, suddenly, that he was still standing in the open doorway.

"Cat?" he said. The green eyes had disappeared. He turned back into the house, closing the door behind him. She was fixing his bed.

"You let Azael out?" she asked.

"Yes," he said. Something better than her, he thought, looking at her—something better here for me. I'll show you, who can handle who, he thought. She was smiling at him, for no reason he could see.

"Don't be hasty," she said, looking at him.

"Who's hasty?" he said.

"Not you," she said. And she had slipped away from him suddenly into the shadows around her bed.

"Turn out the lamp," her voice came back to him. His fingers fumbled with the hot little metal screw; and the brilliant, white-glowing mantel faded. He looked across again at the darkness where she lay, but the firelight danced like a bar between them.

He stepped backwards to his own bed and sat down on its hard, quilted surface. He took off his shoes and socks, listening for the sounds of her undressing—but he heard nothing. He slid in under the covers, still wearing pants and shirt—but after he was covered he thought better of it and stripped off his shirt and dropped it over the side of the bed, leaving his chest naked to the quilt.

He lay on his back, waiting for sleep. But he could not sleep.

The fire danced. He felt at once drugged from

the coffee and quiveringly awake. With the throwing away of the amulet, a weird lightnss and swiftness of thought had come upon him, and a sense of power. Witches or women, he thought, they couldn't match him. Women or witches ... almost he laughed out loud in the darkness at the irresistible fury of his galloping thoughts. The events of the day flickered like a too-swift film before his eyes. He saw the kid, the freight, the old woman over the ridge. Again he climbed the stony, wooded slope and stood at its top, feeling the evil in the sunset. But now he no longer wondered about it. He accepted it, feeling it echo back from some eager sounding-board within him.

The dark fish of his thoughts swam in the black flood of the silent hour surrounding him. The keen edge of his desire for Marie-Elaine, her woman-flesh, was gone. Now something deeper, further, stronger, attracted him. It was a taste, a feel, a hunger, a satisfaction—like that which the business of beating up the kid had brought him. It was as if a mouth within him whose presence he had never suspected, had now suddenly opened and was crying to be fed. Somewhere about him, now, was the food that would satisfy it, the drink that would slake it. He lay still in the darkness, listening.

From the far side of the room came the soft and steady breathing, a woman in sleep ... His wide eyes roamed the blackness; and, as he watched, the room began to lighten.

At first he saw no reason for this brightening. And then he saw the faint outline of the room's two windows taking dim ghost-shape amidst the dark; and, gazing through the nearest one, he saw that the moon was rising above the ridge. Its cold-metal rim was just topping the crest of brush and rock; and he saw light spill like quicksilver from it, down the slope, picking out the points and branches of the dark pines.

He gazed back into the room. Dim it still was, all steeped in obscurity; but by some faint trick of the light, the book on the mantel lay plainly revealed against the wall's deep shadow. Its gold chain lustered in the gloom with some obscure element of reflected light.

The hunger and thirst came up in his throat. He felt a need to do great things, and a feeling of wild joy and triumph swung him from the bed. He stood upright in the room, then swiftly stooped to gather up socks, shoes, shirt and suitcoat and put them on. When he was ready to leave, the book lying above the mantelpiece drew his eye again, like a cask of gold. In three long strides he crossed the room to it and tucked it under his arm. It was heavy—heavier than he had thought; but he could have carried a dozen like it easily, with the wild energy now possessing him.

He went swiftly to the door, opened it a crack, and slipped out, and it was like stepping into another day that was just the negative of the film that sunlight would print when the dark hours ended. Cold light flooded the low places and the hills, and before he had taken a dozen steps from the cabin his eyes had adjusted and he was at home in the night.

He went quickly, seeming to swim through it effortlessly on tiptoe and with the sharpness of the cool air in his lungs, a drunken headiness came on him. The book felt rich with its heaviness under his arm. A warmth from its thick leather binding seemed to burn through his shirt and side, infecting him with a strange and bright-fevered heat. He pressed its shape closer to him, so that the beating of his heart echoed back from it, giving blow for blow. Now running, he went up the ridge between the two hollows with their cabins—but all he did was without effort, as if this was no steep slope, but a plain. And at the top of the ridge he paused— not because he was out of breath, but because he had the book now, *and* the money, and the railroad tracks lay there before him in the moonlight and another freight would be along before the dark was gone. He had won, but at the same time, something pulled at him; and he was reluctant to go.

He stood, irresolute on top of the ridge. The night wind blew coldly in his face; and suddenly the fever that had brought him this far faded out of him, leaving him abruptly cold and clear-headed as if he had just risen from a long night's sleep.

Stunned, dismayed, deprived, he stood blinking. What had happened?

The plain earth, the plain moonlight, and the plain wind, gave him no answer. The dark magic that had lived in them was abruptly gone, snatched away from him as if it had never been; and he stood alone at night on an Ozark ridge with a worn and ancient book in his hands. With fingers that trembled, he tucked the book under one arm and reached into his hip pocket. Stiff paper crackled in his grasp; and he drew it forth to stare at it in the moonlight, slim twenty dollar bills.

"Money!" he muttered. And then, yelling out suddenly in furious disappointment and anger, *"Money!"* he flung it all suddenly from him, far and wide into the night wind. The bills fluttered, darkly falling in the moonlight, lost among the shadows of the two slopes. Snatching the book from under his arm he held it before him, closed, in both hands, heavy and warm from the heat of his body—in both hands. Was this it? Was this the way to their rich and secret life?

His heart beat. In the depths of the hollow behind him, the cabin of Marie-Elaine sent small wisps of smoke from its chimney. Before him the cabin of the older witch lay in equal silence and lightlessness. Under the night sky, they and the whole countryside seemed to beat and shimmer to the beating of his own heart—and to the reverberations of some mighty soundless drum, now far off, but waiting. The book burned his fingers.

"Why not?" he murmured. "Why not?" Slowly his one hand closed over the edge of the book's cover. The taste that had been in his mouth as he clubbed the kid behind the toolshed was with him again. The red fire of the hearth played once more over the curves of the crouching Marie-Elaine. These waited for him behind the cover of the book. He wrenched it open.

Black lightning leaped from the page before him, and blinded him. He staggered back, dropping the book, yet crying out in ecstasy. Blinded, he groped for it on all fours on the ground, mewing.

The distant drumming grew louder. The drummer approached. The landscape melted in the moonlight, swimming around him. He was aware of strange perfumes and great things moving. He crawled in the shadow of a robe and the two witches were somehow present, standing back. But the blindness hid the book from him like a curtain of darkness, and out of that curtain came a Question.

"Yes!" he cried eagerly, yearningly.

And the Question was asked again.

"Yes, yes—" he cried. "Anything! Make me the smallest, make me the littlest—but make me one of you!"

And once more, the Question . . .

"I do!" he cried. "I will! Forever and ever—"

Then the darkness parted, accepting him. And, even as he looked on the beginning of his road, he felt himself dwindling, shrinking. For one last moment it came back to him, the big-muscled, sunburned arms and the proud body lithe and clean, the strength and the freedom; and then his limbs were narrowed to bone and tendon, to thickset fur, his belly sucked in, and his haunches rose and a tail grew long.

And the two witches shrieked and howled with laughter. They stood like sisters, arm in arm, sisters in malice, filling the night sky with their raucous, reveling laughter.

"Fool!" screeched the old one, letting go the other and swooping forward to fasten a leash and collar about his hairy cat's neck. "Fool to think you could match your wits with ours! Now you are my Charon, to fetch and run, an acolyte to our altars. Fool that was once a man, did you think to feed before you had waited on table?"

> *"Character is destiny"* said the ancient Greeks, and drove the point home in their myths.

The Haunted Village

HE CAME TO THE HILL OVERLOOKING THE VILLAGE AND braked to a halt. Below him the still town lay, caught like a mirage of hot air in a shallow cup of the enforested earth. He stared at it as he might have stared at a mirage, not quite certain even now as to how he had found it, for the instructions of the boy at the filling station had been vague and he had seen no one along the way who could give him directions. He had taken County Road number twelve and hunted at random through the small, twisting and rutted trails of dirt that snaked back from it among the pines and birch. Now, as twilight was dimming the hollows with the long rays of a red sunset glancing across the rolling hills of soft, glaciated earth, he had come upon it.

He looked down. In the still, late afternoon, the heat waves still beat and shimmered in the narrow streets and above the dark housetops, giving the town a twisting, insubstantial look. Still as a dream, it lay; and no people were visible about it.

147

He released the brakes and the car rolled forward down the hill, and the first houses, building quickly to a wall on either side of his car, trapped the sound of his car's motor, and magnified it, so that it seemed to clamor in the stillness. He went slowly, searching for a stopping place, until he saw to his right a high, weathered building of brown clapboard with three steps leading up to a dusty porch that bore a HOTEL sign upon its overhang. He stopped his car beside the porch and got out.

A tall dark man with grey eyes large in a thin face appeared out of the porch's deeper shadow, walking toward him.

"Can I help you?" he asked. His voice was deep but muted, as if a sort of weary sadness in him made it a special effort to speak.

"Why, yes," said Barin, mounting the three steps. "I'm looking for a room."

"Oh," said the tall man. "You'll have to ask inside, then."

He waited until Barin had passed him, then followed half a step behind. And Barin thought he felt the slight breath of a sigh on the back of his neck, but it was so light he could not be sure.

He opened the door and stepped into a dim lobby, lit only by the fading light from a bay window. To the left a shadowed passage led away into the gloomy depths of the hotel and about the lobby heavy leather chairs sat cracked and withdrawn. Ahead was the desk. He walked toward it, the tall man behind him.

"Mikkelson?" It was a heavy voice from behind the desk, hoarse and mechanical as the grating of a spade on concrete.

"There's a guest," answered the tall man from behind Barin's shoulder, in his sad, tired voice.

Beyond the counter of the desk, a cubbyhole

reached back into obscurity. At the counter, a pale patch of light from the distant window fell on the grained wood and the stiff white pages of an open guest book—just turned, evidently, to a new page, for there were no signatures upon it.

There was the squeak of a chair from the darkness and the heavy, creaking steps of a large man; a thick form loomed up out of the cubbyhole to stand with belly pressed against the worn inner edge of the counter. Barin looked into a wide face, the face of a man past middle age, heavy-lipped and broad-nosed, above a thick, coarse body loosened only slightly from a younger strength.

"For how long?" The hoarse voice was now directed at Barin.

"A couple of days—maybe three." Again Barin thought he caught the trailing wisp of a sigh from the man behind him. He added quickly, to forestall questions, "I'm a photographer. A writer. I'm doing a piece on the woods up here. I'd like to explore a bit—for a day or two."

"Sign." One thick hand swiveled the guest book toward him. Another passed him the stub of a pencil on the end of a string. He took it and signed. He laid it down and looked up into the face of the man behind the desk.

"I'll be eating my meals in town," he said. "Any idea where—" He left the question hanging, but the man behind the desk did not take it up and a long silence drew itself out between them.

"Certainly you—Rosach—" The voice of the tall man again.

"We can take care of you," said Rosach, abruptly. "Not now. Too late. Breakfast."

"Oh," said Barin; and he tried to sound disappointed, although he did not feel hungry. "Any place else in town?"

"No." Rosach reached under the counter and produced a key.

"Up there," he said, jerking a thumb to his left. "Second door on the right."

Barin turned and looked, seeing what he had not noticed before, a narrow stairway that led up and back from beside the desk.

"Thank you," he said, taking the cold metal of the key into the palm of his hand. He picked up the suitcase he had brought in with him and started up. At the turn of the stairs, he hesitated for a second and looked back. He could see the two faces, the heavy and the sad, upturned to him, caught in the patch of light from the desk and watching after him.

He went on up the stairs, emerging at the top into a long, narrow corridor, lit at the far end by a window which still gave on the fading sky. He moved down it, his shoes giving off no sound against the hall carpet. And, as he went, a girl emerged from one of the rooms farther down the hall and came toward him.

She was dressed in a simple, loose dress of some dark color and the blackness of her hair was gathered together in a bun at the back of her head. Although she could not avoid seeing him, she gave no sign of it and came toward him, looking through and past him, carrying some towels over her arm.

He reached his door before he met her; and turned to insert the key in the lock. It was his intention to stop her as she passed, to ask her some small question about the bedsheets or the location of the bathroom. But her indifference to his presence made him hesitate; and he stepped back out of her way, as her dress passed him.

In the light of the distant window her face stood out sharp and clear. It was unadorned and serious, the pale, white skin thinly stretched over the delicate bones of the face, the lips soft and straight and with two slight shadows under the narrow protrusion of her cheekbones.

He saw her in profile as she went by; and his breath caught, because for a second the shadow below the near cheekbone was gone, the graceful line of the narrow jaw, the smooth, high forehead, outlined against the dark wall opposite—and it was as if he gazed at his secret cameo.

He woke to lethargy, and gazed dully about the dingy room, wondering at himself and his whereabouts in that little uncertainty that always followed his wakening.

He must have gone to bed immediately on entering his room the evening before, because all he could remember were the wild fantasies of his dreams—his dreams about the girl who resembled exactly that cameo about which no one in the world had known, but himself.

It was a cameo he had stolen from a house locked up for the summer, back when he had been a boy. He had kept it secretly to himself and woven about it dark dreams of a strange love of the flesh. He still had it, locked in his safety deposit box, back in the city. Not even Ellen knew about it—Ellen, whom he had now decided to marry, just before he had slipped away on this final trip. It belonged to that dark side of him that he intended to bury forever.

Now there was no thought of Ellen, or the magazine article he had come up here to do. A sullen fire burned in him. Before it, the life he had envisioned with Ellen, and his work, were darkly shadowed. He had come up here on a hint, a breath of rumor from the country about this village. The people outside it considered it to be haunted in some strange way—haunted, in this day and age!

He had laughed. But it had attracted him. A good chance, he had thought, for a humorous article on back-country superstitions. Now, he was no longer interested. It was the girl that demanded all his attention, the girl in the corridor.

He washed and shaved himself quickly in the veined washbowl of the bathroom down the hall, dressed and went downstairs. Behind the desk, the unchanging darkness seemed vacant of all life. He hunted by himself for the dining room and found it at the end of the passageway he had noticed when he had first stepped in. A small room with three square tables and a row of windows along one wall.

He sat down and rang the little bell that stood with its dull silver gleaming the center of the white and threadbare tablecloth. The tiny tinkle sounded in the room and echoed away through the half-open door that led beyond, he surmised, to the kitchen. He lit a cigaret, and waited.

It would, he thought, looking out the window, be another hot day. The haze was already stirring the air above the street; and the hot glare of the sun, reaching him through the glass, was no aid in rousing him from the lethargy with which he had awakened, but reached into him with smouldering sullenness and stirred something thick and hot within the animal part of him. He felt at once dull and eager, with the feverish urge to concupiscence induced by sickness and being long in bed. The smoke from his cigaret went nowhere, but coiled about him, hanging in the still air; and he waited impatiently for his service.

Paced footsteps sounded at last from beyond the door. The girl of the corridor came through its opening and up to his table. Now, in the strong sunlight from the windows, he could see that her dress was grey, but her hair was as black as ever.

"What would you like?" she said.

Now that the question was asked, he found that no more than on the preceding evening had he any desire for food. But he was committed to the ritual of eating breakfast by his demands of yesterday; and moreover, he wanted to prolong his contact with this girl.

"What's your name?" he asked, smiling up at her.

"Dineen," she said without change of expression. "What would you like?"

As she stood there, attendant and silent, her perfect passivity touched sudden flame from the heat within him, like spontaneous combustion in a compost heap. So sharp was the chemical change that he felt his face cool with the shock; and to cover it up, spoke quickly.

"Bacon and eggs. Anything."

She turned and went out, the click of her footsteps fading away behind the door. He sank back into the smouldering of his lethargy.

It was some minutes later when she returned; and he looked at the platter in her hands, startled to remember what he had been waiting for. Picking up his fork, he felt a slight twinge of revulsion from the food. She turned to go.

"Dineen," he said.

She turned, calm and unsurprised. He searched for the color of her eyes; but even in the light from the window, this escaped him.

"Yes?"she said.

"I don't know this town of yours," he said with his lips, still watching her. "How do I get out into the woods?"

"Take any road," she said.

"Any road?"

"Yes." She waited a second further, but the sound of her voice went flying away and away into nothingness in his head, as if it would echo into eternity; and he did not say anything more. When he recovered from the sound of it, she had gone.

He sat, wrung with a desire to follow her that was countered by a feverish inertia like that of the weakly sick. After a little while he turned to his plate and ate automatically, not tasting the food, but feeling it soft and slab-like upon his tongue. It was nothing, but it woke him up. He finished his cold coffee and got up.

He went out; down the dark passageway, through the front door and out into the sunlight. Its glare seized him, blinding and baffling him, and he realized with a start that the morning was already gone. It was high noon. He walked off through the streets at random. . . .

He stood in the hills surrounding the town and looked down on the hot gleam of its rooftops. The air was motionless and under the glare of light, the dancing heatwaves seemed to cause the whole conglomeration of buildings to seethe and boil. The forest about it stood like a protecting rampart. Its coolness held him. It smelled cleanly of natural scents, like his Ellen. And he was reminded of her again and he felt the urge to give up the notion of work here, to pack and drive, and so slip back into the protection of the outside world.

But the impulse was like the distant twinge of a nerve, the prick of a dentist's needle in an area where the novocaine has already gone to work. For, superimposed on Ellen's image came the face of his cameo, the face of Dineen. And the wish to break through the invisible barrier of reticence he felt in the girl, returned to him again and again, like the pounding of a drum, until he could feel the feverish thump and plunge of his heart, beating in unison with it.

It was the town, he thought. The town guarded

her. The unanimity of its conclave of dusty streets, through which he had walked on his way just now to these hills, its solitary figures, just out of hailing distance, its still houses with their blank and eyeless windows, these walled him off from Dineen. He had felt the alien spirit of this place from the first. He had recognized it at the hotel desk and when she had spoken in the hotel dining room. He had felt it on his way to here, passing the houses. Whole and alive, they had stood, lining either side of his way, their windows unbroken and the half-glimpsed hint of a limp curtain here and there behind a glassy edge. But silent, silent—in tenanted silence. He had tried vainly to see women and children peeping from those dead glass eyes.

It was the town, he thought, climbing higher on a little knoll for a better view. It was not Dineen that held him at a distance, but the town. Once within its walls of suspicion and distrust—they were small-town, country people and they undoubtedly knew how the rest of the countryside spoke of them—he would find himself the stronger of the two of them. He could break through to her core, inside.

He struck his right fist suddenly into the palm of his left hand. Of course! The town distrusted him because he was an outsider. They thought he had come in an evening, and would leave in a morning. As long as they believed this, their reticence would hold. But undermine that—and the wall of their defenses would come tumbling down. He would be one of them, not one against many, but one against the one that was Dineen; and in that contest he felt sure he would be superior. That was the answer, to announce that he was staying, that he would be among them henceforward and that there was no point in their standing aloof, for he was in their midst and of them.

So, thinking this, the old emotion of the cameo came upon him, and in the still glow of the sun and the silent wood a haze seemed to form about him so that he felt himself a dream moving in a world of dreams; and near and far off, past, present and future, were all no more than things and shadows of his mind. And, turning, he went back down the slope and once more into the village.

The streets closed once again about him. He drifted on down their dusty sidewalks, past the soundless houses and dead stores. They seemed not so remote now. The figures of townspeople swam in and out of his sight, half a block and a block away. He wandered at random, half-expecting at any moment to come upon Dineen; until, turning around a corner no different from the rest, he came suddenly upon a small blind alley, at the far end of which a tiny old woman, bent and wrinkled, hunched and spat at the sight of him.

"Go away!" she screamed in a cracked voice that struck distantly upon his ears. "Get away from here!"

He looked at her dreamily as she crouched against the wall of the alley's far end. He thought of the answer that should reassure her.

"No, no," he said. "I'm a new neighbor. Just moved in. You should get to know me."

He stepped forward and reached out his hand to her; but she cowered away from him still, and went on screaming, "Get away! Get away!" in her thin, ancient voice.

"Is that any way to treat the citizens?" he said, smiling at her. "A fellow citizen?"

"Get away!" she cried. *"Help!"*

"But I'm settling down here," he said, walking toward her. "I'll buy a house—pay taxes, you know? I'll be settling down with one of your local girls. When Dineen and I—" he hesitated suddenly at the word *married*, as if the crazy old woman would pounce on it and twist it into something mocking or obscene.

"—settle things," he finished, lamely.

She screamed more loudly, a long and piercing wail. He stood right in front of her now, his hands outstretched. And suddenly he was conscious of movement behind him and Mikkelson, the tall, sad man, pushed past his shoulder to take the old woman by her monkey hands and lead her past him and away to a door in one wall of the alley that opened on blackness and took her in.

The door closed and Mikkelson turned back to face Barin.

"She's old," he said in his tired voice, "and not quite right, sometimes."

"I guessed something like that," said Barin. "You know, I was only trying to be friendly. I've just been thinking of staying. Settling down here—" He thought he saw the shadow of a frown beginning to form on the tall man's face. "—Of course, you're right, she's not quite—"

He hesitated. Mikkelson turned and began to lead the way out of the alley. Barin followed, feeling a sudden spurt of anger.

"She ought to be in an institution!" he said.

"Some of our people here," Mikkelson turned his head as he walked, "have ideas brought over from the old country. They don't believe in sending away relatives. They keep them to themselves, in some dark room."

The words struck Barin with an odd ring; but they were back out on the street now and he saw a chance to show his agreement with the spirit of the local people.

"And why not?" he said. "Probably the best way, when you come right down to it. Are there many around here like her?"

"A few," said Mikkelson. "Some. Maybe more than you'd think—by outside standards."

"Oh, not me," said Barin. He made an open gesture with his hand. "It's like the stories about this place. I'll be honest with you. The rest of the country around here seems to think you people are haunted. In fact, that's the article I actually came up here to do. Quaint country superstitions, you know. Well, very possibly it's this practice with the old and senile that's given them that notion about you. After all, it's all relative. Who can tell? Who can set the standards of sanity or insanity? Looked at from one point of view everyone is a little insane. Or everyone is sane."

Mikkelson turned his large eyes upon him.

"That's true," said the tall man. "I suppose you lost your way?"

"Why, yes. That's what happened," said Barin. "Your streets—and I was so busy thinking I didn't notice where I was going." He smiled at Mikkelson. "It was quite easy."

"Very easy," said Mikkelson, "even in a small town like this." He pointed up the street. "There's your hotel, now. I have to turn off here."

Barin looked up and saw the porch and sign of the hotel half a block away. He turned to thank Mikkelson, but the tall man had already turned and was striding off down a street to Barin's right.

Barin went on to the hotel.

In the dining room that evening, he caught Dineen by the wrist after she had brought him his dinner coffee and held her.

"Sit down," he begged.

She looked from his face to his hand, his long fingers enclosing her slim wrist with the white hand limp beyond it. She looked back with no expression on her face and sat down. When he released her arm she drew it to her and out of reach below the edge of the tabletop.

"I love you," he said.

"No," she said, and shook her head.

"You don't understand," he said, leaning toward her. "You think it's impossible, the sort of thing that happens in movies, that I could come in from nowhere and see you once and fall in love. But it *is* possible. It is!"

She shook her head again.

"Listen," he said, putting his face close to hers. "If love is something different to you, it can happen this way. You think I'm just talking—that I'll be going away again. But I won't. I've been looking for a place to settle; and I like it here. You think about that." He put his hands under her elbows and lifted, so that she got to her feet. He pushed her toward the kitchen door. "Go on, think about it."

She went off, turning about like a sleepwalker. He watched her go.

The next morning, the waters of sleep were turgid and heavier, harder to brush from him. He woke to a feeling of heavy dullness and indifference so deep it seemed to hold his body in near paralysis.

He rose and dressed with great effort. Nor, this morning, could he bring himself to make the effort of shaving and washing. Dully, he went out of his room and downstairs.

The front door of the hotel opened under the pressure of the palms of his hands and he stepped out again into the sunlight. He went down the three steps to the sidewalk; and, turning right, began to walk aimlessly through the town.

There was a thought, vague but insistent in his mind, that he should look up some local owner or dealer in real estate. With someone like that, he could go through the motions of renting, or—why not, he had the money—buying a place. But he hesitated at asking directly from Rosach or Dineen where such a man could be found. Dineen might not believe it.

It would be better to stumble across someone like that on his own.

For the first time, now, having walked a little ways, he lifted his eyes from the greyish pavement of the sidewalk that streamed slowly past his plodding feet, and looked around. This day, it seemed, there were more people moving about the village, as if they were all losing their fear of his strangeness. He saw them on every street he turned into; standing, walking or talking, although those who talked were always at such a distance that the sound of their voices did not reach him; and on several occasions, he could see through some magnification of the haze their very lips moving, but could not catch a word.

And of the others, there were many within easy hailing distance, across the street or a few feet away, up on wide, shadowy verandas; but for some reason, he had a disinclination to call out to them, as he might have on his first day here. It seemed to him now that so abrupt and unwarranted an action might easily shatter the fragile web he was weaving to bind himself into the structure of their isolation.

Yet he must ask directions.

He looked around. On a nearby veranda, a woman was sweeping listlessly at the dust on the painted surface of the boards. He took his politeness in both hands, and turned in through the gate in the wrought iron fence that guarded the parched and dying front lawn.

The click of the metal gate, opening and closing,

announced his coming. The woman looked up. Her broom stopped and she stood waiting in silence, defensively, for him to come up.

His feet rang hard on the concrete of the walk and hollow on the wooden steps to the porch level.

"Pardon me," he said. "But I'm looking for a local real estate agent. You couldn't tell me where to find one, could you?"

She looked at him with a face scoured of character and expression by long years of hard work and stifled thought.

"I don't know." Her voice was rusty and uncertain.

"Who might know?" Barin asked. "Do you know somebody who would be able to tell me?"

"I don't know," she repeated dully. "My man, you might ask him."

"And where would I find him?"

"I don't know," she repeated for the third time, wearily. Her hand made a feeble little gesture of vague indication. "Out, someplace. Downtown."

She stopped. Barin waited for her to continue, but she seemed to have forgotten his presence. She made some small, aimless movements with the broom as if she would take up her sweeping again.

"What's his name?" asked Barin, finally.

"His name?" She said, lifting her head, and hesitated. "George. George Monk," she said at last.

"Thank you." Barin gave her a small, half-wave with his hand and turned, going down the walk and out again past the click of the gate, into the street. As he walked away, he turned once briefly to look back over his shoulder. She had gone back to her sweeping.

He walked toward what he took to be the business section. As the shadowed houses gave way to the dusty panes of the store fronts, he came out on a street which was obviously the main one of the village, three blocks of brick and clapboard build-

ings with high blank windows on the second story
and square shop windows below. Under the bak-
ing sun, on this street no one stirred.

He looked about and turned at random to the
nearest store, which had HARDWARE painted in
faded yellow letters above the store front. He opened
the windowless door and went in.

Above his head a bell chimed. A little man came
to meet him between narrow counters piled high
with metal goods and pieces of household equipment.

"Yes?" he said. "Yes, what do you want?"

"I'm looking for a George Monk," said Barin.
"Do you know where I can find him?"

The little man peered up at Barin through rim-
less, glinting glasses. His voice was dusty and crackled like old paper that shatters when crumpled.

"George Monk?"

"Yes."

The little man laughed like leaves rustling across
concrete.

"He's dead. George Monk's dead."

"His wife—" Barin began.

"His wife!" The little man snorted thinly through
his small nostrils. "You've been talking to his wife,
have you?"

"Well, I didn't know," said Barin. "I wanted a
real estate agent."

"Real estate?" The hardware man looked up and
struck the palms of his hands together. "Good.
Good! There'll be a boom yet, you wait and see.
Were you wanting to speculate?"

"No," said Barin. "I just wanted a place."

"Oh!" he chuckled. "A place. That's good. That's
fine."

"I'm thinking of settling down here—" the words
were a little hard, making their way past Barin's
throat. "I might marry. People do, you know." He

tried to give his last words a sly twist, as if joking. Instead they sounded ominous in his own ears. The little man did not seem to notice.

"Well, now," he said. "Well, now, *I* have a place. A fine place just above the store here. That might be just the thing now, don't you think?"

Barin looked around the ancient dirtiness of the store. It was not attractive. But upstairs it might be better, and beggars could not be choosers, and he wanted to rent something to convince Dineen he was serious.

"All right," he said. "If you'd like to let me look at it—"

"Absolutely, absolutely. This way." The hardware man turned and led the way to the store's back, and up a dark staircase to a rickety landing and narrow door. He threw the door open and ushered Barin through it.

"A fine, big place," he said.

Barin walked away from him, through the bare, unfurnished rooms and to the windows in front overlooking the main street. The sunlight slanted through the windows, throwing strong shadows on the floor but without lighting the inside clearly. Standing in the light-glare and breathing the dead, unmoving air, Barin felt coming on him once again the haziness that he had felt on the hill overlooking the town. The walls about him seemed to stretch away to infinity, but at the same time to close about him, so that he felt himself locked like a fly between two panes of glass, caught by the unseen, prisoned-in transparency.

"A fine, big room. An excellent room," the hardware man was chuckling at his elbow; and he, turning, sealed the bargain, paying his fee, whatever the little man asked; and so, not listening to the squeaks and mutterings of the other, turned and went down the stairs and away into the streets of the town. But all in daze, all in a dream, all under the cloak of unreality.

How long this particular fit lasted, he found himself unable to estimate, as he sat on the grass later in the day, opposite a boy perhaps seven or eight years old, perched on the pediment of a stone lion in a tiny park. Thin and close-hunched in khaki shorts and a striped t-shirt faded from much washing, the boy was coloring with crayons the faces of pictures in a coloring book. Barin watched, absorbed, as the boy worked.

"How long will it take?" Barin asked finally, breaking the silence.

"As many days as there are pictures in the book," said the boy. And he held it up to show Barin.

"You see," he said, "everything has to be done just right. Once I make a mistake, there's no fixing it. If the red happens to go just a bit over a line into the blue, the line gets spoiled. When I was just a baby, I used to spoil a lot of pictures. But now I know when you color one, it's for good, and I never make any mistakes."

"I like to color pictures," said Barin, dreamily.

"Then you got to find your own book," said the boy, seriously, without raising his eyes from the page on which he was working. "But remember, it has to be perfect."

He became completely absorbed in his coloring; and, after watching for a little while longer, Barin left him.

The day was fading when Barin came back at last to the hotel. It was the same hour of the afternoon on which he had driven into the town, two days before. The sun smouldered low on the pines of the western hill tops and the lobby of the hotel, when he entered it, was stifled in gloom. The feverish after-effects of his dream-fit were still on him; but in spite of it he felt strong now with the memory of his day's accomplishment, and he strode straight to the desk.

In the dark depths behind it, Rosach stirred, a deeper shadow.

"Yes?" his voice came grating.

"I just thought I'd tell you I'll be leaving tomorrow," Barin said. "I'm going to stay a while in town here. I thought I'd settle down and write. I've rented a place, above the hardware store."

Rosach grunted.

"I'll move early in the morning," Barin leaned a little forward over the counter, trying to make out the expression of the hotel man's face. "I think I'll go to bed early, now. I'm not feeling so well. Would you mind sending Dineen up with a glass of hot milk for me?"

Again Rosach grunted, like some wild pig back in a thicket. It was impossible to tell whether he agreed or disagreed; and Barin, hesitating at repeating his question, turned slowly away and went up the stairs.

The hall above was shadowed darkness, but his room was filled with the clear dimness of the fading twilight seen through the window. Barin lay down on top of the covers of the made bed without even taking off his shoes. The mattress, felt through the sheets and blankets, pressed hard against his back; but he lay back gratefully drugged with tiredness that seemed to clot and impede the nervous muscles of his body. He felt that he did not want to move ever again, but to continue to lie as he was for time unending. Now, indeed, he did begin to feel hot and dizzy and a little out of his head as he might be with fever. He turned his face to the closed door of his room and waited.

After a little while, there was a knock at the door.

"Come in," he said, looking away out the window.

He heard footsteps in the cadence of Dineen's walk, approaching his bed. But he kept his eyes on the glowing oblong of window until he heard the glass of milk being set down on the table beside the head of his bed. Then he spoke.

"Don't go," he said.

The sound of his own voice, bleating and strange, shocked him; and, turning his head at last, he was shocked even more by Dineen's appearance, for she had made no move to go, but stood with lowered head, hands limply at her side like one condemned before the executioner. For a second a thrill of pity cooled him; and then the buried heat of his desire beat up more fiercely. He took her by one still hand, swinging himself up into a sitting position on the edge of the bed. She neither stirred nor spoke.

"Dineen—" he said.

She did not move. And at that he told himself that she had already heard the news of his day's action. Rosach had told her, no doubt. There could be no other interpretation.

"Now you know," he said.

"Yes." Her voice was calm and hopeless, so that he shuddered at it while at the same time it increased his hunger and he tightened his grip on her hand, pulling her toward him. She came, neither helping nor resisting; and the weight of her body fell softly and heavily upon him, pushing him back down on the bed. The last rays of the sun through the window struck him full in the eyes, blinding him; and a surge of triumph like nothing he had ever felt before, washed through and over him.

"Dineen!" he cried wildly, putting his arms around her.

* * *

He awoke gradually, fighting returning consciousness and a feeling of growing sickness that came with it, an abiding ugliness that hung just outside the limits of his knowledge and that increasing wakefulness did nothing to dispel.

He could not remember what had happened the night before, beyond the moment of his calling Dineen's name. There was a vague feeling that nothing had happened, that after a little while she had left him with everything all inconclusive. Forcing himself up to sit on the edge of the bed, he discovered himself still fully clothed, on a bed still fully made. The memory of the evening grew more clear. No, they had done nothing; they had not even talked. She had lain in his arms like a life-size imitation of a woman, a cloth doll stuffed with sawdust—yet the memory of this, just this, was a particular horror. And now, suddenly, he remembered why. It was because, even then, even with her just like that, he had not wanted to let her go.

Now, he wanted nothing but to leave.

At any cost he wanted to pack up and get away from this place. Leave Dineen with the lie of his love and promise, leave the hardware owner with the rent money he had paid down. Leave all, leave everything, but get away before he should be tripped again, to sink once more into the particular foulness he had gone down into the night before.

He thought of Ellen now with the intensity of a drowning man. The image of her was a light, natural and clean as the glimmer of day, far off at the end of this dank and underground tunnel in which he was now groping. He must get back to her, he must get out, at any cost he must get out. Struggling against lethargy, spurred by the sickly fear that held him, he began to dress.

He did not have strength to pack his suitcase.

He left it and went out into the hall. He came down the stairs, slowly and awkwardly, his body protesting against the dreamlike exhaustion that held him in its octopus coils. He walked heavily to the desk.

"Leaving?" said the deep, harsh voice from back in the shadows behind the desk.

"Leaving."

He echoed the word wearily. There was the creak of the chair, the heavy footsteps moving forward and Rosach emerged into the dim patch of daylight behind the counter. He looked at Barin with a hint of obscure triumph on his heavy face. He stood there.

"Well?" said Barin, with a sigh. "How much?"

"Fifteen," said Rosach. He did not refer to the guest book or any ledger; and when Barin painfully laid the bills on the counter between them, he made no effort to pick them up.

"Well—goodby," said Barin.

"Goodby," answered Rosach, still watching him without moving or altering the expression on his face.

Away in the distance, an unfamiliar sound could be heard, the rattling roar of an ancient car breasting the height above the village and starting down the street Barin had followed before.

"Goodby," repeated Barin, almost inaudibly. He turned away from the desk, picked up his suitcase and trudged toward the door. Outside the sound of the car could be heard, coming close. It moved up and stopped in front of the hotel.

He was only a few feet from the door when a patch of shadow near the dusty front window stirred and took on outline. It was Dineen, saying nothing, standing white-faced in the shadows and waiting for him.

He stopped and half-turned to her, a stumbling

apology on his lips. He stepped toward her, but she faded back into the gloom, and was lost. Slowly he turned away.

Behind him, Rosach's heavy footsteps could be heard coming around the counter and toward him.

Barin's gaze went to the window and centered on the weathered convertible that had just pulled up, and on the couple, a young man and girl, who stood at the foot of the porch steps talking up to Mikkelson. For a second they struck welcomely upon Barin's eyes, like representatives of a wholesome world apart. And then it was as if the soft kindness of emotion was wiped away by the acid of a prejudiced and fouled appraisal. The gentle planes of the two young faces became blocky and ugly, the eyes seemed narrow, the pallor unhealthy, the lips sagging and lush and lewd under the sharply seen hairs curling from the nostrils.

They were alien—alien!

Horror mounted in Barin, and repulsion. Against his will, like a strange thing which had ceased to obey orders, he could feel his body shrinking, drawing back from the window, and his mouth opening and widening, stretching at the corners in preparation for letting out the droning, whining bleat that was mounting up from his lungs to his straining throat.

—Then a bear-like arm caught him from behind and Rosach's thick and grainy hand was over his mouth, throttling that madman's wail. He was dragged back from the window and the scene dissolved into a confusion of low voices and the pressure of holding hands as he was dragged backward through obscure corridors and black ways until he felt earth under his feet and a stable smell came up in his nostrils as the arms finally let him go— and he sank into yet greater blackness where his whirling and insane senses departed from him.

Some time afterwards, he came back to himself, lying in muck and dirt, and opened his eyes. Low voices were talking in the darkness about him like voices in a nightmare. But the blackness was relieved, for here and there a chink of light showed as through ill-fitted boards, filtering a greyness into the place. In one lighter portion of the dark, Dineen sat, on something unseen, her face half-turned to him. She sat motionless, her profile a thing of patchwork shade and shadow, like a woodcut.

"Are you awake?"

It was the voice of Rosach, above him.

"Yes," Barin whispered. But it seemed they had not heard him.

"It never happened before," clicked the voice of the hardware man. "Not like this."

"It was . . ." said Barin, and stopped.

"What?" demanded the crackling, high old voice.

"Nothing," said Barin. "Nothing—"

There were confused murmurs from above him, muted argument in which nothing was understandable.

"We have, after all, a duty," said the deep, sad voice of Mikkelson, louder than the rest.

"—And the others passed through?" asked Rosach.

"Directions," said Mikkelson, "that was all they wanted."

"It was the others," said Barin, numbly, "those in the car . . . it's the rest of the world that haunts here."

"Shut him up!" cried the crackling voice, angrily.

"This place is haunted by the rest of the world. Dineen!" cried Barin suddenly. "Dineen, this town is haunted by the real world, isn't it?"

"Yes," her voice came calmly through the darkness. She had not moved.

"Shut her up, too!" screeched the old voice. "How can we think with that gabbling?"

"What sin was it that—" Barin raised himself suddenly on one elbow. "What's that smell?"

"It will be fall in a few months," said Mikkelson's voice, "and with the first snow, the roads—"

"It's goats!" screamed Barin suddenly, scrabbling to his feet. "It's a goat pen in here! You're not going to lock me up with goats—" He made a plunge into darkness, but the arms were around him again.

"There's no goats!" squawked the old voice.

"You can't fool me!" cried Barin, plunging and biting. "I won't be locked up to rot in a pen with goats. I tell you I can smell them!"

"He smells himself, now," said the voice of Rosach in Barin's ear. "Help me get the rope around him and tie him up."

Barin felt the harsh, thick fiber winding around him, but it could hardly hold him. He twisted and plunged in the darkness, butting at anything he felt close to him and bleating his terror, while his churning feet pounded and galloped to nowhere on the hard packed dirt of the ground, like hooves.

On Earth, "men and plants increase, cheered and checked by the self-same sky." Elsewhere they might grow even closer together.

The Three

WHEN THE SUN WENT DOWN THE KLANTHEID STIRRED, unfolding its "petals" until they spilled over the top of the tank in a tumbled mass of green and gold glory, and stretching its slim, fibrous body in the nutrient fluid in the tank. It had slept for a while, but not well, and it was impatient for the woman to come and feed it.

It extended the filaments at the base of its petals, searching the house for her presence. For the filaments were the Klantheid's perceptive organs. With them it saw, tasted, heard, felt and smelled—not as humans do, but in a deeper, more intimate way for which the human language has no words. With them it could even talk, by complex vibrations of the filament tips together—in a sort of husky thrilling whisper. And it talked with the woman often; but with the man only when it had to.

The Klantheids were the dominant life form of Pelao, a small Arcturian planet completely devoid of anything but plant life—a garden planet, a meadow-world and a botanist's dream.

To protect Pelao Central Headquarters, the supreme authority of interstellar and interplanetary human civilization had early set it aside as a government preserve. It was reserved for the botanists and for the research into new fields of organic medicine that grew out of its wealth of plant life and fertile soil. The Klantheids, in particular, were awarded the highest and most strict protection, for before the perambulating, sometimes vicious animal that was man they were helpless. But in late years, the regulations had been relaxed enough to allow the lonely outposts of gardeners and watchers to "fraternize"—that is, take an occasional Klantheid into a nutrient tank in their dwelling quarters and keep it there as a companion, friend or pet.

This, then, was one of those outposts. The man was a sort of gardener-watchman, a flower warden, responsible for several thousand square miles of the garden planet, and gone most of the time on the constant patrol that his job required during the ten-year term of his office. The woman was his wife, brought in to share his term of office with him by special permission. And the house was their home.

All this the Klantheid knew—not as humans know it, but in an odd, personal way. For the Klantheid had senses beyond humans' and the chiefest of these was the ability to respond to emotion.

This, indeed, was the source of its delicateness. There were other plants men had known, on Earth as well as on other planets, who could be hurt and die from slight changes of temperature, who died in the sun, or the sudden damp, or perished at the touch of a finger. The Klantheid was not like these. In its own way it was hardy—able if the need arose to go without food or fluid for a long time, and even to drag itself painfully by great effort from one place to another. Ironically, it was extremely sensitive to smoke; and for that reason cigarettes were *verboten* around it. But generally speaking it was a sturdy life-form, with the single exception of emotion.

IT WAS for this reason that it had not slept well—not this afternoon, nor many afternoons past. This was because the woman was unhappy, with a deep and buried sorrow, and the Klantheid suffered at the touch of her sorrow and did not know what to do about it. In its own way, the Klantheid was desperate, for sorrow, like hate and anger, could kill it, where it loved—and the Klantheid loved the woman, even as it feared and disliked—dislike was the strongest emotion it could summon—the man.

Slowly, these two conflicting emotions were tearing the Klantheid apart. Deeply and hurtingly, as it stirred in its tank and watched the blood-shot purple of the sunset on Pelao through the great curving window that backed its tank, it wished that its basic nature was different, that it did not have to love so deeply. It could ask to leave, and the law would compel them, the man and woman, to take it out into the open meadows again. But it could not bring itself to leave the woman. And it could not change its feelings toward the man. And that last was the hardest thing of all, for the Klantheid was not built to dislike, or indeed to do anything but love. Love was the deep-rooted instinct of its nature, the inner strength and meaning of its existence. Deeply, passionately, it longed to love, not merely the man and the woman, but all things, all humans, all life forms, all planets, all suns, all universes, all time and space. It knew, as humans will never know, the great thrilling sensation of being for one fleeting moment in touch, *en rapport*, with all life within its perceptive circle—that wonderful, ineffable sense of belonging that comes only from a great wave of love and appreciation of the beauty of all things washing out in all directions into the universe and touching response wherever it reaches. The Klantheid had had a few such moments in its life—moments when it felt in tune with all nature, and as far as that part of its existence went, it was satisfied, and ready to meet the rest of what its short dozen years of life might hand it. But it could no more ignore the sorrow around it now, than a human can ignore the killing cold of arctic snows.

Searching, searching, its filaments located the aura of the woman coming toward it. Her heart was breaking and the filaments of the Klantheid curled in agony as it sensed the emotion. In the surge of that reaction it lost what little appetite the last few weeks of trouble had left it. It waved away in protest, with its broad leaves of green and gold, the vitamins and minerals the woman was about to add to the fluid in which it rested.

"You are worried," it wept to her in the soft sussurance of its whispering filaments. "You are afraid, and you hurt. Let me sing to you."

"No," answered the woman, halfway between apathy and sad laughter. "My trouble's beyond singing. You know that."

"Let me tell you a story, then," begged the Klantheid. "A story of long meadows and soft skies and the bud hanging in the wind. A story of peace and contentment."

"No story," said the woman. She laughed a little harshly. "You don't happen to know of any rare old poisons growing wild around here, do you?"

The Klantheid's soft soul quivered in shock away from the emotion behind her words.

"Are you broken, broken, then?" it whispered weepingly, half to itself. "Are you all beautiful gone ugly wrong? Why? Why?"

"You'd know why, if somebody hated you and you learned to hate back," said the woman—but then her mood changed. She became contrite. "I'm sorry, pretty," she said tenderly. "Can't you just shut me out when I get to feeling like this, so I won't bother you?"

"Yes," whispered the Klantheid.

"Then why don't you?"

The Klantheid shivered.

"Shutting out is like dying," it said. "Wrong. No. It is not possible for long. I cannot."

The woman shrugged helplessly. A little silence fell between them, plain Earth-woman and beautiful alien plant.

"He's coming back today," the woman said finally. "His tour is up for this month. He just called me on the visiphone."

The Klantheid shivered and said nothing. . . .

THE man came, at midnight. In the brilliant light of Pelao's twin moons, his tiny flitter sank like a dying leaf to the green lawn surrounding the house; and he stepped out. He came in with instruments slung over his shoulder, scanner and official recording tape, and slung them on the coffee table in the living room, where they clattered and bounced.

"Any news?" he asked the woman.

She was standing by the great curved window and the tank of the Klantheid. She did not turn when he entered, nor when he spoke.

"No," she said.

"The bastards!" he said bitterly. The solid shock of his anger slapped at the Klantheid, making it cower, while its filaments whispered almost noise-lessly in pain. "Do they want me to rot here?"

He glared at the interstel—the wireless communicator that connected with the huge sending station at the planet's pole—the sending station that was his only link with the head office on Arcturus 1, the Headquarters Planet of that Solar System. Two months before he'd applied for an emergency transfer from the service for the reason that he and his wife were incompatible and the psychological situation resultant produced inefficient management of his post. For two months no reply had come.

He turned to his wife.

"Why don't *you* message them?" he asked. "Maybe they'll listen to you."

"What would I say?" she queried wearily.

"Tell them—" he checked himself, baffled. "Hell, tell them anything. Tell them you're sick. Tell them you're going to have a baby."

"And when they check?"

The man cursed, stalked across the room to the liquor cabinet and poured himself a drink. He flung himself into a low chair, broodingly.

"It's your fault," he muttered darkly, after a little while. "You ought to do something."

"My fault!"

The woman's voice was harsh with pain. In its tank the Klantheid whimpered, unnoticed.

"You were the one who was going to make this hell-hole a home—you said," he answered.

"What could I do?" she cried, almost wildly. "What was there to do with you gone twenty days out of thirty? What did you expect?"

The man shrugged his shoulders exasperatedly. He drank.

"I don't know," he said. "Forget it."

But the woman was wound up now.

"Forget it!" she said, furiously, turning on him. "Do you think I don't know what's wrong with you? Do you think I've sat here day after day for the past year and watched you come home month after month just as you are now, without knowing what your trouble is? You were never built to have a home and stay in it. Your life is twenty days steady on the job and then a quick run in the flitter to Pole City and an eight day binge. That's all you wanted before you met me on furlough back on Arcturus 1 and that's all you want now—isn't it?"

He did not answer, sitting frowning at his drink.

"I'm in your way here," she said. "You daren't run off to Pole City now that Headquarters knows you're supposed to be married. They'd declare you psychologically unfit and you'd never get another job with the Botany Service. I'm in your way, aren't I? *Aren't I?*"

He looked up, from his drink to her.

"Yes," he said, slowly, with bitter hatred, "you're in my way. You're breaking me. You're killing me and I'm sick of the very sight of you. Now go hide yourself someplace and leave me alone, damn you!"

The wave of cruel emotion slammed out from him, washing through the room, smothering, washing the Klantheid down through agony into unconsciousness.

WHEN the bruised tenderness of its psyche returned to awareness, the night was far gone, and the twin moons hung low in the sky. The woman had disappeared and the lights were out. In the low chair the man slept with drunken heaviness.

The Klantheid came back to life with a plan, a plan born of the pain it had just endured, and therefore, for it, a plan so monstrous and horrible as to be almost unbelievable. In its own way, the

Klantheid had been driven somewhat insane. The man must be gotten rid of—at least for a long enough while for the woman to be healed and mended. It was impossible for the Klantheid to bring itself to hurt or damage another living creature—but there was another way.

Slowly, awkwardly, in the late moonlight, it began to drag itself over the side of the tank. It teetered for a moment on the edge and fell to the floor. There it rested for a second, then began slowly to pull itself toward the door leading to the lawn outside.

It moved by coiling and uncoiling its broad petals, the weak sucker ends of its roots trailing behind it over the polished floor. Gradually it struggled to the door whose automatic mechanism swung it open before the plant. It dropped one short step down from the sill and fell on the lawn.

Now progress was easier, for the grass of the lawn responded to the controlling will of the intelligent plant, stiffening up beneath it and lying down before it so that it half-rolled, half-slid, looking like some weird skater as it progressed away from the house it lived.

It approached the flitter.

Above, the entrance port of the flitter stood open in the moonlight. The Klantheid reached up with half its broad petals, hooked them over the sill of the port and, with what for it was a tremendous effort, lifted its own weight up and into the flitter. The effort involved was roughly analagous to that of a man chinning himself by two fingers—the little fingers of both hands. It tumbled at last onto the floor of the flitter, and while resting for a moment before proceeding any further, reviewed in its own mind what it must do.

From past experience it knew what the sunrise of the following day would bring. The woman would remain shut in her room. The man, barred from taking off for Pole City and sick with a hangover, would load the flitter with enough liquor to last him for a week and take off to visit one of the other, bachelor, Flower Wardens somewhere else on the planet. To get to another like himself would require an air trip of over a thousand miles, above the park-like planet where landmarks were few and every meadow looked like the next one.

The man would take off, set the automatic pilot and go back to his drinking, leaving to the wonderful mechanism of the airship that was the flitter, the job of bringing him safely to earth at his destination. If the automatic pilot failed him—

The Klantheid inched itself forward. It had been in the flitter only once; but that once had been when the man and woman had first picked it up to bring it to their house, on the occasion of the woman's arrival—and the man had explained the workings of the flitter to the woman as they flew. At the time the words had been meaningless, for the Klantheid had neither mechanical aptitude nor interest. But to a nature sensitive to the slightest whisper of a breeze or the nodding of a blossom, perfect recall was easy. Now it remembered and studied the memory.

The man had said that the automatic pilot was connected to the controls by a single jack plug, and had pointed it out beneath the instrument panel.

The Klantheid inched painfully forward, feeling, tasting, the cold metal all around it, vaguely sickened by it, as a human might be sickened by the taste of the metal of a fork from which the silver plating has been worn away. Memory led it to the jack plug. It closed its petals about it and pulled.

The jack did not stir. It was firmly socketed.

*   *   *

CRYING soundlessly inside itself, the Klantheid wrapped its petals more tightly around the plug, pushed with its tiny, weak roots against the resilient matting of the flitter floor and strained. The roots buckled and one petal tore, sending a spasm of pain through the plant body, but it held on, and suddenly, abruptly, the jack gave, and came sliding out.

The Klantheid collapsed, quivering, on the flitter floor.

For several minutes it lay there, gradually regaining its strength, its hopes brightening. The job was done and there was no harm to it. The man, with a hangover, and perhaps still drunk, would never think of checking the plug. He would set the course and leave the job of guiding the flitter to the automatic pilot. He would drink heavily and sleep again—and wake to find himself lost over the endless meadows and among the countless flowers. No harm would come to him—what harm could on a planet where there was nothing inimical—where the weather was always kind, and where food and drink could be had for the stretching out of a hand by those, who like the man, knew the flora of Pelao.

No harm would be done to the man, but he would be kept away fom the station for a long time and in that time—so the Klantheid expressed it to itself—the woman should shed the blighted petal of her emotion toward him and grow a new one. Weary, but relieved, the Klantheid began its arduous trip back to its tank. . . .

Something had gone dreadfully wrong.

The Klantheid cowered in its tank, trying to understand. Desperately, it went back in its mind, reviewing over and over again the incomprehensible train of actions that had brought tragedy upon the station. Futilely, its alien mind searched for the human thought processes and could not find them—and could not understand.

The day had begun as the Klantheid expected. The man had awakened with his hangover and stumbled around the station collecting his bottles and making ready for his trip. The woman had remained in her room—awake, for the Klantheid sensed her, but pretending sleep so that there would be no more cause for meeting the man before he left. The morning was half gone before the man finally had his gear, and was ready to climb into the flitter.

He came out of the station with the last load, staggering. He had drunk his way up out of his hangover and was continuing now to drink himself on down into unconsciousness again. On his final trip out through the living room, he turned, set down his armload of supplies, and, moving swiftly, but somewhat awkwardly, strode over and rapped on the closed door of the woman's room.

"What?" her voice came to the man and the Klantheid together, muffled by the door panels between them and the woman.

"Come on out here," said the man. "I'm not going to stand here and shout at you."

There was a short space of waiting and then the door opened and the woman came into the living room. Her face was drawn. She had not been sleeping through the long night and the Klantheid sensed the mind-numbing, wire-tense exhaustion that held her.

"What is it?" she said.

"I'm going to Rod Gielgud's station—number fifteen," the man said.

"Number fifteen," she repeated, automatically, tucking a stray wisp of hair behind her ear.

"If Headquarters calls about the transfer, or—" he hesitated, "anything, you tell them I just took the flitter out for a short trip to check on local watershed conditions. Then you call me at Rod's."

"Call you—" she echoed numbly.

THE man looked at her. For the first time the set, staring expression of her thin face seemed to reach through the self-concern that surrounded him and register on his mind. The tight lines of his heavy face, betraying the anger and frustration that lay just under the surface with him all the while, smoothed away for an instant in an expression of puzzlement followed by one of faint concern. He hesitated, looking at her keenly.

"Are you ill?" he demanded with sudden sharpness, pricked to harsh tones by the stirring of a long-buried conscience.

"No," she said dully—but then, as the sense of his words registered, the glaze went from her eyes and a little color crept back into her cheeks. She turned her head directly toward him and for the first time in months they looked openly at each other.

"Yes," she said.

"What's wrong with you?" the harshness was still there, but now his words were actually a question, not merely an indication of his annoyance.

"You know what's wrong with me," she said. "If you'd stay home—"

It was the wrong thing to say. He had begun to open up slightly, but he was not yet ready to have the blame laid squarely on his shoulders.

"Hell!" he said explosively and swung away. "I'm no mind reader."

And, blocking his emotions firmly to any more fair impulses, he grabbed up his last load from the table and went on out the front door. Woman and Klantheid, they watched him go, the possible moment of reconciliation lost and broken.

He climbed into the flitter, and took off. Like a silver bird it rose into the morning sunshine—rose to the height of a couple of hundred feet above the park-like lawn surrounding the station. Suddenly the woman broke. She ran across the room to the communicator and snapped it on to the flitter's wave length.

"What is it?" his voice boomed into the living room from the wall loudspeaker.

"Harry!" she said. "Come back!"

"Why?" The tones of his voice, even filtered through the limitations of the loudspeaker, hinted at a struggle within him. "What for? Why do you want me to come back?"

"I—" she stumbled and stopped, not knowing what to say to make him return. "Just come back and I'll tell you—"

There was a moment's silence, then his voice answered, automatically grumbling.

"All right. Just a minute while I put it back on manual—" He checked himself in mid-sentence. There was a moment when time hung still between the living room and the flitter suspended in the blue sky, and then the short silence was broken by a burst of insane fury from the loudspeaker.

"You—" he choked. "You dirty—," and the hate and resentment in him, spurred by fear came pouring out in a stream of foul denunciations and epithets directed at the woman—ending with, *"I'll kill you!"*

"Harry!" It was a desperate cry from the woman, pleading her lack of understanding.

"Try to get rid of me, will you?" he raved back. "Pull the auto pilot jack and maroon me, eh? What were you going to do—tell Headquarters I'd deserted? Stay where you are. I'm going to come get you and put you in the flitter and disconnect the manual and turn you loose—see how you like it when the automatic takes you out over the hills and cuts its motor and tries to land two thousand feet up in the air. Wait there. I'm coming to get you." And the flitter spun about and headed back toward the station in a vicious, shallow dive.

The whites of the woman's eyes flashed suddenly in abrupt shock and fear. Frantically, she spun about from the set, searching for some kind of refuge. But the station was wide open—neither latches nor locks held its doors and there was no place to go.

LIKE a wild bird beating its wings against the bars of a first cage, she fluttered wildly about the living room. Just as the flitter landed, her distraught eyes came to rest on the equipment cabinet set in one wall. Through its glass door she could see its contents, the medical kit, the communicator spare parts and a signal rocket handgun.

Desperately, she ran to the case, tore open the door and seized the handgun, turning to face the front door as the man came through.

He took two steps into the living room and halted, facing her, his mouth twisted, his shoulders hunched, hands at his sides. His breath came in short ugly gasps.

"Don't come any closer," she gasped. "I'll press the trigger button, Harry."

"Press and be damned," he muttered, taking another step. "You couldn't hit the side of a house."

He stepped forward.

"I mean it, Harry!" Her voice was shrill. His eyes were wild, insane.

"It's not safe with you here," he said, half talking to himself. "You'll be knifing me in my sleep, next. Or poisoning me."

He was almost on her now.

"I should have made you take the psychological

test before we got married instead of letting you talk me into bribing the marriage bureau man into giving us good scores. Then I would have found out about you."

"That was your idea!" she protested—ending on a scream. *"Don't come any closer, Harry!"*

He paid no attention, talking as he sidled forward.

"You couldn't stand the loneliness," he said. "You cracked mentally. Your mind isn't strong like mine. I stand loneliness fine. Put the gun down, Cora—I'm not going to hurt you. Just put you some safe place where you can't hurt me." His eyes said that he lied.

"No," she sobbed, trembling now.

"Yes!" he shouted, suddenly leaping for her. She gave a loud cry as their two bodies came together. A blinding flash of red light filled the room, and the sound of an ear-splitting explosion. Then he was hurled back from her as if by the push of some monster hand, to crumple like a broken doll on the carpet and lie still, a red stain spreading from him, dyeing the carpet where he lay.

The Klantheid screamed, feeling the agony of the man's death.

She dropped the gun and sagged lifelessly to the floor.

FOR two hours now, the room had not changed. The dead man still lay, the woman alive but unmoving. The Klantheid whimpered, helpless in its tank and suffering all that the woman suffered, with all the added torture of not understanding.

As the sun rose to noon, however, it could stand no more. Weakly, tremblingly, it began to sing— not what it wanted to sing, a melody of soothing peace and the healing of hurts—but what it could not help but sing as long as the woman crouched near it, pouring out the tearing, agonizing waves of her emotion. As long as that possessed the room and it, it could sing only what it felt—of death and sorrow. And for a little the pressure went off a bit—the emotion now finding an outlet, flowing through the Klantheid and not damming up there, but turning, fabricating itself into a wire-thin whisper of melodic sound, sweet and bitter.

The sound went out and cried through the room, growing in strength as the Klantheid began to relieve itself of the excess of killing emotion its tender nature had never been created to carry. The song sobbed and wept over the dead man, sorrowed over the woman and looked beyond and beyond into tragedy and sorrow everlasting.

The sun passed its zenith. Gradually, as the song went on, the woman began to stir. Like a somnambulist hypnotized by the music, she raised her head to look at the Klantheid. And, after a while, she got to her feet. The Klantheid watched her, aching for her and wanting to sing her comfort, but unable to do anything but echo the emotion that she herself was putting out—that was feeding on the very music it sang, and growing, and which possessed the plant. Into her soul it sensed, and sang a great, great longing for peace, utter and final peace—and the Klantheid cheered up as this new note crept into its music, for it thought that the woman was feeling better at last.

So it threw its whole self into its singing and sang of peace. And the woman turned away from it and walked over to the equipment chest and took from the medical kit a hypodermic filled with a strange brown liquid, which she injected into the big blue vein inside her right elbow. And while the Klantheid still watched and sang hopefully, she sat down in one of the big chairs and died.

With her dying, present peace came to the Klantheid, for it was not human, and to it death was the final solution and end to all things. As far as its own sensitive feelings were concerned, the man, and later the woman, disappeared when they ceased to think and feel. It only retained a memory of the woman and the beauty it had sensed buried deep in her and remembrance of having loved her. The plant felt a great emptiness within it and a need for healing.

So, slowly, tiredly and laboriously, it climbed over the edge of its tank and down onto the floor. Weakly, it dragged itself across the threshold and out into the soft light of afternoon, into the warm light, into the bright light.

Before it the meadows fell away unendingly under the afternoon sky, and the grass, pushing and relaxing beneath it, helped it along as it moved slowly away from the station, leaving it behind. The bright light warmed it and the air was heavy with the constant whisper of living, growing things that the Klantheid could hear and feel deep within it. As it traveled, gradually its tense, rolled-up petals unfolded and spread themselves to the sun; its filaments rose and swayed in the breeze and the gentle motion of its travel. On every side the outspreading wash of its appreciation and affection was returned a thousandfold. Happy, the Klantheid vibrated its filaments together and sang a paean rejoicing in the end of all unhappiness and sorrow.

> *If alternate realities balance like yin and yang, one world's misfit might become another's hero.*

Walker Between the Planes

FOR A MOMENT HE LET DARKNESS AND AGONY TAKE HIM. Then, like a soundless shock wave, reaction flared. Something like panic, but too hard for panic, which he had lost along with fear somewhere back among the scarred rough years since his youth.

Fighting the spasms from the deadly gas, he worked the pill from under his tongue and up between his teeth. As he bit down, a liquid oozed from the capsule and fumes spread through his mouth and toward his brain.

He floated, half-conscious on the hard chair. Suddenly he seemed to be dreaming. Events piled up in his mind—mostly ugly. Thirty years of being alone and friendless has to be ugly. Even the man he knew as Uncle Jim had acted from outmoded pride, not from any love for him . . .

The aged face of the man who called himself James Rater Bailey had worn a snarl when they left him alone in the cell with Doug. His gnarled fingers clutched at the tattered charms he always wore about his throat and he muttered something, as if praying to the devils it had been said he worshiped.

"What a place! If your grandfather had lived to see it . . ."

"I didn't ask you to come," Doug Bailey told him stiffly.

Doug had never sought help, knowing he could expect none. It had been a fair fight after he was attacked, and the hoodlum's death had been an accident. Doug could have escaped if he had not called for an ambulance. But he had not asked for mercy even after he had learned the drunk was the son of the state's Governor. When they had lied and then had thrown the book at him, he had faced their gas chamber without pleading. He was not ready to plead for sympathy now.

"Your family may mean nothing to you," Uncle Jim lashed at him. "But in my day, no man escaped his family responsibility."

Doug nodded bitterly. Maybe the old man was right. Once, according to the books, the family and not the government had been the basis of society. But that was before people thought they had a right to be supported and to be paid for hours, not work. And family ties were weak at best. Certainly they had never meant much to him. He had been an orphan at ten.

"Doug." The old voice was urgent. "Doug, I didn't come to quarrel but to help you—for your grandfather's sake."

Doug snorted. "Miracles don't work against cyanide."

"Doug, listen. You won't believe me—nobody ever did. But listen!"

For a moment, the appeal cut through Doug's cynicism. Maybe Jim deserved some last-minute respect. He had always been a weird shadow, spoken of in whispers for dark beliefs and practices no one could detail. He was supposed to cast spells and deal with witches, according to some accounts.

"All right, I'll listen," Doug agreed.

"Then take this." A tiny capsule fell from Jim's crooked hand into Doug's palm. "Put it under your tongue and bite down on it just before ... It's a powerful antidote, boy—maybe too powerful. But you'll have a chance."

Now the dream-events were beginning to fade and slow, to draw themselves out into long, hollow sounds here in the gas chamber. The taste of the capsule was again in Doug's mouth and he felt himself being wrenched and flung—as if across some great, unimaginable distance of time or space ...

... Into whiteness.

IT was white sun-glare without a sun, dry white mist all about him and powdery whiteness under him. It was a strangely filled emptiness, without direction. Then abruptly, a small darkness soared over him and passed on.

Instantly he felt cold. No, he felt emptied, suddenly weakened—robbed, as if something had been stolen from his integral self. His eyes turned to his right and downward like steel balls drawn by a magnet.

Crouched there, lost in the dazzle, was a thing black and blurred. Something man-sized but which gave an impression of being crow-like and burdened with what had just been stolen from inside Doug. Too heavy to fly now, the creature flopped to its feet and began walking away, and the robbed feeling came back to Doug with hovering anger.

He dug into the stuff in which he stood and gave chase. But the new emptiness about him sapped his strength so that he could not gain on the Walker.

He followed it. But suddenly before him, shining against even the dazzle, hovering in mid-nowhere, loomed a bright and terrible disk—a kind of doorway casting a circle of blinding light.

Instinctively he halted, daunted by the circle of brightness.

The Walker went on, carrying its stolen burden into the circle. Soon it was lost to sight in the forbidding, blazing radiance. As it disappeared, the emptiness expanded around Doug. The doorway was too bright, he was too tired—he could not follow. All he wanted was to relax into the emptiness now swallowing him ... which was death, after all. Yes, that was easiest. Simply to die, to turn away, from that terrible doorway and let the Walker go. To give up—

But he could not. All his life, a cross-grained stubbornness had driven him, had been his master. It would not let him surrender now.

He stumbled onward. The radiance engulfed him—and then it was gone. He seemed to fall, down through darkness forever.

Horror smothered him. For the darkness was not so much like the absence of light as like being blind. He would not endure it! The fury that had driven him toward the radiant circle rose wildly in him again, became a white flame inside him.

He was falling ... endlessly falling. And he fought.

Abruptly, there was a faint light. And through it he could see the Walker approaching him. He reached out a hand but the Walker went striding past. Then it stopped and pointed once, and moved on.

Now the light strengthened into a small glow ahead. He willed himself toward it—and found it nearer. There was another circle of brightness, but fainter and less forbidding. He burst triumphantly through it, feeling the momentless moment of his passage slip away from him.

For a second, it seemed that the Walker was back and that a dark hand touched Doug. Then he was through, again in real time and space . . .

HE emerged to a roar of voices, the howling of a crowd at some wild sport event—and to a deep, sharp pain in his chest. The sun overhead was strangely white and fiercely bright. Ranks of faces surrounded a circle of bare paving fifty feet across. Just above the paving two outlandish figures like man-sized fighting cocks sparred in mid-air with silver-flashing spikes at their heels. As Doug watched, one of the fighters tumbled, wings flailing, to the pavement.

He looked down at himself, at a wide brownish chest that surely must be his own although he did not recognize it. A male face with folded wing-crests behind it was stooping over him. A three-fingered hand danced before his eyes and something like an invocation sounded in his ears.

In panic, Doug tried to shout but his voice was frozen. As the gesturing fingers moved back, Doug saw that his own hands were manacled by chains to a broad belt around his waist. His feet were clamped together at the ankles and he lay on some boardlike surface at a forty-five degree angle with the pavement.

Directly in front of him, one of the fighting creatures was on the pavement now. The other hovered above it, poising long metal spurs for a killing downstroke.

"Mount! Mount . . ." the circling crowd of faces was clamoring at the fallen figure. But the fallen one seemed stunned and helpless.

"There he goes ..." muttered someone behind Doug's head. "Out, duLein!"

The last words cracked commandingly in Doug's ear. Then, without warning, he was no longer watching the fighting figures. He was one of them.

He was the one lying on the pavement, wings spread out behind him and staring up at the descending spurs of his enemy.

A dizziness like the after-effect of a heavy blow on the head clouded his thinking, but not his reflexes. Twenty years of practice in legal and illegal sports had made him a maverick among his own people—but a maverick who could react. Reflex sent him rolling out of the way of the descending spurs.

THE down-stabbing spur-points aimed at Doug slammed into the pavement where he had been, sending sparks flying. His opponent crumpled on the flat surface, moaning, clutching a broken leg.

Reflex still drove Doug like a set of emergency controls. Without thought, he scrambled up and started running.

He careened blindly into the packed throng. They parted conveniently before him, leaving an avenue through which he could see streets between stony buildings five to ten stories in height. Still operating on instinct, he pounded down the corridor of escape opening before him and turned into the closest street.

As he rounded the corner, the roar of the crowd behind him diminished. The cliff-like buildings on either side swam past him as he turned right at the first cross-street, left at the next.

Gradually his blurred vision was clearing, bringing his surroundings into focus. The monolithic buildings were like giant slabs of gray rock. He passed no openings, no doorways or windows at

street level. It was only at two or three stories of
height above him that he saw openings piercing
the walls—unglazed openings which were the only
evidence that these shapes he passed were not
solid blocks of stone.

He turned down another street and staggered,
almost falling. He was close to the end of his
strength.

He stumbled to a halt at the intersection. Leaning against a building wall in a little patch of
sunlight, he looked back. There was no one to be
seen behind him and he had passed no one since
he had left the crowd at the fight. It should be safe
to rest for a moment.

Strangely, it was not his breath that had given
out but his legs. He was not even breathing hard.
His chest pumped as slowly as if he were sitting in
a chair, reading. But his legs trembled uncontrol-
lably and threatened to fold at the knees.

He looked down at those legs. They were thin
brown limbs almost lost in the shadow thrown by
the huge wings on his back. As he noted the wings,
he became aware of a deep ache in their joints—
the toll of his rolling over upon them. And he
realized the top-heaviness of his body he now
inhabited—wings, powerful shoulders, deep chest,
all supported by the thin, trembling legs. He shivered, conscious suddenly that he wore nothing more
than a thin pair of trunks and here, in the deep
shadow between the building walls, the air was
chill—

"Kath—*ang*! Kathang duLe—*in*! . . ."

Faint and sad, like a wild bird's cry of two notes
repeated in descending series, a voice sounded high
overhead.

He looked up. Outlined against the white-blue,
cloudless sky in the crack of space between the

buildings was a small figure soaring on great gray wings.

"Kathang duLe—*in* . . ."

He bolted to the end of the street and around a corner into another way between high buildings. Staggering to a stop against the nearest wall, he looked up and saw only cloudless sky.

For a moment he felt the relief of having escaped. Then, without warning, the figure swung again into view above and steeply dived for him.

SIDESLIPPING into the narrow space between the buildings, the flying figure reached to the pavement perhaps three yards in front of him, turning up sharply at the last moment to land on its feet. For the first time he saw that it seemed to have no arms. There were only the undersides of the great spread of dove-gray wings that filled the street, their feathers reaching to the shoulders, and a pair of legs like his own—but even shorter and more fragile. He looked at the body and saw it was female. It was clothed, except for the wings, in close-fitting silver-metallic cloth and a wide black belt from which things like medals dangled.

The flyer stared up at him with enormous eyes. She was a good head-and-a-half shorter than he. Now her arms appeared, unclothed, from among the feathers, where apparently they had been stretched out and moving as part of the wings. As he watched, the wings themselves folded up slowly on her back.

"Kathang!" Her voice was musical, low-pitched in the contralto range, but tense with concern. "You can't just run around the streets like this. The Cadda Noyer will have men out after you any minute now."

Doug stared at her. Her features were tanned, small and narrow, with enormous dark-brown eyes.

She was not pretty by any human standard—but, just as he made that judgment about her, he felt his body expressing a strange disagreement. His human mind might not find this female attractive but his winged body clearly did.

"Kathang—" she said again, and started toward him.

He stepped back. She halted, cocking her head to one side.

"I'm not Kathang," he said without thinking, and was shocked by the hoarse bass voice that came booming out of his chest.

"Not—" She stopped. "Kathang, are you out of your mind? I was there at the fights! I saw the soul transfer when the fighter you'd bet on went down—" She broke off, staring narrowly at him. "Don't you know me?"

"No," he said hoarsely.

"The transfer spell must have been incomplete," she said. "Your soul isn't firmly bound yet. But can't you remember? I'm Anvra—Anvra Mons-Borroh, Water Witch, your contract-mate. Kathang, don't you remember anything?"

He shook his head.

"My name is Bai—Bai—" His different lips and tongue stumbled over words they had never before formed. "I'm DougLass Bai—"

"You've had a reaction, all right." Anvra Mons-Borroh stepped forward quickly before his trembling legs could back him away again. She caught him by the arm. "Never mind. My self-obligation to you holds. I'll get you hidden away somewhere. I'll call on my own Water Witch Aerie for temporary mate-sanctuary for you. Now, you see what it comes to—gambling away your Brotherhood rights? Come on! The Cadda Noyer is probably after you already. There's a catapult just two streets away—"

Stumbling along on his worn-out leg muscles,

Doug let himself be led down another street to the right.

This new street was short and buildings flanking it were no more than three stories tall; thus a narrow strip of white sunlight reached one side of the pavement. Suddenly that sunlight was momentarily interdicted by two shadows flickering across it.

Automatically Doug stopped and stared up. Overhead, above the buildings, he saw two soaring figures, male-sized, wearing tight suits in a sort of livery pattern of red, black and orange squares.

"Cadda Noyer," cried Anvra sharply. "Run!"

She set off down the alley. Doug followed, willingly now and at a better speed than before. The pause had rested his legs.

Jogging, Doug and his guide passed one intersection, arrived at another that broadened into a kind of plaza. In its center was a strange-looking structure with a track projecting into the air and a small platform at the foot of the track. The other end of the street opened into a wide square of pavement on which a number of figures were walking, wings folded, while flyers soared in the air above them. Anvra caught Doug's arm and pulled him toward the deserted plaza with its strange mechanism.

Doug jerked free. If the two figures circling above were indeed enemies, he wanted to meet them out where there was room to dodge and run—and possibly where the presence of other people would make the hunters cautious or slow them down. He ran for the large square, Anvra calling him back.

She ran after him, but in a burst of speed he pulled away from her. Once out in the square, however, he stopped. What energy was left in his legs clearly must be hoarded for the fighting—if it came to that.

AND clearly it was going to come to that. The strollers in the square were making no effort to interfere. They had drawn into a loose circle around him. As he paused to look up at the threat overhead, Anvra broke through their ranks. She whistled so loudly, so shrilly, that his ears momentarily deafened.

"Water Witches!" she was trilling as she swung about to face the watchers. "Water Witches . . ."

She whistled again, despairingly. Doug detected no response from anywhere. A shadow flickered over him. Glancing up, he saw the two pursuers zoom lower. They looked a little like clowns in their checkered tricolor suits. But they were both heavy-chested males. They wore no sharp metal spurs on their heels. But where the spurs might have been were what looked like blunt dowels of dark wood, some eight inches long and an inch in diameter.

Doug was sure an assault would soon begin. But it was on him so swiftly that he barely had time to brace himself. The two hunters swooped suddenly, one a little in advance of the other, like hawks upon a rabbit. And Anvra, spreading her wings and leaping upward, tried valiantly to beat her way into the air and intercept them.

"Mount, Kathang!" she cried. "Mount—"

It was clearly all but impossible for her to take off from a level surface. Yet she managed to gain half her own height in the air and meet the first attacker. He struck out at her—not with the polished dowels on his heels but with one of his wide wings. His wing and hers came together with a booming sound like the note of an enormous kettledrum. Anvra tumbled backward in mid-air, fell to the ground.

She was out of the fight. But at least she had diverted one of the enemy. The second came diving through the air, dowels-first, at Doug's head.

He ducked, crouching under the driving dowel-ends, then leaped swiftly to catch a sweeping wingtip in both hands and swing his weight on it.

The attacker floundered and fell, giving a hoarse, gargling shout. He rolled on the pavement, threshing reflexively with the wing Doug had not touched. The other hung rigid, propped at a strangle angle, half-dragged out of its socket.

Doug looked for the first attacker, could not see him. Once more he ducked—and probably saved his life. A tremendous double hammer seemed to smash into his head sending him half-unconscious to the pavement. On hands and knees he saw the first attacker, still airborne, circling to strike again.

Doug was recovering his wits. Crouching, he saw the attacker swooping upon him now, swelling suddenly large before him. Gathering himself for a supreme effort, Doug waited until the last second— and sprang.

He cleared the in-driving dowel-ends, his body slamming hard against the attacker. The creature's flailing wing caught on the pavement. Both went down. Rolling over on the winged man, Doug stiffened his hands for a karate blow and chopped downward with it, edge-on.

He had aimed at the point where the side of the other's neck met the collar bone, but he missed his target and slammed hard instead into the ribs of the upper chest. A sudden wave of agony shot up his arm.

He looked at his hand in amazement as he rolled free of the attacker. The smallest of three fingers was bent in against his palm at an unnatural angle. When he tried to move the other fingers, a needle-like twinge of pain ran up his arm.

The man he had struck was now lying back on his half-folded wings, shuddering slightly. The whole right side of his chest was caved in, as if by a sledgehammer. A bloody froth showed on his lips.

Staring from the obviously dying man to his own ruined hand, Doug made an effort to get to his feet, remembering something about birds back on Earth . . .

"Bones . . ." he croaked to himself. "Hollow . . ."

Now upright, he moved toward the dying enemy to find out if this were true. But at the first step, sky and square tilted and went around him as if he were on a carousel. The next thing he knew, he was lying on the pavement, looking up into the face of Anvra. On his other side stood an old winged man dressed in black, his face lined and narrow.

". . . he bet himself on one of the fighters," Anvra was saying, looking up at the man in black, "and the fighter was forced to the pavement. So they prepared Kathang for transfer. But after his soul was transferred, he dodged the kill-blow and the other fighter hurt himself on the pavement. The other wasn't able to rise but Kathang was—and that made him winner. But he was in the body of the fighter he bet on."

"Nonetheless, mistress," said the old man, slowly and deeply, "the body he wears belongs to the Cadda Noyer. It's their fighter's body."

"It was a beaten body—a dead body until he saved it."

"That goes beyond present discussion." The old man shook his head. "It will have to be decided by a full panel of the Magi. I'll set a date."

He looked down at Doug.

"Kathang DuLein," he said, in his deep voice,

"the Cadda Noyer can't be restrained from attempting to recover the body you inhabit. As a Magus, I can give you no protection. I recommend you to the protection of your Aerie Brothers."

"He has none," said Anvra quickly. "He gambled away his Brotherhood rights in the Sorcerers. But I'm a Water Witch—I can find him mate-sanctuary temporarily in one of our Aeries."

"Then I recommend you, DuLein," said the old man, "to the protection of your contract-mate, Mistress Anvra Mons-Borroh."

He turned and stepped away, revealing two other winged men wearing silver and black, like that of Anvra's costume.

"Can we help you, Sister?" one of them asked.

"Where were you when I whistled?" began Anvra sharply, then checked herself. "Forgive me, Brothers. I'm still wound up from the attack. Help me get him to our nearest Aerie, will you? I can't carry him alone."

Anvra's voice and the scene about him was lost in a sudden flooding of nothingness, with only a brief shadow-glimpse of the Walker watching him.

II

He woke gradually. He squinted and raised his right hand to brush the haze from his eyes.

But his right hand was heavier than it should be. With an effort he heaved it up and saw a clumsy lump of something that looked like a ball of cloth soaked in concrete. A cast, he realized.

He remembered the fight with the two winged men then, and jerked himself up on one elbow to see about him.

He lay on what seemed to be a bed in a semi-circular room open to the air all along its flat side. Several backless armchairs stood about and from the chipped stone of the wall extended objects looking like water-faucet handles in either silver or black. Nowhere in the wall was any door visible.

His bed was at the open edge of the room—almost overhanging it in fact. There was no barrier or guard rail. He turned to look out . . .

He stared down at the tops of toylike buildings several hundred feet below him, stretching away like a sea as far as the horizon. Rising out of this sea at something like quarter-mile intervals were huge towers—and it was plain that the room where he lay was a tower.

It was an impossible scene, like something discovered in a nightmare. Were those buildings below him the structures among which he had been running?

A faint click made his head turn.

The wall had opened to reveal a door. Coming through it was Anvra Mons-Borroh. The door closed behind her, its outline becoming invisible once more.

"You woke early," she said. Her voice was rather cold. It lacked the concern that had been in it when she had first warned him about the Cadda Noyer. "Kathang wouldn't have recovered from the sedative that fast."

"You know I'm not this Kathang, then?" he asked, gazing up at her curiously.

"I don't *know* anything!" Her voice sharpened. "Except that Kathang was my contract-mate, and that my self-obligation holds until I have proof you're someone else."

"You don't need proof," he said emptily. "I'm not your Kathang."

"You could be, and not in your right mind." She stared at him brilliantly out of wide brown eyes. "Who did you say you are?"

"My name's Bai—" Once more the pronunciation defeated him. "Anyway, I don't know how I happened to be in what's-his-name's ... Kathang's ... body. But where I come from we don't have wings."

HE told her all of what had happened to him as he remembered it. She listened patiently. When he was finished, she nodded.

"Yes," she said. "It's what you said under sedation."

She turned from him and walked back to the wall, which opened before her.

"Sirs," she said. "Will you come in now?"

Two winged men answered her invitation. The first was small for a male, and dark-haired, his right wing deformed and patently useless. Doug's vision seemed to blur again as he looked at the smaller winged man. But it was not a general blurring, he noticed. The others, the rest of the room, remained sharp and clear. Only the small man was blurred in features and outline—and stayed that way. Doug looked over at the larger newcomer. His body was as big as the one Doug himself was now inhabiting. Both visitors wore close-fitting suits of dark red with a yellow lozenge over the heart.

"Mistress ..." said the smaller one, bending his head briefly to her. "May I present our Master of Aerie 84? Master Sorcerer Jax duHorrel."

"Sir." She bent her head. "Will you both sit?"

The two picked up backless armchairs and carried them to Doug's bed. They sat down, staring at him. Anvra remained standing.

"Kathang," said the smaller man with the deformed wing, "don't you know me? We're Aerie Brothers. You must remember me—Etam duRel? And Jax, our Aerie Master?"

"No Aerie Brother of ours, Brother. No longer," said the man called Jax grimly. "Remember that, Etam!"

He turned to Anvra.

"I could wish you a better contract-mate, mistress," he said.

"Thank you," she said. "You heard him tell about himself?"

Jax nodded. "It's the planet of the damned he's fantasy-making about, all right," said the big Aerie Master of the Sorcerers. "It's real enough, even if it is on another plane. They're all wingless there, slaves crawling about the surface just the way he describes it. It's exactly the sort of self-torturing fantasy a weak man like Kathang *would* pick."

"Sir!" Anvra's voice had an edge to it. "The name of duLein is an honorable one. It's my contract-mate you're speaking of."

"Apologies, mistress," said Jax stiffly. "But you've no self-obligation to a man you believe not contracted to you."

"Until I have proof," snapped Anvra, "my self-obligation holds. We women don't shed our contract-duties as lightly as some men shed the duties of their Brotherhood."

As they glared at each other, Anvra's wings half-spread, Doug Bailey found his tongue.

"Wait a minute," he said "Let me hear that again—you *know* where I come from?"

Anvra and the two men turned back to face him. "Kathang . . ." Etam duRel patted Doug gently on the arm. His blurred features leaned down toward Doug; his voice sounded blurred but understandable in Doug's ears. "Don't you remember how we were two of the workers on the construction of the Portal? Think! There were other planets we opened the Portal to besides Damned World. Remember the world that was all shadow ocean, and the

transparent bodies of the water-creatures we recovered from it?''

"What's the use of trying to explain to a madman, Etam?" grumbled Jax. "To remember what
you ask, he'd have to abandon his fantasy. He's
incurable. He should be quietly put out of the
way—"

"That decision's not yours to make, Aerie Master," said Anvra. "When he sold off his right to
protection by the Sorcerers, he also took back the
right of Sorcerers to judge or condemn him."

"Yes, if he's Kathang," Jax admitted. "You got
us here because you think he actually is from the
Damned World. Isn't that right?"

"I don't believe—or disbelieve," said Anvra stiffly.

Etam spoke. "Why do you doubt he's Kathang,
Mistress?"

"Because of the things he's done," Anvra answered. "Things I, as contract-mate, happen to
know Kathang would not do. For example, Kathang
was no public coward; not, at least, to the point of
having his wings cut off and being sentenced to
the sewers. But there were braver men—"

Her gaze flashed suddenly, warningly, at Jax.

"I can say that about Kathang, Aerie Master,
because my self-obligation still holds," she interrupted herself. "You cannot, in my presence, because your Brotherhood is broken. I say, frankly,
that there were braver men than Kathang duLein,
even if he is the last to bear the ancient and honorable name of the duLeins. This man I aided against
two Cadda Noyer is one of the bravest."

JAX rose from his chair.

"And this is all you have to tell us, then?" he
asked Anvra. "You brought us here simply because
you think Kathang is acting more courageously
than he used to?"

"Look at what he did," blazed Anvra, ruffling her wings, glaring up at the big man. "Kathang's soul was legally transferred into the body of a fighter about to die, so that the fighter could be preserved in Kathang's body. But Kathang didn't perish with the dead body. Instead he activated the body and defeated a professional fighter! Kathang—who in the gym never wore anything but padded dowels!"

"Even that can happen by accident—"

"Then how about the two Cadda Noyer bullies?" she demanded. "He also defeated them. He even killed one—"

"I understand you helped."

"I?" Anvra laughed scornfully. "A small woman? I tell you he defeated them both himself. He actually crushed one's chest, ruining his own hand in the process. What ordinary man—let alone Kathang—could strike a blow like that? Sirs, you're blind if you don't see something more here than a man out of his mind with the effects of an incompleted transfer spell."

Jax shook his head.

"As Kathang must have told you when he was sane and a Sorcerer," Jax said, "only dead specimens can be recovered from other worlds through the Portal."

"But a soul—" she began.

"Can only be transferred from another plane by a spell operating on that plane."

Jax held up his hand to Anvra as she was about to interrupt him passionately.

"We know," he said, "that Kathang was in his own body before the spell was begun. We know the spell sent him into the body of a fighter facing what looked like certain death. He had to obey that spell. So—he went into the fighter's body."

"That has to be true," put in Etam, rising also

from his chair and speaking earnestly to Anvra. "Kathang couldn't have moved into the fighter's body unless the fighter were already dead—or anticipating death so strongly he was as good as dying. The soul in any healthy, living body is too strong to be ousted—you know that. That's why we can't pull anything but dead or dying animals through a Portal. All right, the fighter was essentially dead. If you're correct in what you think, that left two bodies and two floating identities—Kathang's and the stranger's."

"What's your point?"

"Well, mistress, if the stranger beat Kathang into the Fighter's body, that left Kathang with only one place to go—back to his own body, which was perfectly usable, since the transfer spell only drives out the soul temporarily. If you're right, and a stranger from the Damned World is inhabiting this body here with us, then Kathang also has to be alive and in his own body somewhere. But I was told Kathang's body died immediately and was carted away by the Cadda Noyer for disposal. So Jax is right, you know, mistress. Your idea of a stranger in Kathang's body is an impossibility. It has to be Kathang on the bed here—even if he is insane and doesn't recognize himself."

They left, the door of the room opening and then shutting behind them. Anvra stood staring after them, her wings ruffling slightly.

"What was that?" demanded Doug. "That business about if I'm crazy, I ought to be put out of the way quietly?"

Anvra turned.

"The insane can't be allowed to live at large and become a danger to the community, Kathang," she answered in level tones.

"You know that. You may not have a Brotherhood to take the responsibility of amputating your wings and locking you up—but the Magi will do it, if necessary. Unless you can be made sane."

"I never felt saner," he told her. "Come to think of it, I never felt more alive—" He broke off suddenly, staring closely at her. "If you don't think I'm Kathang, you're going to a lot of trouble to help a stranger."

"A stranger?" Her eyebrows lifted. "Kathang, you know better than that!"

"But I'm not Kathang and I don't know," he answered goodhumoredly. "That's right, isn't it? Think about it for a minute. If I wasn't Kathang, I wouldn't know—is that correct?"

Anvra thought it over. "All right, I'll talk to you as if you really are a stranger from some other place. What I'm doing isn't for you. If you're Kathang, you know that I wasn't going to renew our contract anyway—and you know why. If you aren't Kathang—" She hesitated. "What I'm doing, I'm doing out of respect to my honor and my duty of self-obligation. They demand of me that I help my contract-mate."

"But you don't believe I'm Kathang?" he pressed.

"No, I don't," she snapped at him. "Still, I'm not infallible. If by some wild chance I'm wrong and it should turn out I'd abandoned you though you really are Kathang, my contract-mate, then I'd have failed in my self-obligation—and everything I believe in."

"I see." His thoughts raced. Whatever had happened to him during the transfer of souls, one thing was certain. He had been shaken up more by it, mentally and emotionally, than he had been by anything else in his life. His old bitterness, his indifference to death, were gone. He wanted to live—in fact, he intended to live.

"Help me, then," he said to Anvra.

"How?" She stared at him strangely. For all her

snappishness and disclaimer of any interest in him other than as an insane Kathang, her eyes at times held a curious softness for him.

"Talk to me as if I were a stranger. Tell me things."

"For example?"

"What was I doing at that fight in the first place?"

"You had already gambled away all you had," she answered, "except your apprentice-fee in the Brotherhood of Sorcerers. You mortgaged that in a bet and lost it. Then you had nothing left except your life. So you bet that. You bet your body as a replacement for the fighter whose corner you were in. If he had won, you would have won—enough, that is, to buy back into the Sorcerers. But he lost."

"The Cadda Noyer," he said. "Who are they?"

"They run the fights—among other things," she said. "One of the gray Brotherhoods. I'd never contract-mate myself to a Cadda Noyer. Some day the Magi will declare them outlaws for any member of the community to kill on sight. But for now they're tolerated. It was the Cadda Noyer from whom you stole that fighter-trained body. They'll be waiting outside this Aerie now for the six days of grace to expire. Then my Brotherhood will have to make you leave. Your own Brotherhood could have given you sanctuary indefinitely. They could even have bought off the Cadda Noyer— maybe."

"Maybe." Doug added, "So you can change bodies any time you want, in this world of yours?"

"Change—" The sharp note in her voice brought his eyes back to her face. She was all but glaring at him, as she had glared at Jax. Suddenly conscious of having to look up to her, he swung his legs over the side of the bed and rose unsteadily to his feet.

"Sit down," she said, catching his shoulders and pushing him.

The edge of the bed caught the back of his knees and he sat down heavily. "No, people can't change bodies any time they want," she said. "The person giving the body has to have signed his life away according to the law under the Magi. A fine thing it would be if a person could change bodies whenever he wished! A criminal could disappear from the eyes of justice any time he felt like it. The Magi have to approve each transfer, don't you see?"

DOUG'S mind was clicking off conclusions. "Where do these Cadda Noyer—where's their headquarters?"

"Their local Aerie? Or their Chief High Aerie?"

"The one nearest to that Sorcerer Aerie where Kathang used to work—where that Portal is."

"You mean the local Aerie," she said.

She stepped around his bed and pointed off at a tower perhaps five miles distant. He stared at it. There was an illusory shadow hand before his eyes. It blurred fantastically. He seemed to see telescopically, shadowedly, into the very interior of the tower, where two figures lay still in an underground room.

"How do I get there?"

"You?" Once more there was that strange softness mixed with the sharpness of her voice and gaze. "You get there by flying fifty feet out beyond your bed. Half a dozen of the Cadda Noyer will escort you personally to the Aerie. I told you that they're waiting—"

Baffled, he stared at the tower. Like a huge gray finger it pointed upright in the distance, half threatening, half beckoning.

"What happens to dead bodies?" he asked.

She frowned at him.

"They're held several days to make sure all life is gone. Then a Magus is called in to certify to the death. The individual's name is removed from both

Brotherhood and community rolls. Then the body is burned." Anvra continued to frown. "Why?" she asked. "Why did you want to know that?"

"I have a body around here somewhere—the real body I was born with." He added thoughtfully. "There must be some way of getting into that tower."

"The Cadda Noyer Aerie? You want to get in there? Well, you're not Kathang, that's clear." She shook her head impatiently. "Do you think Aeries are built so they can be gotten into? What use would an Aerie be if anybody could get in without the permission of the Brotherhood owning it?"

He was still gazing at the tower. It seemed to him that his mind had never been so clear and swift-moving. The shadow hand was gone but the blurred image of the two motionless figures in the room flashed in and out of his brain.

Doug swung on her.

"You're a Water Witch, you said." He watched her. "Doesn't that tower have water and sewer connections?"

"Of course," she answered. Then she paled and seemed to shrink from him. "You're not thinking of invading the aerie through the underground piping?"

"I'm in no position to be finicky—"

"Finicky!" She shuddered. "No, you're not Kathang. You're not even a normal human being!"

The horror in her face went beyond ordinary squeamishness at the thought of passage through a sewer. She was plainly shaken by some deeper emotion.

"What's so bad about your pipes, Anvra?"

"They are . . . underground. Underground! Away from the light and the air. Away from the sky!"

Then he understood. He remembered the note in Jax's voice when Jax had spoken about Earth's people as wingless, about the Earth as the Damned World. To a flying people, being without wings would literally be hell. And being forced underground—where they could not use wings, where they were locked from their natural open environment—would be double hell.

All the better, thought Doug grimly. If such were the case, there was that much more chance he could travel through the piping unobserved.

"As you say." He rose again to his feet, fending her off as she tried to stop him. "I'm different. Let's see if you can't find me a route to their tower through its water or sewer pipes."

III

LESS than an hour later, his thin brown legs were encased in hiphigh boots of some thin rubbery material. He was clothed, all but his arms, in an insulated one-piece suit of the same stuff. Anvra had found the garments for him.

Doug stood beyond a water-tight door at the top of three steps leading into a tunnel perhaps ten feet in diameter. He was in the subbasement of the Water Witches' tower. The tunnel—a great metal pipe—seemed lit by a phosphorescence covering all the surfaces above the ankle-deep water. The pipe ran straight, losing itself in brilliance both far ahead and far behind.

The pipe was not one of the sewers, Anvra had said. It was part of the storm-drain system. In case of a flash rainstorm, anyone in the drain would be swept away and drowned. But this was not the time of year for thunderstorms. Now only a bare trickle of water was pumped into the drains to nourish the fungus that coated the drain walls and illuminated their interiors for the benefit of the slave working crews.

Doug stepped down into the drainpipe and felt the water tugging at his ankles. A splashing behind him made him turn. Anvra, carrying the pipe-charts for the area between this tower and that of the Cadda Noyer Aerie, had entered the water behind him.

"All right." He reached for the charts. "I'll take those."

"Will you?" she said, holding on to them. "And how are you going to read them?"

He saw that she, too, had on a pair of the rubbery wading boots.

"You aren't going with me?"

"I am," she said. "You can't read the charts. You're no Water Witch! You can't even read the pipe markings. You'd never get there."

He respected her courage. A flying woman, she was forcing herself to go underground, swallowing her horror.

"Your self-obligation at work again, I suppose?"

"That's right." She was tight-lipped.

"Well ... thank you," he said. He started forward. The rounded surface underfoot obliged them to walk single file and he heard her splashing along behind him.

Doug was genuinely touched. Kathang must have been a damn fool not to have appreciated this female more than he had. Loyalty such as Anvra showed was something to admire.

THUS began the long wading trip through the phosphorescent corridor. They said nothing except when they came to an intersection or a branching. Then Anvra would stop briefly to compare her charts with the markings on the pipe wall at that point. She would give directions and they would move on.

She had explained earlier that there was no direct route from the Water Witches' tower to that of the Cadda Noyer. In effect, the distance to the tower would be almost doubled by the route they had to take.

Doug had held himself to a slow, steady pace from the start, remembering how his legs on occasion had threatened to betray him. In spite of his precautions, after a time he felt his thigh-muscles beginning to ache. The ache woke him to the fact that had not previously registered on him. The water through which they had been wading had deepened gradually until now he was slogging through in knee-depth. Also, there was a new, strange ache—across his back. He discovered that he was, instinctively, holding his wingtips high above the wet.

A sudden, different sound of splashing sounded behind him. He swung about—to see Anvra stumbling, going down into the water. He moved to catch her just in time. She was a limp weight in his arms. Looking down at her in the eerie light of the phosphorescence, he saw that her eyes were closed.

Her face looked like a death mask in old ivory. Her wings were soaked clear to the feathers of their top joints. Plainly, the massed feathers took up water like a sponge. Anvra, being shorter and weaker, had not been able to hold her lower wingtips out of the water as Doug had done. She felt heavy in his arms with the added weight of liquid, and she was icy cold.

"Anvra!" He had noticed that her hands were empty. She must have dropped the charts.

He shook her. Her eyes fluttered open.

"Anvra," he said. "where are we? Are we headed for the tower?"

"Straight . . . ahead . . ."

Her eyes closed again.

"How far?" he demanded. "How far, Anvra?"

But she was no longer answering.

He lifted her in his arms—one hand up under her wing-sockets, one hand under her knees—and waded heavily forward. After forty or fifty steps his arms began to tremble with the load. He was forced to stop.

Supporting her with an effort, he pulled off one by one his two hip-length leg-coverings. The thin material was as easy to handle as cloth. He knotted the feet together and the tops to each other to form a loop. He put this loop around his neck. Lifting Anvra into it as into a supporting sling, he moved forward once more.

But soon the weariness of his legs became pronounced. He stopped to rest, leaning against the cold side of the pipe, then went on, stopped a little later, went on and stopped again . . . he was staggering forward more by a reflex of the survival instinct than anything else.

SUDDENLY Doug tripped over some steps at the side of the tunnel and sprawled off balance to his right, spilling Anvra through an open door to the stone floor of a room above water-level.

He dragged himself up beside her. It was some little time before feeling began to come back to his water-numbed legs. He set about rubbing some circulation back into Anvra's limbs, too. After a while her eyes opened.

"All right," he said. He gathered her still-chilled body to his warmer one. She made no sound. He held her until he suddenly became conscious of a new dampness against his chest.

He looked down, startled. Her face was as expressionless as if she were yet unconscious, and her eyes were closed. But from under the closed lids, tears were streaming down her cheeks.

"Anvra—" he blurted. "What is it? Are you hurt?"

"I failed you," she said dully.

"Failed me? You got your wings wet. That wasn't your fault."

"At the last, I couldn't help you ..." It was a terrible, soundless weeping. He realized that in spite of what she said it was not him she had failed. It was that stern personal code of hers—that creed of self-obligation.

He hugged her to him comfortingly. After a while, she stirred and lifted her head.

"Don't forget," he said, "I'm not Kathang. You don't really owe me a thing."

"You're many times what Kathang was," she said, not looking at him. "And I owe you all I've got to give."

She rose to her feet, then. He stood up also, and for the first time he looked about him. They were in a small bare room that was almost the twin of the one at the Water Witches' tower behind the water-tight door through which they had entered the drainpipe. Floor and walls were of what seemed to be concrete.

He could hear a faint rushing sound. It seemed to come from the corridor off a room they could see beyond the open inner door of the room they were now standing in.

"Blowers," said Anvra. "The Cadda Noyer must have many deep-rooms under this Aerie." She turned her face to him. Though it was still white from chill and exhaustion, her eyes glowed. "There might—I mean, it's possible they have something to hide from the Magi. If so, maybe you can dicker with them to leave you alone as the price of keeping your mouth shut."

She started toward the inner door. He followed.

THE corridor led past several other bare rooms to end at last in a chamber no larger than a walk-in closet.

"An elevator," Anvra explained. She touched its wall. A small panel slid aside, uncovering a vertical row of square studs. Apparently Anvra's people did not like their devices or controls to be out in plain sight.

The doors of the elevator closed and she touched the bottom-most stud. He felt the familiar, stomach-floating sensation of a rapid elevator descent.

The doors opened again before them. They stepped into still another room. A room with no doors other than the one through which they had emerged.

Anvra made a sharp but barely audible sound like a curse and jumped back into the elevator. Her fingers ran rapidly over the area of the studs and a facing panel fell off, revealing a tangled maze of small transparent tubes filled with green liquid.

"It may fool a wingless slave," Anvra whispered. "But I'm on the Secrets Committee of my own Aerie—"

She twisted and pinched a couple of the small tubes together. They melted into one another and the green liquid drained from the section of transparent tubing below the pinched spot in the vertical one of the two tubes.

One whole wall slid aside. Beyond it lay a brightly lit expanse as immense as an aircraft hangar, filled with equipment.

"Space!" murmured Anvra with relief. She ran into the huge room and pirouetted, unfolding her wet wings, stretching them out until they were extended to their full, sweeping width, the feathers still dark with water.

Instinctively Doug joined her, felt himself extending his own wings. He reacted without thinking, shaking the stiffness and moisture from the appendages. His feathers clacked and rattled.

Anvra's hands caught his shoulders where clavicle and scapula came together in the great double-socket that allowed the winged people to use their arms either separately or as a reinforcement to the heavy wing-muscles themselves. Anvra's own wings folded around Doug's, holding them still.

"Kathang," she whispered fiercely, "are you crazy? You know they're bound to have listening devices here."

"All right," he said harshly, but remembering to keep his voice down. "It was just a reflex. I didn't know. I'm not Kathang, remember?"

She stepped back from him, folding her wings. Her large eyes peered uncertainly at him. He settled his own pinions, turned from her and began to walk among the devices filling the floor space.

He stopped before an apparatus consisting of a metal hoop some six feet in diameter, surrounded by strange jewels and odd curlicues. He could swear he had never seen these shapes before—but they blurred as he looked at them, and suddenly they seemed familiar. He stepped forward, feeling his hands lift and begin tracing an ordered pattern in the air.

Anvra was puzzled. "What are you doing?"

He ignored her. His fingers touched the jewels in a quick combination.

Soundlessly and magically, the metal hoop was replaced by a disk of blinding radiance—a circle he remembered.

He ducked back instinctively.

Through a disk like this one had gone the dark thing that had stolen some essential part of himself. And though such a disk he had come to this place of a winged people.

Behind him, Anvra made a small choked sound.

"Kathang?" she said, softly and almost timidly. Her voice shook. "Do you remember who you are now?"

"I repeat," he said. "I'm not Kathang!"

"But you—" She turned to stare at the glaring radiance. "You activated the Portal. Only a Sorcerer like Kathang, who had worked on it, would know how to do that. If you're a stranger in his body, how did you know?"

"It must have been reflex," he muttered. "Like using the wings. I don't know what I did. I just let my fingers work by themselves."

But she still stood back from him.

He gave up the thought of trying to convince her. He laid his hands on a jewel. The disk of light vanished, leaving the hoop of metal as cold and harmless-looking as before. He walked on among the machines.

He looked ahead, at the room's far wall. His vision blurred, then cleared. He saw a door that pierced the wall, and he approached it. He pushed the door open and stepped through into a dim, smaller room—like the room his blurred vision had seemed to show him when he had looked at this tower from the open room of the Water Witch's Aerie.

Before Doug were four table-like pieces of furniture. Two were bare. The other two bore the figures he remembered seeing—each a dead body dead some little time. One body had wings while the other had not.

The one without wings was his former self.

The body was dried and shrunken inside its clothes. The skin of the face was gray-white and fallen in upon the bone beneath it, so that the broken nose and scarred jaw seemed emphasized. The hands were as bloodless and dry as the face. And their knuckles were like massive bony knobs swelling the dry-dead skin.

"So . . ." said Anvra softly beside him. "It's you. That's what you looked like."

He turned to her, suddenly bitter.

"You're sure it isn't just one of your slaves?" he snapped. "With his wings cut off?"

"A Cadda Noyer slave it would be. Not mine," she answered. "But look at it. That body was never born on this earth."

She turned to the other dead winged figure, the one with wings.

"Kathang," she began, her eyes glowing. She broke off and seized Doug's arm with fingers that dug in. "What's your name—your real name? I can't call you Kathang any more!"

"Doug—" said Doug. There was no point in trying once more to wrestle with the unpronounceability of the rest of it.

"Doug . . ." she said. "Look at this body. Look! It's Kathang! The body of Kathang!"

Doug frowned.

"Look at his neck," said Anvra. "Jax said that if you had the fighter's body, Kathang wouldn't have any place to go but back to his own!"

Doug looked. He had not noticed it before because the wings had propped up the head, but the neck itself was at an unnatural angle to the shoulders.

"The Cadda Noyer must have killed him right there at the fights, under cover of the confusion of you running away." Anvra said. "Of course! They couldn't risk leaving him alive. If they had been able to kill you, too, they would have done it right then—to make sure you couldn't talk. Don't you see? That Portal machine back there has to be unregistered with the Magi!"

She broke off, the color suddenly draining out of her face.

"I was wrong," she whispered. "No matter what you know, the Cadda Noyer can't afford to make a deal with you. They've got to hide the fact you ever existed—or be declared outlaws if the Magi find out about the unregistered Portal!"

"What I can't understand," he replied, "is this. With all the knowledge you people have about things like that Portal, nobody but you wants to believe I could be from another world."

"Nothing living ever came through a Portal," she said. "Until you. If the Cadda Noyer have found a way to bring souls from other worlds to ours, no wonder they—"

A BRAZEN voice, amplified beyond the power of any flesh-and-blood throat, rang out in the big room behind them.

"*Anvra Mons-Borroh!*" it thundered. "*Anvra Mons-Borroh! Leave this aerie immediately by the route you came, and you can go unhindered. Anvra Mons-Borroh, leave alone, at once, and leave safely. The elevator and corridor by which you entered will remain clear for you three minutes more . . .*"

"I won't leave alone," Anvra shouted at the walls. "I'm a contract-mate. I'm self-obligated. The Water Witches will call you to account for any harm you do me."

"You have trespassed on territory of the Cadda Noyer," roared the walls. "The Water Witches have no authority here."

The voice stopped abruptly as if the power source activating it had been interrupted.

"Quick," gasped Anvra to Doug. She ran back into the large room and Doug followed her. They twisted and dodged at a run through the maze of equipment and reached the small room where the elevator waited—just as the elevator doors opened. Standing within the box of the elevator, facing out, were three winged men.

Doug stopped at the sight of them, then took a menacing step forward.

"No," screamed Anvra, catching at his arm with both her hands. "They've got interferers."

Doug saw that each of the three held something like a black cone six inches long and perhaps four in diameter at the base.

While one stayed back in the elevator, holding his weapon on them, the two other Cadda Noyer walked out. Methodically they proceeded to tie up both Doug and Anvra, binding each in rope so that their wings were held in folded position. Doug also found his hands clumsily but effectively roped tightly against his sides.

"All right. Into the elevator," said the Cadda Noyer holding the weapon.

The ride up was longer than Doug had expected. When the doors opened, he understood why. They had reached a large room with one open side. Looking out, Doug could see that they were now high in the tower, the city spread out below them.

"Release the woman," said a voice.

Doug turned. The speaker was standing behind a long table. Seated on either side of him were two other winged men in Cadda Noyer livery. There was a darkness of age to their still-unlined faces, and the long primary feathers of their wings were gray-brown.

"And rack those interferers," added the standing Cadda Noyer, as the last coil of rope fell from Anvra. "Do you want it said we held a Sister of the Water Witches at weapon-point?"

"Are you trying to pretend that isn't just what they did?" blazed Anvra.

"Mistress," said the standing official behind the desk, "the Cadda Noyer has no quarrel with the Water Witches." He turned and gestured toward the open side of the room. "The sky is yours. Why don't you leave us now to our business?"

"Because it's my business, too," said Anvra. She had her temper back under control and spoke coldly. "I'm self-obligated."

"To a man who gambled his body away to the Cadda Noyer?" said the winged man. "There's nothing for you to obligate yourself to. Kathang duLein is legally dead."

"As you said," answered Anvra quickly, "Kathang's legally dead. I chose this man to take Kathang's place as my contract-mate. My self-obligation lives."

The smile vanished from the lean face behind the table.

"Remarry a legally dead man? Don't talk like a fool, mistress!"

"I so declare it. Who's the fool now?"

"You, woman!" exploded the Cadda Noyer. "Do you think this is some little trespass that we'll overlook for fear of offending another Aerie? If you declare yourself contract-bound to this man and your self-obligation leads you to interfere, we can kill you, too. There'll be no question of criminality to be raised against us by the Magi. All your Brotherhood can do is sue for damages. And even if we have to pay those, it won't matter. We're not a poor Aerie now."

Doug's vision blurred, briefly. A curious feeling of understanding woke in him.

"*Now,*" he said.

The single emphasized word turned every eye toward him. For some moments there was a curious silence in the room.

"Now?" echoed the Cadda Noyer official softly.

"I think you must know what I mean," said Doug.

"Yes," said the Cadda Noyer, stroking his chin with a narrow forefinger. "I'm afraid I do. You're a fool, too. You could have died quickly. But you've made it necessary for us to know all you know before we set you free of life. There's a madness in you and the woman both."

He turned back to Anvra.

"Mistress," he said, "think before you answer me—for your own sake. Do you know what this man is talking about?"

Anvra was staring at Doug.

"No," she said. "But if I did, don't think I'd be afraid to admit it."

"Then you don't know," said the official with relief. "Good. The Cadda Noyer have their secrets, mistress. But bravery and pride is as honored among us as among your own Water Witches. I'm glad we can save you from yourself, after all."

HE turned to the three who had captured Doug and Anvra.

"Two of you take the Mistress Water Witch into the air, away from the tower, and hold her until I've shut the wall. Then let her go."

"No!" cried Anvra as a pair of winged men approached. Her wings were half-spread and cupped.

"Don't touch her," Doug said softly, "or you'll regret it."

The two who had been closing in on Anvra stopped, confused.

"Anvra," said Doug, "pay no attention to what I'll be doing. Get one of those weapons. Now. Don't ask questions."

For a fraction of a second, Anvra hesitated. Then she spun toward the wall where the three interferers had been pushed into slots.

The three guards lunged for her. Doug took two quick steps after them, stopped and half turned, balancing on his left foot with his body tilted over to the opposite side. His knee drew up to his chest like a spring—and lashed out.

His lightly shod foot, flat soled, thudded into the spine of one of the guards. There was an ugly crack. The guard dropped and lay still.

Doug staggered, off balance with the effort and the untrained muscles of his body. He managed to get his kicking foot down on the floor and kept himself upright. He kicked again, this time toe-up in conventional fashion. The point of his shoe drove into the neck of the closest of the other guards. The man flipped backward to crash, wings half-spread, on his back. His hands were at his damaged throat as he fought for breath.

The remaining guard drove hard into Doug in a kind of a high tackle. They both went to the floor.

"Stop!" It was Anvra's voice, high-pitched and fierce. But Doug drove a knee hard into the winged man's middle. The Cadda Noyer grunted. His grip relaxed and he rolled away. Doug jumped to his feet.

A black cone in her hand, Anvra was covering the three winged men behind the desk. The guard with the crushed throat was still fighting for air. The one who had tackled Doug was struggling up.

"Don't move," Anvra said tensely to the men of the Cadda Noyer. Covering them with her weapon, she walked to Doug. Her free hand went to work on the ropes that bound him. When they fell away, he flexed his released arms and stretched his wings.

She turned and plunged out into the air. The guard now on his feet hurled himself courageously at Doug, wings partly extended and cupped to strike. Instead of retreating, Doug stepped forward inside those wings and struck a quick, short blow at the other's face with the cast enclosing his broken hand. The man dropped.

"Stand still," shouted the voice of Anvra from empty air behind him. He saw that the three Cadda Noyer behind the desk had moved to attack him, but her words froze them. Anvra was hovering with spread wings upon a warm current of air fountaining up the side of the tower.

"Doug," she shouted. "Come on!"

He looked out and down at the dizzying depth of air separating him from the ground. Furiously he took his instinctive fear in hand and flung it aside. He jumped blindly out into the unsupporting space.

IV

HE had just time for one flash of panic as the wall of the tower flashed up past him. Then, with a wrenching muscle effort and a boom of suddenly trapped air, his wings opened. All at once he was wing-spread and soaring, circling out and up.

Anvra was only a little higher than he, wings moving in what seemed to Doug to be camera-work slow-motion, beating up and away from the Cadda Noyer tower.

He tried to follow her, and the flight reflexes of his body responded. He found that both his arms were extended. His cast-enclosed right hand fitted its wingbone-niche awkwardly but it adequately locked itself in among the underfeathers of his right wing. His left hand was no problem. Arm and wing muscles were moving together in great, slow, heavy wingbeats that rowed him upward into the air.

He had always thought of birdflight as something effortless—but this was not. Against the great area of his wings the air pressed with a mass that felt as heavy as water. He lifted himself with each double down-stroke of his pinions as if he were laboriously rowing a boat.

He felt the breeze of his movement cold on his face and neck. He was sweating. He looked back and down. Behind him and far below, four figures in the clown-colors of the Cadda Noyer were circling upward. He turned his eyes forward again to search for Anvra.

She was high above him. She had stopped beat-

ing her wings and was now soaring, circling higher
and farther away from him by the second. He
struggled to lift himself faster—and then he felt
the updraft Anvra had already caught.

Suddenly his body seemed weightless. He turned
reflexively into the updraft, circling higher and
higher—and all at once the glory of being airborne
was upon him.

SMALL movements of his wingtips directed him,
tilting him into the rising column of air. He was in
full effortless sail across the sky—falling upward,
gracefully and effortlessly upward.

"Doug," called Anvra.

She was waiting for him to join her. But he
could not let go of the ecstasy of riding the updraft.

"Doug!" Her voice rang in his ears. She had
coasted nearer. A second later she flashed upward
from below him, turning to face him as they all
but collided.

"This isn't the time to get soar-drunk," she said.
"The Cadda Noyer are gaining."

He looked down. The parti-colored figures were
still a good distance below them but climbing rapidly. A cold shock of common sense cleared from
him the emotional transport of flight.

"Where to?"

"Home," she said. "My Aerie. If you're not
Kathang, then you have to be a Brotherless man,
entitled to unlimited sanctuary with the Water
Witches as my contract-mate."

He looked ahead and down at the distant, fore-
shortened tower of the Water Witches' Aerie for
which they were headed. The scene blurred. Far
and away through smoke-like layers of double images, he saw a room in which stood a tall winged
man, an old man, clad entirely in black. The distortion vanished from his vision. He saw the scene

below, again sharp and clear. Decision firmed in him.

"That's no good," he called to Anvra. "I can't just sit there, locked up forever. Let's go find those Magi you talk about. Let's tell them the story."

"No," she called back over her shoulder. "There's no Brotherhood to speak for you. You'll never convince the Magi on your own. I won't take you to them."

He gazed at her sailing beside him and a little ahead on the long downward slant. Below, the scene blurred momentarily. Again he glimpsed the old Magus he had seen after he had beaten the two Cadda Noyer bullies in the plaza.

"Then I'll find them by myself," he said.

He tilted away from her, aiming himself toward the closest tower he saw along their flightpath.

"Doug ..." her voice was a wail behind him now. "That's an Aerie of the Numerologists. All right. Wait! I'll take you to the Magi. But they won't believe. They won't!"

He followed her toward a tower some miles off. They flew hard for several minutes. Then he glanced back over the wind-combed feathers of his stiffly extended left wing. The four figures in Cadda Noyer livery were gaining faster now that Anvra had altered course. But from the fund of instinctive flight knowledge in this body Doug wore came an instant calculation. The Cadda Noyer were gaining, but he and Anvra should reach their objective before the pursuers could catch up.

Soon the tower they sought rose close below. They fell rapidly toward a small circular area on the tower roof. Several black-clad figures were peering up at them. Suddenly he and Anvra were landing in the protected circle.

Rather, Anvra was landing. Lulled by the easiness of instinctive flight, he had forgotten that his flying abilities were only reflexes. Wings thrashing, he sailed into Anvra and into several of the waiting black-clad figures, who tried to duck out of his path but were too late.

He felt a collision of bodies and the back of his head slammed against something cruelly hard. And that was all he knew for the moment.

HE opened his eyes to see faces gazing down at him. Anvra's was concerned. But the other faces—all of males in black or Cadda Noyer-colored clothing—were either blank with astonishment, or set with anger.

Climbing to his feet, Doug looked around him. There was a dull throbbing in his head. His wings felt bruised and heavy.

"Magi?" he asked, gazing at the black-clad men.

"Who else serve the Brotherhoods?" answered one, a thin and elderly man with a pinched, frowning face.

"Sirs, I told you, just now!" broke in Anvra urgently. "He can't know that you're Magi. He doesn't even know how to use his wings. Didn't you see how he landed?"

The thin man's frown became a scowl.

"To chambers," he said, and swung about on his heel.

An elevator took them down to a room somewhat larger but otherwise resembling the room in the Cadda Noyer tower from which they had escaped.

There was even a similar if unoccupied table at one end of the room. Doug shut his eyes, trying to will his headache out of consciousness. It faded, but would not go away completely.

The thin Magus who had answered Doug walked behind the table. He sat down, passed his hand across the bare surface directly in front of him, then stood up. Instantly a silence and a quiet shuffling of position took place in the room.

Doug found himself and Anvra, with a black-clad Magus beside her, standing before the table. The Cadda Noyer official was standing beside another Magus a little to Doug's left.

"Well?" demanded the thin Magus behind the table. Obviously he was a man of authority.

"Elector, sir," said the Cadda Noyer official, "our Brotherhood has already entered a claim to the body of this individual. He belongs to us."

The Magus now had his head cocked on one side, listening to murmured sounds that seemed to come from the table top. The sounds were completely audible to Doug's ear, but they made no sense. It was as if they were words in some foreign tongue.

When the murmurs ceased, the Elector raised his head.

"I see," he said to the Cadda Noyer. "We also have a report of the individual in this body defending himself so well against two of your bullies that he disabled both of them without leaving the ground. A hearing was set on the rights of that encounter. Because of your claim, the hearing has been put off until two days from now."

"Why a hearing?" demanded the Cadda Noyer. "Kathang du Lein gambled his body to us and lost—"

"There's no question that the body is yours," interrupted the Elector.

"Then what is at issue?"

"The question concerns the body right of the soul of Kathang duLein. I assume the Cadda Noyer are planning on dispossessing the duLein soul and replacing it with the first Cadda Noyer soul that needs a new body?"

"Yes," said the Cadda Noyer. "Why not?"

"Because a question of inherent justice concerns

itself here," said the Magus dryly. "You may be entitled to the body, but not to the right of dispossessing the soul currently inhabiting it. The evidence seems to show that the body was considered lost at the time duLein was transferred to it—and that it survives now only because of his efforts."

The Cadda Noyer stared.

"Even if so—" he said. "What of it?"

"Kathang duLein may be entitled to lifetime tenancy of the body," said the Magus, "in which case, you could take possession of it, and put it to use— say, as a wingless slave. But you would not be entitled to give the body for use by another identity."

"That's ridiculous—" The Cadda Noyer began, then changed his tune. "What are the alternatives?" His voice was strained.

"If you don't deny—and if evidence appears at the hearing to show the Cadda Noyer guilty of any criminality against the associated Brotherhood Aeries—then the punishment can be no greater than a fine on the Cadda Noyer and their surrender of responsible members, such as yourself, for slavery or execution."

"And if we deny—and evidence of criminality appears?"

"Then the Cadda Noyer must be declared outlaw, its members unprotected from death at the hands of any lawful individual, and its Aeries shall be cast down and destroyed."

The Cadda Noyer official stiffened.

"Self-obligation gives me no choice," he said. "I must put my Brotherhood first. We shall accept the hearing."

"Very well," said the Elector. "In two days, then."

He turned toward the Magus standing with Doug.

"Lock up this individual—" he began, pointing

at Doug. But Doug spoke before the sentence could be finished.

"I'm not Kathang duLein," he said.

"Quiet," said the Magus. "You've got no voice in this matter. Take him—"

Doug felt something hard jammed against his right side.

"I repeat," said Doug steadily, ignoring the weapon and staring back at the Magus behind the desk. "I am not Kathang duLein."

"He's insane," said the Cadda Noyer swiftly.

"No," snapped Anvra.

The Magus turned to look squarely at her for the first time.

"What do you know of this, mistress?" he asked.

"I was Kathang's contract-mate," said Anvra hastily. "This man is not Kathang."

"Sir," blurted the Cadda Noyer, "the woman has nothing to do with the case—"

"Be quiet," said the Elector without turning his head. To Anvra he said, "If this man—this identity—isn't your contract-mate, what interest have you in him?"

"Oh, he is my contract-mate—I mean, he's my new contract-mate, now that Kathang's dead. Sir," Anvra pleaded, "I've seen proof he's not Kathang duLein. Let me speak."

"If you're now the contract-mate of the identity within the body of this man," the Elector said slowly, "you must know there's a question to be asked before any testimony from you can be heard. Tell me, mistress, is your self-obligation to this identity such that you'd lie to the Magi in order to protect him?"

Anvra hesitated. For a moment she gazed at the Elector eye to eye. Then her fierce stare wavered. "Yes," she whispered.

"Mistress," said the Elector, "I honor you for

your sense of self-obligation. But I refuse to consider any testimony of yours. Remove this individual as ordered—"

"I am not," Doug said clearly, "Kathang duLein."

The Elector turned and stared at Doug.

"You keep repeating that," he said at last, "as if
it were a statement that ought to have some meaning for me. Actually, it has no meaning at all. Why
do you think I should pay attention to it?"

"Because," answered Doug, looking steadily at
the Elector, "if there's the slightest chance that
I'm not Kathang duLein, you must stop and wonder what others in your Aeries and Brotherhoods
also might not be who you suppose they are."

The Elector stood up.

"I'll have to think about that," he said, half to
himself. He nodded at the other Magi. "Take him
away."

This time Doug let himself be herded out of the
room into the elevator. They dropped a long distance to a narrow corridor leading to a room that
had no open side and felt as if it were deep within
the lightless earth.

SOME hours later the door opened. The same thin
Magus came in, shutting the door firmly behind
him.

Doug got to his feet from the bed on which he
had been lying. They faced each other.

"Tell me," said the Elector abruptly. "If I offered you the chance to prove you aren't Kathang
duLein, how would you do it?"

"Anvra Mons-Borroh knows the proof as well as
I do."

"Her testimony is worthless."

"All right," said Doug. "Let me take you to the
underground section of the Cadda Noyer Aerie,
near here. I'll show you—"

"I have no authority to enter the Aerie of another Brotherhood without invitation."

Doug took a deep breath and tried his only remaining hope.

"Do you know what a Portal is?"

Thoughtfully the Elector touched the top of his narrow chin with one frail forefinger. "I know."

"When I speak up at this hearing—"

"You aren't going to speak up." The dark eyes in the narrow face of the winged man were dispassionate but closely watching Doug. "As you certainly should be aware, by Kathang's own doing there's no Brotherhood to speak for you."

"Can't I speak for myself?"

"Again, you should be aware that you can't. This is a civil case concerning the right of dispossessing a soul inhabiting a body owned by the Cadda Noyer. You have no more voice in the Hearing than some inanimate object of value claimed by two different individuals."

"I see," said Doug. "All right, I can't testify. But I'll be questioned?"

"If necessary—to provide information not otherwise available."

"Then I want someone there who can explain how those Portals work. Say, one of my ex-Brothers in the Sorcerers' Aerie—preferably the Aerie Master, Jax duHorrel. Can you order that?"

"I can't order," said the Elector. "I can ask if any wish to attend, and perhaps the Aerie Master, if not others as well, will do so."

The Elector turned and left abruptly, closing the door behind him.

After that Doug went through another timeless period of waiting, punctuated only by the occasional arrival of food. When at last the door suddenly opened again, he guessed that at least two full days had passed.

*   *   *

Two people walked in. One was a Sorcerer—Etam duRel, the lean, blurred, dark man who had been Kathang's friend. The other was Anvra.

"Doug—" She stepped quickly to him ahead of duRel and half lifted her wings as if to sweep them around him. But the space of the room was too small. She dropped her feathers and stood back, looking at him yearningly. "Your hearing takes place in just a few minutes. I brought Etam to see you."

Her eyes seemed to be trying to deliver some message. He gazed back at her searchingly. There was both love and anguish in her gaze.

She sighed. "I can't stay," she said. "I'll see you at the hearing, Doug."

She left. The door closed behind her.

"Listen now, Kathang," said Etam, rather gently, and Doug turned back to the winged man. "What I have to say will not please you. There's but one way to save your life and keep you from the Cadda Noyer. You'll have to risk the loss of your wings and your freedom. It's your only chance."

Doug blinked. Before his eyes the blur that was Etam shifted and almost resolved itself, becoming a simple double-image. There was the dark face and short figure of Etam haloed by the ghost of a larger shape with two good wings and lighter-colored hair.

"What does Anvra think?" Doug asked.

Etam made a deprecating gesture with his left hand.

"Well," he said, "she believes in self-obligation the way dying men believe in reincarnation. I did tell her that I was going to urge you to plead insanity."

"Insanity!"

Etam smiled sadly.

"It would be a fair enough plea, old friend," he

said. "You really are insane, you know. This whole belief of yours about the Damned World is a fantasy I watched you build, bit by bit, as we worked on the Portal. You've even got Mistress Anvra half-convinced your fantasy is true. That's why she wants you to let me help you—to save your life. And at the same time, that's why she doesn't want you to take my help. Because she thinks you'd be pretending insanity only to save your life—the worst sort of cowardice and breaking of self-obligation."

"I see," said Doug. "But if I really am insane, it's all right?"

"If you're insane . . ." Etam shrugged. "It's not a matter of right or wrong. How can an insane man understand self-obligation?"

"How about you?" demanded Doug. "How does your self-obligation face up to helping me with something like this?"

"I've got as much sense of self-obligation as any other man. My family . . ." He broke off, relaxing. "Of course, this violates my self-obligation to the Magi—even to the Sorcerers. Never mind that. Are you willing?"

"To say I'm insane?"

"Not just to say it. That's what I let Mistress Anvra think I was going to suggest. But you'll have to do more than that. You'll have to demonstrate that you're insane."

He reached into a pocket under the yellow lozenge on his red tunic, pulled out a triangular sliver of metal six inches long and about two wide at the base. He handed it to Doug.

"Hide this up your sleeve," Etam said. "And before the hearing gets really under way, try to escape. When you make your break, head for me. Slash me with that blade I just gave you."

"Slash you!" Doug frowned.

"That's important," snapped Etam. "Just an attempt to escape will not convince them you're insane. But if you harm me—your Brother and friend—"

"They will want to know where I got the blade."

"After you slash me, I'll grab you. During the struggle, you'll drop the knife over the side of the tower. The Magi will never find it—and they won't worry about it, because the fact of your insanity will be self-evident."

"I see," said Doug.

He took the blade. A greenish stain tinged the point. As he looked away from it, the double-image effect that held the man before him seemed to expand to affect the whole room. The walls became as transparent as thin gray smoke. Doug stared out . . . and out . . . into a white vastness where the Walker's dark shadow lurked.

Then abruptly the room was again solid about him. Carefully he slid the knife up under the tight silver sleeve of the garment Anvra had given him.

"Good," said Etam, dark eyes watching Doug out of the double-image. "As a lunatic, you'll have to lose your wings. But I'll do my best in testifying to sway the Magi into making the rest of it just confinement rather than slavery. Courage, old friend!"

He gripped Doug's bulging double shoulder-joints firmly with his hands, then departed.

ONLY a few minutes passed before two black-clad Magi came for Doug. They led him to an elevator and rose with him to a large three-sided chamber. The fourth side was open to the elements.

Doug saw that the time was late afternoon. The weather was now nippingly chill. A cold wind blew freely into this tower room from its open side. But no one present seemed to notice. Beyond, the sky was cloudless and ice-bright. The sun slanted in at

an angle that lit only the edge of the open side and
left the rest of the room, by contrast, in deep
shadow.

In this shadow, five of the Magi waited behind a
massive table. Only the middle one—the thin
Elector—was standing. Each of the five had a black
scarf bound tightly around his head.

Along the wall opposite the open side of the
room were other black-clad Magi but without the
head scarves. Near the open side stood the clown-
suited Cadda Noyer official Doug remembered and
two others wearing the same livery. There also sat
the small silver-suited figure of Anvra. Etam duRel
lounged beside Jax duHorrel, both wearing the red
livery and yellow lozenge of the Sorcerers.

The two Magi guards had Doug stand before the
center of the table. The Elector's cold face briefy
examined him, then turned to the others.

"Nye duBohn, you were a witnessing Magus at
the professional fight on which Kathang duLein
wagered his life?"

A young-looking Magus moved to stand almost
beside Doug.

"I was," his tenor voice rang reedily. "The Magi
in hearing may be sure I am aware of the rules. No
transfer of soul from one body to another is per-
mitted without a license issued by the Magi, and
without Magus present to witness and record the
transfer."

"It was all in order?"

"As I recorded it. I examined the individual, this
Kathang duLein, before the fight started and I was
satisfied with his freely made contract. I remained
with him until the spell was cast. And I sensed his
soul depart for the body of the downed fighter."

"And afterward?" The voice of the Elector was
toneless.

"My attention was caught by the surprising survival and escape of the supposedly beaten fighter. When I finally turned back to the body of Kathang DuLein, it had already ceased breathing."

"You examined the body?"

"I felt under the right armpit. There was no pulse."

"May we have," said the Elector, looking along the wall, "the second member of the Magi to have been involved with the identity of Kathang duLein."

"But he wasn't—" began Doug.

"The identity at issue will remain silent," said the Elector.

A BLACK-CLAD figure detached itself from the wall and walked toward Doug. Doug recognized the old man who had peered down at him after the fight near the catapult. In his slow bass voice, this witness gave his account of being called to the scene by bystanders. He had found the two Cadda Noyer conquered and Doug unconscious.

"Were you surprised to learn that the individual had defeated two bullies wearing wooden spurs?" asked the Elector.

"The individual was dressed and spurred as a professional fighter," answered the witnessing Magus. "It was only when I was composing my report later that something struck me as odd. Why should an untrained entity, even in a trained body, win such an encounter?"

"I note here," said the Elector, examining what to Doug seemed the bare tabletop, "your mention of that oddity in your report, together with a recommendation for investigation."

"I did so recommend," said the old Magus.

"And the Cadda Noyer rejected investigation," said the Elector. "I see. You may stand back."

There was a faint cough from the open side of the room. Glancing over, Doug saw that Etam had stepped back between the Magus on one side of him and Jax on the other, so that his double-imaged face was hidden from all but Doug. Sharply, Etam jerked his head in a signal to Doug to act.

"Very well," said the Elector. "The Cadda Noyer may now state their claim upon this body."

The sound of the Elector's voice brought Doug's eyes back to the table. The Cadda Noyer official was stepping forward.

"We have already submitted our claim to the Magi," the Cadda Noyer said. "Together with a list of pertinent documents, such as the original request for permission to transfer the entity of Kathang duLein—a request made by Kathang duLein, himself, as is customary. But to review our position . . ."

The Cadda Noyer spoke on. Once more Doug's eyes wandered to the blurred face of Etam. The man jerked his head again in imperative signal. His dark forehead gleamed slightly in the late sunlight. Before the table, the Cadda Noyer was elaborating on the claim of his Aerie to the body Doug inhabited.

". . . The Magi," he concluded, "cannot deny the Cadda Noyer use of a body which belongs to them."

"That remains for this Hearing to determine," coldly responded the Elector. "It is a fighter-slave body, with which the Cadda Noyer may ordinarily do as they will. But what is in doubt is the right of the Cadda Noyer to evict its current resident soul."

"Kathang duLein gave up any right to his life when he bet and lost it on the fight," cried the Cadda Noyer official.

"But the fighter—the body of the fighter he bet on—did not lose the fight," said the Elector impassively. "Therefore Kathang did not lose, either."

"Having already submitted freely to the spell, he had abandoned his body-right and life-right.

Technically, from that moment on he was a dead man."

"He is a dead man!" cried Anvra desperately from the sidelines. "I saw his dead body, myself. Kathang duLein isn't in the live body at this Hearing. Kathang is dead!"

"Alive," growled the Cadda Noyer official. "But legally dead."

"Silence!" The Elector paused. Then he turned slightly, and for the first time his eyes met Doug's.

"Alive?" asked the Magus. "Or dead?"

"The Cadda Noyer," Doug answered slowly, "honestly believe that Kathang is alive in this body I wear. Mistress Anvra Mons-Borroh honestly believes him dead. Both are wrong."

Doug took one step back from the desk and turned so that he could see clearly past the figure of the Cadda Noyer official.

"One man knows the truth," said Doug. "One man other than myself."

He turned back to the table. Reaching into his sleeve he drew forth the knife, tossed it to the polished surface.

"I was given this by a visitor to my cell," he said. "I believe that the tip is poisoned—so that even the smallest scratch would kill."

The Elector and his flanking Magi stared at the knife. They did not touch it. The Elector raised his gaze but sat without a word, as if waiting for something to happen.

Doug and everyone else in the room now were watching Jax and Etam.

Out of the blur of superimposed faces, Etam's dark forehead seemed to shine strangely. Doug attributed that to the beads of sweat he could see on the Sorcerer's brow.

Doug spoke up loudly in the silent room.

"The one who came to me," he said, "knew I was not Kathang, that I was from the Damned World. So he didn't think I would understand the concept of self-obligation. But I do. I know that while some persons may lose their self-obligation entirely, there are others who never completely lose it, no matter how they try. In the end—"

Etam exploded into movement. His left elbow jerked back into the midriff of the guard beside him. He snatched the black cone from the guard's belt.

"Stop!" he shouted, waving the weapon threateningly.

Doug took one step toward him. "I'll take that gun," he said.

"Stand back." The voice from the small, dark blurred figure with its one crippled wing was high and cracking. Etam turned and shouted at them all, "I cheated my Aerie. I lied to my Brotherhood. But I will not dishonor the name of duLein. For I am Kathang! Kathang duLein! The man from the Damned World tells the truth."

With a choking sound, he threw the weapon to the floor and flung himself over the room's open edge into emptiness.

Doug hurled himself between the bodies of Jax duHorrel and the guard, stopped at the edge to gaze down. Below he saw Kathang-Etam spinning with one wing outstretched, falling without any effort to save himself.

"This Hearing will resume," said the Elector tonelessly.

Doug was suddenly aware of Anvra standing beside him at the open side of the room. They both stared downward at the distant dark slit of a street in which the body of Etam duRel had disappeared from sight.

"He did well at the last, though," she whispered to Doug. "He made his end a good one . . ."

"It now becomes necessary," the ranking Elector was saying coldly, "to inquire more fully into the situation."

His steady eyes swung to the Cadda Noyer official, who had taken up a position beside Jax duHorrel. The Cadda Noyer's face had gone pale.

"The Cadda Noyer," he said, "in self-obligation, consider that their Brotherhood may be responsible for an indiscretion by some of its members. We are prepared to admit that there now seems a possibility that the man whose body has just died— Etam duRel—may have approached some of our Brotherhood with a scheme to build an unregistered Portal to the Damned World."

"For what purpose?" asked the Elector.

The Cadda Noyer hesitated. His face regained color, hardened.

"I am no Sorcerer," he said. He glanced at Jax duHorrel. "Perhaps the Aerie Master would be willing to venture a theoretical explanation . . ."

"Not I," said Jax. "The Brotherhood of Sorcerers has been doubly shamed here today." He looked at Doug. "Also we owe gratitude to this being from the Damned World." He added in a different tone, "Sir, what do we call you rightly?"

"Doug," said Doug. "Or Doug duDamned World, if you prefer."

"Perhaps," said Jax, "you would like to be the one to explain what Etam and Kathang were up to."

"Only Etam—originally," said Doug, and glanced at the Cadda Noyer official.

"Sir," said the Cadda Noyer swiftly, "we also owe you gratitude. We offer you whatever recompense is judged proper."

The thin face of the Elector changed slightly, as if a smile were struggling to emerge.

"Then it seems beyond our duty to demand further explanation in this case," he said. "So if all parties are satisfied and provided guarantees are made . . ."

He glanced from Doug to the Cadda Noyer.

"The Magi," said the Cadda Noyer official stiffly, "have the word of the Cadda Noyer, upon their self-obligation as a Brotherhood Aerie, that any illegal machinery on their premises shall be destroyed."

"Then this Hearing is dissolved," said the Elector.

The room immediately began to empty. The Cadda Noyer official and his companions were already launching themselves into the air, away from the tower.

V

DOUG found himself standing with Anvra at his side, facing Jax duHorrel and the gaunt Elector.

"Doug duDamned," said the Magus, "unofficially, we would be grateful to hear your further explanation of this matter."

Doug nodded. "Sure. But tell me something first. I gather a Magus can sense when an exchange of souls between a couple of bodies is taking place, even if afterward there's no way to detect the change. But can he sense whether more than one pair are exchanging if all the exchanges take place at the same moment?"

"Why . . ." The Elector hesitated. Then he frowned. "No!"

"That's what I thought," said Doug. "You see, Etam set up a portal system for the Cadda Noyer so that while a legal transfer was going on, an illegal transfer could let a third party shift to another body undetected. The explanation is a little complicated. Have you got something I can write on?"

The Elector touched the table behind him. A drawer opened to reveal something like a classroom pointer, two feet long, narrowing from a butt perhaps an inch thick to a pencil-like tip. He picked it up and traced with the tip on the table surface. Where the tip passed, a glowing yellow line appeared.

He reversed the pointer and passed the butt end over the line, erasing it. Then he passed the pointer to Doug.

"Thanks." Doug stepped to the table. "Look. This is the transfer as it was legally planned to be, between Kathang and the fighter."

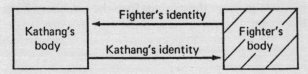

"The crossed-out box," he said, "represents a body scheduled to be dead shortly after exchange is accomplished. Now, on that pattern Etam planned to superimpose secretly the illegal transfer of two other identities, of which one was to be a dying man—dying, so that he could be brought body and all through the Portal. And Etam himself was to be the other. Etam had already discovered on my world a place where a man would be dying at the required instant. He set up a transfer pattern timed to coincide with the legal transfer between Kathang and the fighter, like this . . ."

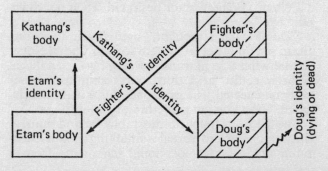

"But you've got Kathang marked to end up in a dead body," protested Jax. "He wouldn't have agreed to that if he were in the plot with Etam!"

"Kathang was not in the plot. All he knew until the moment of his transfer was that Etam had been stealing equipment parts from the Sorcerers' laboratory. He said nothing about it because he considered Etam his friend. Actually, Etam was afraid that sooner or later Kathang would realize that Etam had built an illegal Portal. The fight must have been rigged, too. Etam wouldn't want to gamble his whole scheme on the chance Kathang's fighter might win."

"But Kathang ended up in Etam's body, not the other way around," said Anvra.

Doug smiled briefly at her.

"Yes," he said. "But it wasn't until Kathang found himself in the room under the Cadda Noyer tower with the illegal Portal that he figured out what had happened. Seeing a chance to escape all the troubles he had brought on himself as Kathang, he decided to sit tight in Etam's body and say nothing. He knew there was no way now to prove he wasn't Etam."

"But the fighter, alive in Etam's body—" began Jax.

"Etam must have had plans to dispose of him, too," said Doug. "Plans the Cadda Noyer must have agreed to, privately. There must have been a lot at stake. I assume there were certain individuals to whom they could have sold illegal body transfers for a good price."

"Shamefully, yes," said the Elector. "Such people exist in every generation—in spite of all watchfulness."

"Anyway," put in Jax, eyeing Doug curiously, "it didn't work out the way Etam planned it. Why not?"

"Because of me," said Doug. "You see, I wasn't really dying when Etam pulled me through the Portal. For certain special reasons I was being poisoned by gas—but I'd taken measures to save myself. This brought me close enough to death for Etam to pull me into this world—but by the time he had transferred my identity into the body of the fighter, I was already reviving. That's what tangled things up."

He pointed to the second pattern he had drawn on the table.

"I was supposed to transfer identities with Kathang," said Doug. "And Kathang's identity, finding himself in my dying body, would have no choice but to die also. Meanwhile, Etam's healthy soul would have no trouble ousting my dying one from Kathang's body. The fighter's soul, leaving his own dying body behind, would find Etam's healthy body open for occupancy. That was the plan. But here's what actually happened."

He drew a third pattern on the table:

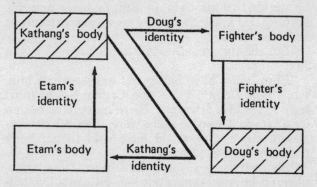

"You see, by the time my reviving soul reached Kathang's body, it was already stronger than Kathang's," Doug said. "Consequently, I ousted him. But I occupied his body just in time to hear the spell for Kathang to change bodies with the fighter. The figher's soul had already left his body—so I ended up there, instead."

He paused, looking in turn into each of the three faces watching him.

"You know the rest of it," he went on. "I won the fight and the body survived. The Cadda Noyer attendants, seeing the fighter still alive, apparently thought the whole scheme had misfired. They broke Kathang's neck under cover of the general confusion—to keep him from testifying to what had been tried. But by that time Etam had already occupied Kathang's body. So it was Etam who died.

"Meanwhile Kathang, ousted by the spell and my own stronger identity, moved instinctively into the nearest healthy but unoccupied body. That was Etam's body, back in the Cadda Noyer underground lab. Evidently Kathang occupied it just before the fighter tried to, and the fighter, dispossessed, was left with no place else to go but my own original body—now actually and irreversibly dying from shock and identity-abandonment. Instinctively he entered my dying body, and died with it."

"But how could you know it was Kathang in Etam's body?" demanded Jax. "And what made you so sure he'd admit it?"

"I relied on his sense of self-obligation," Doug told the big Aerie Master. "It almost drove him to admit who he was earlier, after he saw me in his body in Anvra's Aerie. Then, just before the hearing, he tried to trick me into killing him so that his shame would be buried with him. I knew then his self-obligation could be made to drive him to acknowledge his name."

"You knew? Sir—" Jax checked his verbal explosion. "No offense—but what does someone from the Damned World know about self-obligation?"

"As it happens," said Doug wryly, "it's not unknown where I come from." He smiled to himself. "Actually, it was just Etam's bad luck that he imported someone with it—a maverick like myself."

"Mav-er-kkk ..." Jax's tongue stumbled over the unfamiliar sounds.

"That's close enough," said Doug. "It's from the Damned World's language—a word meaning someone without the ownership mark all his herd-followers wear burned into their bodies. Every society has a few mavericks—even yours. You can tell us by our habits, if you know what to look for. For one thing, we refuse to live by the herd rules, so we're forced to make up our own rules instead."

"But we're talking about self-obligation," Jax said.

"That is self-obligation," Doug replied. He shook his head as the Aerie Master opened his mouth protestingly. "Never mind, I know you can't see it yet. You're as blinded by your society as my people are by theirs back on the Damned World. It's as if my people were all blind in the right eye, and you folks here all blind in the left. They see only the virtues that exist in the social mass. You see only the ones existing in the individual."

"Sir," said the Elector, "without the safeguards to individual freedom embodied in the Brotherhoods and the Magi, all but a handful of men would enslave the rest."

"No they wouldn't," said Doug. "But you won't believe that until you see it for yourself. That's why I'm going to go back and open up communication between my people and yours. They need to see that to make a society work, the individual doesn't have to be swaddled in protection from birth to the grave.

"Doug—" the word came from Anvra's throat like a catching of breath. He turned and smiled at her.

"Don't worry, I'm not going to stay on the Damned World. How can I? I inhabit one of your bodies and my old one is a ruin. But I've got a responsibility—"

"Responsibility to whom? Those wingless, crawling slaves back there?" demanded Jax.

"To them and you, too," said Doug. "I'm the only one in both societies with what amounts to full vision. Even physically, two eyes see more than one, you know. They allow binocular vision—depth perception. I can see things you can't even begin to imagine—like the advantages to both worlds in getting to know each other—"

"Doug duDamned," said the Elector, "I'm not sure we could approve this."

"Maybe not—but can you stop me?" Doug laughed. "I didn't set up the rules of this society of yours—you people did. Does anyone in your whole civilization have the right to stop me from doing what I want?"

"Stop you?" echoed Jax. "We won't stop you—we just won't help you. You need a Portal to get back to your own planet. Also a poison and an antidote that works on your present body the way whatever you took on the Damned World worked on your old body."

THE room shadowed about Doug for a moment. For a moment again, as when Etam-Kathang had been living, Doug seemed to see through the walls around him as if they were made of smoke—out and out until his vision ranged into the whiteness among the planes of eternity.

"You don't understand at all, do you?" He focused down to the three of them watching him, and the walls became solid once more. "No, Jax duHorrel," he said gently. "I don't need a Portal or any special help—any more. I told you I can see things none of you will be able to see until you acquire this new perception of mine. For example, you asked me how I knew Kathang was in Etam's body. Well, I saw him there—first as a blur and then, just before the Hearing, as a recognizable double-image. And just as I can see now how to get back to the Damned World—even taking this body along with me—by an effort of mind alone."

"You!" Jax choked on the words he had been going to say, took a deep breath and made an effort to lower his voice. "You don't understand what's involved in what you're talking about! Do you think your plane's just the other side of some magic space, four inches thick within the ring of a Portal? It's not just inches thick, that Portal. Its other surface is dimensions and qualities away, on the world of its destination—there are elements to the equation that change value second by second."

Doug laughed. "It doesn't matter."

"Nonsense. Utter nonsense," snapped Jax.

"No, not nonsense," said Doug, sobering. What he had seen during that terrible momentless moment of distanceless passage through the planes of interdimensional space formed again in his mind's eye. "There's something else I didn't tell you. You all assumed Etam brought my body and soul here together. He didn't. Maybe it was because of the drugs in me, but my identity was left behind. It could have stayed behind and died an easy death. But some instinct in me wouldn't let it."

Jax stared at him.

"From the moment my identity entered interdimensional space, my new vision began to operate," said Doug. "What I saw then seemed all blurred and out of focus. But I've since had time—

and maybe help—to strengthen it and bring it into focus. The last confusion ended when I saw Etam Kathang an hour ago. I remember—and I understand now. There are many, many roads between the planes, and all of them are roads I can travel."

Jax stared at him, unconvinced. "You'll still need help."

"And maybe I'll get that, too," Doug said, smiling at Anvra.

"Love will not be enough," muttered Jax.

But Doug was looking outward, beyond the Magus and the Sorcerer and the Water Witch, beyond the room—and beyond what the others could see. He was staring at a dimensionless brightness through which a dark thing strode. And as he looked, it turned toward him.

The Walker lifted a lumpish arm. And this time, the hand beckoned.

> *The saint who said, "All the way to heaven is heaven," did not envision the converse being equally true.*

The Last Dream

HE MEANT IT.

A couple of days back, or perhaps it was a week or so ago—it was too much trouble now to keep track of the calendar—a reporter had got into his hospital room. They had found the man, of course, and hustled him out again; but not before he had had time to ask a few questions. Most of them were the same old questions ... what did it feel like to have run through thirty million dollars of inheritance, would he do it all over again, etc. But there was one question that hadn't been asked before. How did Tommy feel about dying?

"I'm looking forward to it," Tommy Harmen had said.

The reporter had made a note of that answer—with pencil on some thickly typewritten paper, sheaved together. A newsy point? Well, thought Tommy, I meant it. It wasn't something he had said merely for the shock value. After all, he was ninety-four. At ninety-four, dying wasn't something

you considered academically. It was right there in
the room with you, like a piece of furniture. Maybe
it wasn't sprung or padded just to suit you, but
it was something to sit on anyway, and you planned
on sitting on it. What the hell! Tommy Harmen
chuckled at the profanity in his thoughts. Funny.
Old people shocked others as children did when
they swore. You were supposed to be above such—

The chuckle, he realized suddenly, had also been
in his mind. It was too much effort to chuckle
aloud. They had him in an oxygen tent now. It
made the room seem wavery and unnatural, seen
through the plastic. Which reminded him—he
needed that nurse. Damn it, they took better care
of the babies in the nursery ward, he'd be bound.
With an effort as large as that in hauling back on
the rod when there was a big blue on the end of
the line, he groped for the button. Where was the
damn thing . . . ? No matter. He gave up. After all,
it was the hospital's good name and odor that was
at stake, not his.

He lay still, exhausted by the effort, lapsing into
a light doze. Bet that reporter hadn't believed him,
knowing the things he'd done, the places he'd been,
the things he'd . . . all over the world, too. There
was that little island down in the West Indies . . .
and Antibes . . . and . . .

"How about the jereboam?" asked Winkie.

"Jereboam, hell," he said. "Let's have in the
Methuselah."

. . . His vision cleared. He was sitting at a small,
round table with a marble top—a real marble top.

"Didn't know they made them any more," he
said, testing it with his fingernail.

"You have to know the dealer," said Winkie.
Tommy looked up. Winkie was tipping back on
two legs of the elegant occasional chair, with his
collar open. Drunk as usual. No, not drunk. Tight.

Tight as a lord. Square jaw hanging down, curly hair mussed. Handsome devil, Winkie.

"You've taken off weight," said Tommy.

"Polo," said Winkie. "Makes all the difference." He winked. "Second story polo."

Tommy laughed and finished his glass. It was one of the good ones. Piper Heidsieck? He looked about for the bottle, and then remembered they had just ordered in the new one. He glanced around the room. It was a drawing room, large, with comfortable furniture, but rather too many tables to sit at and a small plush bar over in one corner. He felt a sudden access of delight.

"Why, it's a house!" he said. "A real house!"

"Exclusive," said Winkie. "Very."

He looked back at Winkie.

"You're looking damned young," he said. "Where've you been all these years?"

"Living it up," said Winkie. "Here comes the champagne."

And it was coming. They were wheeling it in on a sort of cart, like he hadn't seen since—when was it? In the south of France, somewhere. And there was the Methuselah, a great-granddaddy among champagne bottles.

"Pop it," said Tommy to the black-tied waiter, who was releasing the wire from the bottle's cork. "I don't care what it does to the bouquet. I want to hear it bang."

"Yes, Mr. Harmen," said the waiter, his lean, bony face lit by a happy, conspiratorial smile. Tommy peered suddenly at him.

"Why, you're Caesare," he said. "What're you doing on this side of the world—after all these years?" Tommy frowned. "Why, that was back in the thirties—no, the twenties—"

"Twenty-five and twenty-six, Mr. Harmen," said Caesare. The cork flew suddenly from the bottle and the impelling tips of his thumbs with a sound like a cannon shot. Applause burst out, around the room. Glancing up and about him, Tommy saw the room was now filled to overflowing with good-looking women and men in all sorts of costume, from evening clothes to hunting outfits. The faces of old friends leaped out at him everywhere his eyes fell among the crowd.

"Winkie!" he said.

"What, Tomser?" said Winkie, pushing a glass of the champagne from the methuselah into his hand.

"All the gals," said Tommy. "All the guys. I know them all. What is this? Some kind of party?"

"Graduation party," said Winkie, winking. "Five guesses for who."

"Me!" cried Tommy, shot through suddenly with delight. "Damn you, Winkie—oh, damn you!"

"Think nothing of it," said Winkie, winking like mad.

Tommy tossed off his glass of champagne. It went bubbling through all his veins bringing fire to his body in every part of him.

"Fill her up!" shouted Tommy. "Fill up, Winkie! Fill up, everybody! Let's kill the old gent. Let's have a party!"

Chattering and laughing, the surrounding crowd poured in around their table and the bottle. Champagne danced and sparkled in Tommy's throat—the best, the best, the very best he'd ever tasted. Good-looking women sat on his lap, leaned over his shoulder, twined their arms around his neck. And he knew them all; and they were beautiful, beautiful—more beautiful than ever. And the canapes were the tastiest, and the waiters the happiest, and the bartenders—there were dozens of them—the jolliest; and the music (it came from somewhere hidden behind the crowd) all the things he liked. And the party went on and on and on; and nobody grew tired at all; but gradually, by some beautiful, natural, group assent, they began to slow down, to quiet down, to a sort of wonderful, companionable silence.

"Bless you," said Tommy, looking at them all with a last glass of champagne in his hand, and sniffing in spite of himself, "Bless you all, damn your eyes. I'm going to miss you."

"Miss you too, Tomser," said Winkie. And then, as if Winkie's words had been a signal, they all got up and began to file by, one by one, and shake his hand before going back to their seats or stations (in the case of the bartenders and waiters), where they lapsed into silence and stillness once again.

At the last, there was only one man who had not come by; and he was a slim, nondescript looking chap in a business suit and the sort of ordinary face people have trouble remembering.

"Who's he, now?" said Tommy to Winkie, peering at this last man, who was sitting at a table by himself, with no drink, but a briefcase laid out on its marble top before him. Winkie did not answer; and, looking over at his old friend and drinking companion, Tommy discovered Winkie had fallen into the same sort of brown study that had claimed all the rest.

Tommy looked back over at the slim man, and found him standing before his and Winkie's table.

"I'll sit down, if you don't mind," said the slim stranger, and pulled out a chair and took it without waiting for an answer. Tommy, seeing this, lifted his champagne glass for a last time to his lips—and found it empty. He put it back on the table; and recognition came belatedly.

"Oh," he said, "you're the reporter guy."

"Yes, and no," said the slim man, in the judicial

tone of a good lawyer. "Yes . . . and no." Tommy's eyes slowly widened.

"Don't slip and slither around with me," said Tommy. He sat up suddenly a little straighter in the chair. "I know who you are now; and I settled my problems with you sixty years ago when I got tossed by that rhino—the one in Uganda. I didn't see my way clear to making any changes then; and I'm not about to go back on that decision now. Never did in my life and I don't intend to at this late date."

"Changes," said the slim man, and coughed, "are not exactly a topic for discussion at this point." He had been busy opening his briefcase, and now he withdrew from it a thick sheaf of papers bristling with paperclips, interspersed with smaller slips of colored paper. He laid the sheaf before him.

"I just want you to know," said Tommy. "It was my money and my life, and I don't regret a dollar or a minute of it. Nobody lived it up like I did. It was one long circus and if you people've been warming a spit for me all these years, why lead me to it. I don't say," said Tommy, touching the empty champagne glass a little sadly, "that I'm exactly looking forward to it. But I always paid my bills; and I bought this and I'll pay for it."

"Yes. Indeed. Well," said the slim man with another dry cough, tapping the sheaf of paper before him, "I have your complete record here. It establishes beyond doubt that, among the other things, on innumerable occasions you have proven yourself a profligate—"

"Right," said Tommy.

"—a drunkard—"

"Yes," said Tommy, glancing with a touch of nostalgia at the now-empty methuselah.

"—and an engager in illicit relationships with the opposite sex. Nowhere," said the slim man, "is it recorded that you did as much as one honest day's work, that you sought to improve the world you lived in, or change your fellow man in any way for the better. An unparalleled, a unique, record, in which all the entries of a lifetime fall on one side of the ledger." He tapped the sheaf of paper with one dry forefinger and glanced sharply at Tommy. "I hope you realize this makes you a special case."

"And what's that supposed to mean?" growled Tommy, for he was beginning to get tired of all this and the fumes of the champagne were fading from his head.

"Just this," said the slim man, and made a sweeping outward gesture. "Here you see gathered—" Tommy looked up and discovered that the room in which he sat had strangely and subtly expanded; it stretched now to fantastic distances, and everywhere that he could see, it was filled, stuffed and jammed with silent people—"All the people, living and dead, whose lives your own life affected. Look at them."

Tommy looked again; and it was true. There were armies of waiters and waitresses and bartenders, regiments and companies of men and women he had known, even back to those that had populated the shadowy early beginnings of his childhood. They all looked at him now with silent, waiting gazes.

"Hey, lads and lasses," murmured Tommy, gently. "Good to see you one more time."

He had almost whispered the words; but some trick of the now vast room picked them up and amplified them and sent them rolling amongst all the watching multitude. And a wordless, rustling stir answered back from their formless ranks.

"We can dispose of your case very quickly," said the slim man, "provided any one of these people will produce an indictment," he turned his head to the room and raised his voice. "Anyone having just cause to condemn Thomas Nicholas Harmen will now speak up!"

His words like Tommy's, boomd out through the watching crowd. But no sound came back. . . . And Tommy, staring in incredulity from face to remembered face, his glance dancing like lightning from remembered features to remembered features, met here a friendly wink, there a grin, and there again a surreptitious thumbs-up gesture, there a tenderly remembering smile, there a beam of gratitude, there again and once more a glow of pure, remembered jollity and happiness.

"Will no one, no one out of all this man's life time," said the thin man, speaking up again, "find some cause for indictment against him?"

Silence made answer, a happy, stubborn silence.

"Well then," said the slim man, returning the sheaf of papers to his briefcase, with a wash-my-hands air and standing up. "That concludes the matter." He looked at Tommy. "Shall we go?"

"Go?" said Tommy, looking up startled; and then back again at the crowd for a second, before returning his gaze to the slim man. "But I thought—"

"The other place, the other place," said the slim man with some asperity, frowning. "It has to be one or the other."

"The other place!" said Tommy, astonished and set up in his chair. "Now who'd have thought—" He started to get up, then sank back into his seat.

"Well? Well?" said the slim man, checking himself in midstep away from the table.

"This other place," said Tommy slowly; "just what's it like?"

"Why, it's like whatever you wish," said the slim man. "That's why it's a place of reward."

"Oh," said Tommy. "Well—"

"Well what?" said the thin man. "Surely you don't object to that?"

"Well, you see—" said Tommy, slowly still, "about this business of rewards. You might put it that I've been being rewarded all my life long, right here where I've been. And I enjoyed—" Tommy's voice got firmer— "every damn minute of it. I don't mean to have you think I didn't. I wouldn't take back a glassful or a moment of it. But—" his voice slowed again—"all the same . . ."

"All the same—what?" said the slim man.

"Well, it's been one hell of a fine life." Tommy looked up at him. "But you know, I'm ninety-four; and sometimes I think nowdays, even if I could drink another bottle just like the ones I used to, and feel the way I used to—perhaps I'd just as soon sit back instead and remember the bottle I did drink, than put another one on top of it. There's some kind of quote about that—" He wrinkled his brow. "The pitcher going to the well once too often, or some such—no, that isn't right. The point is, the first times are really the best times for everything. After a while it gets to be just comfortable, instead of being all skyrockets and New Year's Eve."

He stopped and looked up at the slim man again.

"You remember when you came into my hospital room," he said. "I told you I was looking forward to the end of the book, here. And I meant it. It's all been so fine all these years and I wouldn't want to spoil it now by taking the pitcher to the well too many times. . . . What I mean is—" he looked at the slim man almost appealingly— "other place, or no other place, if my reward there is simply going to be more of the same, I think I'd just as soon pass. It just isn't worth it—" he looked out once more over the waiting multitude—"it just isn't worth it to spoil what I had."

"Don't worry," said the slim man, and for a second his voice sounded quite unbusinesslike, "we hadn't an eternity of parties scheduled for you. It was something rather different. We've got a comfortable chair reserved for you in the library of a rather exclusive club. A club full of old characters like yourself who like to sit around and talk."

"A club? A club? What characters? Who?"

"Who?" said the slim man, almost smiling. "Why, there's one named Bacchus, and another called Don Juan, and a rather fat one named Diamond Jim Brady."

"Oh," said Tommy.

"So you see," said the slim man, looking at him. Tommy was nodding his head slowly and emphatically.

"I see," he said. "I should've known it. Sorry I was so suspicious. Give me a hand up, will you?"

The slim man gave him a hand up.

"Lean on me," said the slim man.

"That champagne," said Tommy apologetically, as his knees rubbered a little. "Drank it a little too fast. But it was a great bottle to end up on."

"Pleasure to be of assistance," said the thin man; and together they went up through the crowd, and out of the door, and into a sunlit world beyond, where the skies were as bright as Memory.

DAHUT, Book III

Dahut is the daughter of the King, Gratillonius, and her story is one of mythic power . . . and ancient evil. The senile gods of Ys have decreed that Dahut must become a Queen of the Christ-cursed city of Ys while her father still lives. 65371-7 $3.95

THE DOG AND THE WOLF, Book IV

Gratillonius, the once and future King, strives first to save the surviving remnant of the Ysans from utter destruction, and then to save civilization itself as barbarian night extinguishes the last flickers of the light that once was Rome! 65391-1 $4.50

ANDERSON, POUL
THE BROKEN SWORD

Come with us now to 11th-century Scandinavia, when Christianity is beginning to replace the old religon, but the Old Gods still have power, and men are still oppressed by the folk of the Faerie.

65382-2 $2.95

ASIRE, NANCY
TWILIGHT'S KINGDOMS

For centuries, two nearly-immortal races—the Krotahnya, followers of Light, and the Leishoranya, servants of Darkness—have been at war, struggling for final control of a world that belongs to neither. "The novel-length debut of an important new talent . . . I enthusiastically recommend it."—C.J. Cherryh 65362-8 $3.50

BROWN, MARY
THE UNLIKELY ONES

Thing is a young girl who hides behind a mask; her companions include a crow, a toad, a goldfish, and a kitten. Only the Dragon of the Black Mountain can restore them to health and happiness—but the questers must total seven to have a chance of success. "An imaginative and charming book."—*USA Today.* "You've got a winner here . . ."—Anne McCaffrey.

65361-X $3.95

DAVIDSON, AVRAM and DAVIS, GRANIA
MARCO POLO AND THE SLEEPING BEAUTY
Held by bonds of gracious but involuntary servitude in the court of Kublai Khan for ten years, the Polos—Marco, his father Niccolo, and his uncle Maffeo—want to go home. But first they must complete one simple task: bring the Khan the secret of immortality!

65372-5 $3.50

EMERY, CLAYTON
TALES OF ROBIN HOOD
Deep within Sherwood Forest, Robin Hood and his band have founded an entire community, but they must be always alert against those who would destroy them: Sir Guy de Gisborne, Maid Marion's ex-fiance and Robin's sworn enemy; the sorceress Taragal, who summons a demon boar to attack them; and even King Richard the Lion-Hearted, who orders Robin and his men to come and serve his will in London. And who is the false Hood whose men rape, pillage and burn in Robin's name?

65397-0 $3.50

AB HUGH, DAFYDD
HEROING
A down-on-her-luck female adventurer, a would-be boy hero, and a world-weary priest looking for new faith are comrades on a quest for the World's Dream.

65344-X $3.50

HEROES IN HELL

created by Janet Morris

The greatest heroes of history meet the greatest names of science fiction—and each other!—in the greatest meganovel of them all! (Consult "The Whole Baen Catalog" for the complete listing of HEROES IN HELL.)

MORRIS, JANET & GREGORY BENFORD,
C.J. CHERRYH, ROBERT SILVERBERG, more!
ANGELS IN HELL (Vol. VII)
Gilgamesh returns for blood; Marilyn Monroe kisses the Devil; Stalin rewrites the Bible; and Altos, the unfallen Angel, drops in on Napoleon and Marie with good news: Marie will be elevated to heaven, no strings attached! Such a deal! (So why is Napoleon crying?) 65360-1 $3.50

MORRIS, JANET, & LYNN ABBEY, NANCY ASIRE,
C. J. CHERRYH, DAVID DRAKE, BILL KERBY,
CHRIS MORRIS, more.
MASTERS IN HELL (Vol. VIII)
Feel the heat as the newest installment of the infernally popular HEROES IN HELL™ series roars its way into your heart! This is Hell—where you'll find Sir Francis Burton, Copernicus, Lee Harvey Oswald, J. Edgar Hoover, Napoleon, Andropov, and other masters and would-be masters of their fate.
65379-2 $3.50

REAVES, MICHAEL
THE BURNING REALM
A gripping chronicle of the struggle between human magicians and the very *in*human Chthons with their

demon masters. All want total control over the whirling fragments of what once was Earth, before the Necromancer unleashed the cataclysm that tore the world apart. "A fast-paced blend of fantasy, martial arts, and unforgettable landscapes."—Barbara Hambly
65386-5 $3.50

EMPIRE OF THE EAST
by Fred Saberhagen

THE BROKEN LANDS, Book I
A masterful blend of high technology and high sorcery; a unique adventure in a world on the brink of ultimate change; a world where magic rules—and science struggles to live again! "The work of a master."
—*The Magazine of Fantasy & Science Fiction*
65380-6 $2.95

THE BLACK MOUNTAINS, Book II
East meets West in bloody conflict on a world where magic rules, but technology is revolting! "A fine mix of fantasy and science fiction, action and speculation."
—Roger Zelazny
65390-3 $2.75

ARDNEH'S WORLD, Book III
The gripping climax of the "Empire of the East" series. "Ranks favorably with Tolkien. Exceptional in sheer unbridled zest and imaginative sweep."
—*School Library Journal*
65404-7 $2.95

SPRINGER, NANCY
CHANCE—AND OTHER GESTURES OF THE HAND OF FATE
Chance is a low-born forester who falls in love with

the lovely Princess Halimeda—but the story begins when Halimeda's brother discovers Chance's feelings toward the Princess. It's a story of power and jealousy, taking place in the mysterious Wirral forest, whose inhabitants are not at all human . . .

65337-7 $3.50

THE HEX WITCH OF SELDOM (hardcover)
The King, the Sorceress, the Trickster, the Virgin, the Priest . . . together they form the Circle of Twelve, the primal human archetypes whose powers are manifest in us all. Young Bobbi Yandro, can speak with them at will—and when she becomes the mistress of a horse who is more than a horse, events sweep her into the very hands of the Twelve . . .

65389-X $15.95

To order any Baen Book listed above, send the code number, title, and author, plus 75 cents postage and handling per book (no cash, please) to Baen Books, Dept. CT, 260 Fifth Avenue, New York, NY 10001.

To order by phone (VISA and MasterCard accepted), call our distributor, Simon & Schuster, at (212) 698-7408.

THE KING OF YS
POUL AND KAREN ANDERSON

THE KING OF YS— THE GREATEST EPIC FANTASY OF THIS DECADE!

by Poul and Karen Anderson

As many authors that have brought new life and meaning to Camelot and her King, so have Poul and Karen Anderson brought to life a city of legend on the coast of Brittany . . . Ys.

THE ROMAN SOLDIER BECAME A KING, AND HUSBAND TO THE NINE

In *Roma Mater*, the Roman centurion Gratillonius became King of Ys, city of legend— and husband to its nine magical Queens.

A PRIEST-KING AT WAR WITH HIS GODS

In *Gallicenae*, Gratillonius consolidates his power in the name and service of Rome the Mother, and his war worsens with the senile Gods of Ys, that once blessed city.

HE MUST MARRY HIS DAUGHTER— OR WATCH AS HIS KINGDOM IS DESTROYED

In *Dahut* the final demands of the gods were made clear: that Gratillonius wed his own daughter ... and as a result of his defying that divine ultimatum, the consequent destruction of Ys itself.

THE STUNNING CLIMAX

In *The Dog and the Wolf*, the once and future king strives first to save the remnant of the Ysans from utter destruction—then use them to save civilization itself, as the light that once was Rome flickers out, and barbarian night descends upon the world. In the progress, Gratillonius, once a Roman centurion and King of Ys, will become King Grallon of Brittany, and give rise to a legend that will ring down the corridors of time!

Available only through Baen Books, but you can order this four-volume KING OF YS series with this order form. Check your choices below and send the combined cover price/s to: Baen Books, Dept. BA, 260 Fifth Avenue, New York, New York 10001.

ROMA MATER • 65602-3 • 480 pp. • $3.95 _____
GALLICENAE • 65342-3 • 384 pp. • $3.95 _____
DAHUT • 65371-7 • 416 pp. • $3.95 _____
THE DOG AND THE WOLF • 65391-1 •
544 pp. • $4.50 _____

Here is an excerpt from Mary Brown's new novel
The Unlikely Ones, coming in November 1987 from
Baen Books Fantasy—SIGN OF THE DRAGON:

MARY BROWN

THE UNLIKELY ONES

After breakfast the next morning—a helping of
what looked like gruel but tasted of butter and nuts
and honey and raspberries and milk—the magician led us outside into a morning sparkling with
raindrops and clean as river-washed linen, but
strangely the grass was dry when we seated ourselves in a semicircle in front of his throne. Hoowi,
the owl, was again perched on his shoulder, eyes
shut, and he took up Pisky's bowl into his lap.
Although the birds sang, their songs were courtesy-
muted, for the Ancient's voice was softer this morning as though he were tired, and indeed his first
words confirmed this.

'I have been awake most of the night, my friends,
pondering your problems. That is why I have con-
vened this meeting. We agreed yesterday that you
had all been called together for a special mission,
a quest to find the dragon. You need him, but he
also needs you.' He paused, and glanced at each
one of us in turn. 'But perhaps last night you
thought this would be easy. Find the Black Mountains, seek out the dragon's lair, return the jewels,
ask for a drop of blood and a blast of fire and Hey
Presto! your problems are all solved.

'But it is not as easy at that, my friends. Of your
actual meeting with the dragon, if indeed you reach

him, I will say nothing, for that is still in the realms of conjecture. What I can say is this: in order to reach the dragon you have a long and terrible journey ahead of you, one that will tax you all to the utmost, and may even find one or other of you tempted to give up, to leave the others and return; if that happens then you are all doomed, for I must impress upon you that as the seven you are now you have a chance, but even were there one less your chances of survival would be halved. There is no easy way to your dragon, understand that before you start. I can give you a map, signs to follow, but these will only be indications, at best. What perils and dangers you may meet upon the way I cannot tell you: all I know is that the success of your venture depends upon you staying together, and that you must all agree to go, or none.

'I can see by your expressions that you have no real idea of what I mean when I say "perils and dangers": believe me, your imaginations cannot encompass the terrors you might have to face—'

'But if we do stay together?' I interrupted.

'Then you have a better chance: that is all I can say. It is up to you.' He was serious, and for the first time I felt a qualm, a hesitation, and glancing at my friends I saw mirrored the same doubts.

'And if we don't go at all—if we decide to go back to—to wherever we came from?' I persisted.

'Then you will be crippled, all of you, in one way or another, for the rest of your lives.'

'Then there is no choice,' said Conn. 'And so the sooner we all set off the better,' and he half-rose to his feet.

'Wait!' thundered the magician, and Conn subsided, flushing. 'That's better, I have not finished.'

'Sit down, shurrup, be a good boy and listen to granpa,' muttered Corby sarcastically, but The Ancient affected not to hear.

'There is another thing,' said he. 'If you succeed

in your quest and find the dragon, and if he takes back the jewels, and if he yields a drop of blood and a blast of fire, if, I say . . . then what happens afterwards?'

The question was rhetorical, but Moglet did not understand this.

'I can catch mice again,' she said brightly, happily.

But he was gentle with her. 'Yes, kitten, you will be able to catch mice, and grow up properly to have kittens of your own—but at what cost? You may not realize it but your life, and the life of the others, has been in suspension while you have worn the jewels, but once you lose your diamond then time will catch up with you. You will be subject to your other eight lives and no longer immune, as you others have been also, to the diseases of mortality.

'Also, don't forget, your lives have been so closely woven together that you talk a language of your own making, you work together, live, eat, sleep, think together. Once the spell is broken you, cat, will want to catch birds, eat fish and kill toads; you, crow, will kill toads too, and try for kittens and fish; toad here will be frightened of you all, save the fish; and the fish will have none but enemies among you.

'And do not think that you either, Thing-as-they-call-you, will be immune from this; you may not have their killer instinct but, like them, you will forget how to talk their language and will gradually grow away from them, until even you cross your fingers when a toad crosses your path, shoo away crows and net fish for supper—'

'You are wrong!' I said, almost crying. 'I shall always want them, and never hurt them! We shall always be together!'

'But will they want you,' asked The Ancient quietly, 'once they have their freedom and identity returned to them? If not, why is it that only dog, horse, cattle, goat and sheep have been domesticated and even these revert to the wild, given the chance? Do you not think that there must be some reason why humans and wild animals dwell apart? Is it perhaps that they value their freedom, their individuality, more than man's circumscribed domesticity? Is it not that they prefer the hazards of the wild, and only live with man when they are caught, then tamed and chained by food and warmth?'

'I shall never desert Thing!' declared Moglet stoutly. 'I shan't care whether she has food and fire or not, my place is with her!'

'Of course . . . Indubitably . . . What would I do without her . . .' came from the others, and I turned to the magician.

'You see? They don't believe we shall change!'

'Not now,' said The Ancient heavily. 'Not now. But there will come a time . . . So, you are all determined to go?'

'Just a moment,' said Conn. 'You have told Thingmajig and her friends just what might be in store for them if we find the dragon: what of me and Snowy here? What unexpected changes in personality have you in store for us?' He was angry, sarcastic.

'You,' said the Ancient, 'you and my friend here, the White One, might just do the impossible: impossible, that is, for such a dedicated knight as yourself. . .'

'And what's that?'

'You might change your minds . . .'

'About what, pray?' And I saw Snow shake his head.'

'What Life is all about . . .'

432 pp. • 65361-X • $3.95

Here is an excerpt from Heroing *by Dafydd ab Hugh, coming in October 1987 as part of the new SIGN OF THE DRAGON fantasy line from Baen Books:*

Hesitantly, Jiana crawled into the crack.

"It's okay, guys," she called back, "but it's a bit cramped. Toldo next—wait! —Dida, then Toldo. I want . . . the priest in back." She felt a twinge of guilt. What she really wanted was the boy where she could reach out and touch his hand when needed.

Dida whimpered something. Jiana turned back in surprise.

"What's wrong?"

"Oh, love . . . are we really going—into *there?*"

"Dida, it's the only way. Are you a mouse? Come on, warrior!" He pressed his lips together and crawled toward her hand. When she touched him, she felt him trembling.

"Don't fear. I came through here, remember?"

The tunnel smelled as fresh as flowers after the stench of sewage. Jiana could breathe again without gagging.

The ceiling of the passage sank and sank, until she was almost afraid it would narrow to a wedge and block them off. But she remembered her harrowing crawl from the prison, her heart pounding with fear, feeling the hot, fetid breath of *something* on her neck, and she knew the passage was passable. At last, they were scraping along with their bellies on the floor and their backs against the splintery ceiling. Jiana wondered how Toldo Mondo was managing with his prodigious girth.

Suddenly, she knew something was wrong. She crawled on a few more yards, then stopped. Dida was no longer behind her. She heard a faint cry from behind her.

"Jiana, help me—please help me . . ."

"Lady Jiana," called out Toldo, "I think you had better come back here. The boy . . . seems to have a problem." Jiana felt a chill in her stomach; Toldo sounded much too professionally casual.

"What's wrong?" She turned slowly around on her stomach, and inched her way back to where the two had stopped. She stretched out her hand and took Dida's; it was clammy and shaking. With her fingers she felt his pulse, and it was pounding wildly.

"I can't do it," he whispered miserably. "I can't do it—I just can't do it—all that weight—I can't breathe! —I can't . . ."

"What? Oh, for Tooqa's sake! What next?"

As if in answer to her blasphemy, the ground began to shake and roll. Again she heard the scraping, grinding noise, only this time much closer. Dida continued to whimper.

"Oh gods, oh gods, oh please, let me out, oh please, take it away . . ."

"Too close," she whispered, trying to peer through the pitch blackness.

"Oh my lord," gasped Toldo Mondo, "don't you hear it?"

Again the ground shook, and this time the scraping was closer yet, and accompanied by a slimy sucking sound.

For a moment all were silent; even Dida stopped his whimpering. Then Jiana and Toldo began to babble simultaneously.

"I'm sorry," she cried, "I'm sorry, o Ineffable One, o Nameless Scaly One, o You Who Shall Not Be Named! I never meant—"

Toldo chanted something over and over in another language; it sounded like a penance. The fearful noise suddenly became much louder.

"Toldo! It's coming this way! Oh lordy, what'll we do? Crawl, damn you, crawl, crawl! And push the kid along—I'll grab his front and drag!"

"You fool! It's here! Don't you hear it? Am I the only one who hears it?!"

"Shut up and push, you fat tub of goat cheese!"

In a frenzy, they began to squirm away from the sound, dragging Dida, and Jiana discovered that the tiny crawlway was as wide as a king's hall, though the ceiling was but a foot and a half off the floor. Dida was no help. He was in shock, as if he'd been stabbed in a battle. He could only move his arms and legs in a feeble attempt at locomotion, praying to be "let out."

After a few moments, Jiana realized she was hopelessly lost. Had they kept going straight from the hole by the river, they would have found the next door. But they were moving to the right, and she did not know how far they had gone in the pitch black. In fact, she was not even sure which way they were currently pointing; the horrible noises had seemed to change direction, and they had concentrated on keeping them to their rear.

"Oh gods, I've done it now," she moaned; "we won't ever get out of here!" A sob from Dida caught at her heart, and she cursed herself for speaking aloud.

"We shall make it," retorted Toldo Mondo. "There must be *something* in this direction, if we go far enough!"

Soon, Jiana herself began to feel the oppression of millions of tons of rock pressing down on her. She had terrifying visions of being buried alive in the blackness by a sudden cave-in caused by the movements of whatever was behind them. With every beat of her heart it got closer, and the shaking grew worse. She could clearly hear a sound like a baby sucking on its fist.

"Jiana, go!" cried Toldo in a panic. "Crawl, go—faster, woman! It's here, it's—Jiana, I CAN SMELL IT!"

"How does it squeeze along, when even we barely fit?" she wondered aloud. *You're babbling, Ji . . . stop it!*

She surged and lunged forward, not letting go of Dida, though he was like a wet sack of cornmeal. And then, there was a rocky wall in front of her. There was nowhere left to crawl.

Coming in October 1987 * 65344-X * 352 pp. * $3.50

To order any Baen Book by mail, send the cover price plus 75 cents for first-class postage and handling to: Baen Books, Dept. B, 260 Fifth Avenue, New York, N.Y. 10001. And ask for our free catalog of all Baen Books science fiction and fantasy titles!